The Pirate's Legacy

by

Sarita Leone

The Lobster Cove Series

This is a work of fiction. Names, characters, places, and incidents are either the product of the author's imagination or are used fictitiously, and any resemblance to actual persons living or dead, business establishments, events, or locales, is entirely coincidental.

The Pirate's Legacy

Cover Art by *Debbie Taylor*

The Wild Rose Press, Inc.
PO Box 708
Adams Basin, NY 14410-0708
Visit us at www.thewildrosepress.com

Publishing History
First Vintage Rose Edition, 2016
Print ISBN 978-1-5092-0802-9
Digital ISBN 978-1-5092-0803-6

The Lobster Cove Series
Published in the United States of America

The way a man handles a car

is a good indication of how he loves a woman. She'd been watching him drive, taking the curves in the coast-hugging road with confidence and control. Most of the time he just used his left hand, resting the right either on his thigh or the shift stick.

"Did you really grow those flowers?" The first lull in conversation; it gave her too much time to consider how the man "drove" in bed, so she said the first decent thing that popped into her head.

A low chuckle. "You sound surprised."

"I am. A little bit. I mean, it's not every day you meet a guy who knows his way around a garden."

There was a small vegetable patch at the house, in the only corner the huge oak didn't shadow. It produced enough tomatoes, lettuce, and cucumbers for salads in the summer. And, an occasional watermelon. But she'd always been the one to tend it. Uncle Ted kept far from it; his only comment had been that he'd help with it when she grew something he could smoke. So far, that hadn't happened.

"Ah, so it's the old flower power stereotype, is it? You think I'm a girly man for stopping to smell the roses?"

Teasing felt natural, so she gave it right back.

"I should've known."

"Okay, I'll bite. Should've known what?"

"That you have a thing for roses, too." A long, dramatic sigh. "That's it. I'm out. Now that I know there're roses to be competed against, I'm pitching the white towel in."

Dedications

For my father, the man who inspires me to do my best,
always. His strength, love and support have lifted me
high, and if I fly, it's because he's shown me
how to use my wings. I love you, Pop.

~*~

And, for the man who stole my heart
all those years ago. Sempre.

Chapter 1

1979

Morning came softly to the old house. Birdsong, carried on a warm breeze, swept through the windows and stirred white lace curtains. As day chased night, its occupants began to stir. Bare feet padded down hallways. Water made old lead pipes bang in protest. Creaks and groans, wood across wood as doors were thrown wide and stairs navigated.

Not for the first time, Chloe wondered how much longer the beloved place was going to hold up. It had seen better days—much better days—and expecting it to hang on indefinitely without some serious greenback infusion was just plain delusional. What could anyone expect from a house, though? Hell, it was only made of wood and nails—and most of those nails were the old, square-headed ones, at that.

The softness of a new day came to an abrupt end.

A crashing door was her alarm clock. Had she not been out so late the night before, she would have been downstairs already, taking care of the man who, now that he'd slammed his bedroom door, could be heard greeting the others already in the kitchen. Two floors down, and she could still hear him. Part of the sound carried through the vents placed in the floorboards which were handy during the winter months when heat came up through them but decidedly intrusive when one half-deaf man wanted to get his point across.

And Uncle Ted always had a point to get across.

Tooth brushing would have to wait, along with face washing. Grabbing the shorts she'd tossed on the floor just hours earlier, she hurried from her room into the hallway. It was not big, more a glorified landing with two other doors leading off it, than a proper hallway like the one on the second floor. She stepped down, out of her room, onto the rectangular landing. Then, up, into the bathroom. No one else lived in the other bedroom right now, so she did not bother to shut the bathroom door. Being too damn hot, right up under the roof, was both advantageous and bothersome, so unless the place was jam-packed, she had the floor to herself.

Now, she pulled her long hair into a loose ponytail and secured it with a double-bobble hair holder while she sat on the throne and did her business. Mornings like this, slightly fuzzy headed and sleep deprived, made a hard start to a day.

Chloe stepped into the shorts, shimmied them up to her hips and did up the snaps. Then, she turned and surveyed the yellow water.

To flush, or not to flush, that is the question, she thought. Shakespeare could not have guessed his line would be used thusly, but every time she stood in the tiny tiled room, the thought passed through her mind.

She closed the lid, went to the white porcelain sink and twisted the cold water handle. *Clank. Clank. Clankety-clank.*

Water finally fell from the faucet, so she wet her fingertips, slid them along the bar of Ivory in the soap dish, and lathered. Rinsed. Twisted the handle. As she swiped her hands dry on a worn pink towel, she counted the drips.

Just as it nearly refused to give water when prompted, the faucet begrudgingly stopped the flow when the handle was turned off. One. Two. Three. Four drips.

Chloe's heart fell. Four drips? A bad sign.

She counted, holding her breath.

Finally, the faucet stopped dripping. She tossed the towel over the rack, breathed a sigh of relief, and headed for the stairs. She took them two at a time, hit the second floor hallway with a barefoot thud, and went down the wider staircase even more quickly.

The living room was empty. The dining room, as well. She passed her uncle's closed door, then the open bathroom door, on her way to the kitchen.

She paused in the doorway. Scenes like this pushed all thoughts of questionable plumbing, hit-or-miss wiring, and termites from her mind. Who cared about the mundane when everyone looked so happy?

Uncle Ted, dressed in a washed-too-often black-turned-gray Keep on Truckin' T-shirt and frayed Levi's sat at the speckled Formica table, a mug of joe cradled in one hand. Across the table, two women half his age, both listening to him as intently as if he were Jimi Hendrix back from the grave playing the Star-Spangled Banner.

Hard not to listen when every word was a near-shout.

He saw her then, and stopped mid-sentence, the whole weed-as-sedative discussion forgotten.

"Morning, Sunshine. Sleep well, or was the sedative too much of a one-two punch last night?" He chuckled good-naturedly when she went around the table, kissed him on the cheek, and gave him a playful tap on the shoulder. He seemed so strong, the way she remembered from childhood. But she knew better, so kept the touch gentle. "You know I'm just fooling you. Hey, no one's more up on legalizing the shit. But The Man, now he's got a whole different attitude on that one…"

Gabby gave a serious nod. "Ain't that the truth? The Man? He needs a straight-up dose of reality, is what I think." She turned, meeting Chloe's gaze with a knowing nod. Dropping her voice, she said, "He's doing a-okay today. Seems to know what the hell is going on. So, good morning, Sunshine."

"Morning. Thanks for being so fast to get in here. You the one who made coffee?"

"Nope. It was our little bookworm. I don't think she even went to bed." Gabby raised her voice, so the man across the table could hear the conversation resume. She raised her own mug of coffee in small salute. "Isn't that right, Ted? I was telling Chloe that I think Reva has been up all night again."

"She has. I got up to use the john about four, and it's a good thing I saw the light on in here, or I might have given her a free show." He winked, but they all knew better. A man did not open his home to women without learning to close the bathroom door. "She should have been out, like the rest of you, last night. Having some fun. Smoking some reefer—"

Reva, the only one still in college, called out from the enclosed back porch where she—and her books, presumably—spent most of their time. "I can hear you. And you know I don't smoke anything, so give it a rest.

4

I'm going to pass the Bar Exams next year, and then you're all going to have to worry about what goes on in this place."

Gabby looked over at Ted, who turned to raise an eyebrow at the quiet, obviously very hung over, blonde beside him. "What do you think, Jules? Getting set to worry?"

Julia blinked twice. Her eyes were so bloodshot they looked painted red. Her hair fell in a tangled mess around her shoulders, and if Chloe wasn't mistaken, the woman's left shoulder showed sand burn.

One of them had had a tough Saturday night. And it was no surprise who that was. When she walked past Julia's chair, she gave it a bump with her hip. Just enough to let the other woman know that even though she stunk of Pabst Blue Ribbon and sex, she still needed to answer the man waiting beside her.

"Uh, yeah." A harsh hacking sound accompanied the throat clearing, but Julia made her voice louder and turned to Ted with a ragged smile. "I'm probably the one who should worry the most."

"You think?" Gabby tapped her Saturday night manicure on the table. She was so polished, despite the clock showing it hadn't even hit eight yet, that by contrast Julia looked even worse.

Chloe poured two cups of coffee. She left Julia's black and splashed some milk into her own. She took both to the table, set one cup in front of the other woman and claimed the seat beside Gabby.

She took a long swallow, letting the hot liquid soothe her throat. Messing with Julia too much when she had been no angel the night before was wrong. Bad karma, so she kept her mouth shut.

Her gaze shifted to her uncle. He seemed content, surrounded by the ever-changing parade of women he referred to as his girls. Chloe was a constant, of course, but others came and went. The three in the kitchen had all been with them over a year now, making for a comfortable environment. More like family than strangers.

The stability helped with Ted's condition. To look at the man, no one would guess that at forty-nine, he was nearing the end of his life. Any day now. That's what the doctor had been telling her for the past six months. Each day that wasn't "the day" was one day more she had with him.

Had she been a praying woman, she would have begged a pardon for the man. But she had used up all her prayers when Aunt Ginny had needed them. They had proved futile, then, and wasting energy praying for an impossibility wasn't something she planned to do again. Ever.

He was all she had, and even though the future intruded on the present, hanging like a noxious cloud over her head, she refused to pray—or to think too much about it. Today was all they had, so every today was one she was going to be grateful for.

"Hey, Reva?" She waited for a reply. The scholar, as they called her, was too polite to ignore the call.

"Yeah?"

"You going to study all day? Or do you have time to hit the beach with us?"

"I can't…"

"Yes, you can," Gabby called out. "Come on, let's have some fun."

"I really shouldn't…"

Julia shook her head and gave a disgusted snort. Holding her right temple with her hand, she turned so she faced the open doorway to the porch. Just beyond the doorway, a foot dangled over the arm of a wide, wicker rocker, swinging lazily.

She cleared her throat again, and once more the sound was enough to make Chloe and Gabby both cringe. They exchanged looks, each mirroring the other's wide-eyed expression.

"Listen, Bookworm, it's Sunday. Family time. And, we are family—that's right, even me, who drank that asshole Brent Carlyle under the bar last night down at The Dockside." She paused, gave a little snort, and added, "Before I went off with his best friend—who, as it turns out, is not such a great friend to anyone."

Uh oh. It wouldn't be the first time Julia, the looking-for-love-in-all-the-wrong-places chick had gotten tangled up with a jerk. A stab of remorse ricocheted in Chloe's midsection; she had been fast to judge the other woman's sand scrapes, thinking the romp on the beach was a pleasurable moment.

By the sudden sheen of tears in the bloodshot eyes, it seemed doubtful the interlude would be repeated.

Julia tossed her hair over her shoulder. A tired, sarcastic chuckle, then, "I'm going to take a shower—wash that man right out of my hair. Then, we're all going to have some fun. Including you, Reva. Don't make me come out there and burn those books of yours."

The foot stopped mid-swing. After a long moment of silence. "No need, I could use some time with the family."

Contentment bloomed in Chloe's midsection. They

might be an unlikely family, but they were all any of them had at the moment. Uncle Ted loved Quinn Beach, the day was gorgeous, and they were all aware they might not get another chance to show him a peaceful day. No sense wasting borrowed time.

Julia stood. She swayed a little but found her balance. "Be down in ten."

"Take fifteen, honey." Ted smiled at her back as she left. If he knew something was amiss, he did not let it show.

Gabby met his gaze when Julia rounded the corner onto the stairs. "I'm going to make sandwiches. Want to help?"

He nodded. "Peanut butter and jelly?"

"Is there anything else worthy of filling our basket?"

"Nothing I can think of." Ted smiled, finished his coffee, and stood. It hit Chloe again that he looked as strong now as he did when she came to live in this house. She'd been six then, and he seemed invincible.

Reva would, everyone knew, study up until the very last minute.

Gabby put a hand on Chloe's shoulder as she went around her chair. "What about you? What's up your sleeve?"

"Wrench, probably. I'm heading to the basement. Those pipes…"

"I know. The second floor toilet took three flushes. Sorry." Gabby opened the bread drawer, removed the red-and-blue-bubble wrapped Wonder Bread and put it on the countertop. Ted already had the Welch's grape jelly waiting, along with wax paper and two knives.

"Don't be." She stood, leaving her mug on the

table. The coffee had gone cold, but she didn't care. It would taste just fine when she returned from the dirt-floored hole where all the house's failing systems were located. It would wash the taste of cobwebs from her mouth. "The faucet...a seven-drip morning."

The other woman's eyes widened. "Seven? Say it ain't so!"

"I wish I could, sister. But seven—you know what that means."

Trouble, with a capital T, Chloe thought. That's what a record-drip morning meant. And, trouble? It never seemed to have a hard time finding her, no matter what.

Chapter 2

Lobster Cove was a sleepy place where time almost stood still. Quaint shops lined neat streets where potted geraniums hung from lamp poles, trash cans never overflowed but were always used and most cars never blew past the only Stop sign in the village square. Neighbors knew each other, people slept with their doors unlocked and the keys in the ignitions of the cars parked in their driveways. No one worried they might lose something off a porch.

Two cops kept the peace, which meant they dealt with rare outbursts from drunken summer tourists, directed the most sunburned to the village pharmacy for pain relief and popsicles and kept a watchful eye on Main Street. Ken and Tate Humphrey were brothers who had grown up in a house not far from the town park, gone to Vietnam with every other able-bodied man, and had been fortunate enough to come back to the place they loved. Both had married their high school sweethearts, and each now had one child. A boy for Ken and Cecilia, and a girl for Tate and Becky. That was the way of the Cove; people stayed when they could. It was too pretty a place to leave, for most, anyhow.

Quinn Beach was more crowded than usual, with summer in full swing and tourists in abundance. They chose a spot further down the beach than most families with small children ventured toward, near the rocky outcropping that reached into the Atlantic like a big stone toe.

Chloe kept her steps slow and walked beside her uncle. He smiled at everyone, greeted families as they passed their blankets or beach chairs, and patted wet heads when sandy children stopped him to say hello.

A tow-headed boy of two or so ran toward the shore. His mother, her nose stuck in the latest issue of Ladies' Home Journal, did not even see the toddler escape from beside her. A red Tonka truck lay forgotten and half-buried in a small hole, along with a blue plastic shovel. The kid whizzed past them, cutting right between Gabby, who walked about ten feet ahead of them, and Chloe and Ted.

Lightning-fast, her uncle stepped forward and caught the little boy, who laughed so loudly his mother looked up from the magazine.

"Whoa, my friend. Where are you going so fast?" He bent down, so his face was closer to the child's.

"Water!" The boy pointed a chubby finger toward the ocean. "Wanna come?"

The mother had finally followed him. She looked down at the child and waved her own finger. "Mikey, didn't Mommy tell you to stay by her chair?"

"Water!" The grin was heart-melting.

The mother glanced up at Ted, then shot Chloe a look, before she turned back to the man who'd just kept her son safe. She licked her lips, ran a hand through her short, blonde hair and practically purred. "Mmm, why, thank you. You big, strong man, you kept my baby from drowning."

"You're welcome, but I hardly think the tyke was

about to—"

"Oh, he was! Just inches away from drowning!"

The other woman was close to Chloe's age, and certainly young enough to be Ted's daughter. While the attention may flatter her uncle, it made her want to retch.

"He was nowhere near the water." When the woman ignored her, she looked down at the little one. "Were you, Mikey?"

The kid was cute, but she didn't feel the longing for one of her own that all her friends described feeling. It bothered her sometimes, that she never thought children would be part of her life. She didn't have anything against them; she simply didn't see herself with one. Or two. Or, God forbid, three.

Mr. Cutie Pie cemented her feelings when an unmistakable odor reached her nostrils. Amazing that something that adorable could make such a god-awful stink.

Taking a step back, she put a hand through the man's arm and gave a gentle tug.

"The others are all the way over by the boulders already. Damn, I hope they don't start the orgy without us." She grinned sweetly up at his startled expression. Then, with a wave of her free hand, she started walking.

When they were a few feet from the stinky child and his stunned mother, he began to chuckle. "I can't believe you just did that."

"Damn straight I did. She practically had her claws in you."

"Got something against free love, my dear?"

"Nope. I do, however, have something against my uncle getting a dose of the clap."

He shook his head as they reached the others. "Unbelievable."

Gabby looked up. She straightened the edge of a tie-dyed blanket, anchoring it with her pink flip-flops. "What's so unbelievable? Did I miss something?"

Reva's canvas carryall spilled books onto the sand. She opened two woven lawn chairs, positioned one beneath the striped umbrella already in place, and motioned to the man. "Take a load off. And spill the beans—what's unbelievable?"

She watched her uncle as he sat. He looked fine, not even out of breath, so she dropped the picnic basket into the shade of the umbrella.

With a snort, he said, "My niece doesn't want me to get a dose of the clap, as she so eloquently puts it. Hell, but her aunt must be rolling over. The clap, indeed!"

Reva giggled. She made no ploy to hide the fact that she was a virgin and planned to stay that way until after marriage.

Julia flat out laughed. She'd improved greatly after her shower; even her eyes were less bloodshot behind her dark glasses. "Shit, I think your wife would be thanking her for that. Who has the clap, anyway?"

Chloe shimmied out of her cut-off shorts and adjusted the bottom of her lime green bikini.

"No one has the clap," Uncle Ted said. "I just had a word with a nice lady over there, and right away Chloe here got concerned about my love life and how the heck anyone could tell if someone has the clap I don't know…"

"X-ray vision." Reva dug in her bag and pulled out a big, fat book.

Chloe read the book's spine. "*Judicial Law Practices and Theory*? Goddamn, I think I'd rather get the clap than read that."

"Is there something you should be telling me?" The voice behind her was familiar. Too familiar. Years and years worth of familiar.

The others must have seen Neil's approach, but no one warned her. She stuck her tongue out, a general gesture to those who now grinned at her, all looking as if they'd enjoyed every second of watching her make a fool of herself.

She turned to face the man who stood barely a foot away. If she wanted to, she could lean in and bring them chest to chest.

"Nope."

When he smiled down at her the rest of the world fell away. His eyes, bluer almost than the ocean, sparkled. Full-on mischief, always, in those eyes. So many times, his schemes—and those eyes—had landed her in hot water. Or, in his arms.

He looked over her shoulder and winked at the others. He was tanned almost golden. Tousled sun-kissed hair fell to his shoulders in waves any woman would give her eye teeth to have. He had a body to die for. The guy was hot—and he knew it. And, the personality inside the sex-on-a-stick wrapping was genuinely all-American hero.

He stirred her, but it was pure lust. Love had diminished long ago.

"I dunno; it sounds like I might have to get you a big dose of Penicillin, or something. I'll have to ask— well, I'll ask one of the guys what the medic gave him for that when he was in Saigon. He'll know what to do about your...ah, condition."

She slapped his shoulder. His skin was hot to the touch, raw energy over taut muscles. Damn, but the man pushed her buttons!

"Don't you dare. What's the deal, sneaking up on me now?"

He sighed, holding his hands up in surrender. "You got me. I snuck up on you, right in front of all these tourists. I did it, I can't deny it—and I planned to give you a big hug from behind, but then I heard the conversation and decided to keep my hands to myself." He smiled, and her belly did the strange little floppy thing it had always done when he smiled a certain way. She suspected he knew exactly what he was doing, too.

"That's a good thing, then. Keep your hands to yourself." It took every ounce of self-restraint not to throw herself into his arms. Wanting something but knowing better...such a drag, on so many levels.

"It's not my hands that I'm worried about."

Behind her, Uncle Ted snorted. The others were quiet, and she knew they ate up every word. Later, at the house, she'd suffer the good-natured ribbing she was sure they were already concocting in their minds.

"Worry about everything, buddy. Everything."

Neil stuck a thumb toward the water. "Swim?"

In the Cove, most kids learned to swim before they were out of diapers. Chloe had gotten a late start, but she could hold her own.

"You know it." She turned to check on her uncle. He'd tipped the chair back and covered his face with his NY Mets baseball cap—the picture of relaxation.

Reva glanced up from her book. She looked at the sleeping man, then met Chloe's gaze. She gave a don't-worry-I've-got-this nod.

"Come on, Mama Hen." Neil grabbed her hand and gave a fast squeeze. "Everyone's fine. Time for you to have some fun."

She faced him. For the first time all day, her shoulders didn't feel heavy. Life might not be smooth sailing, but it wasn't that bad. She didn't have her shit together, but at least she knew where it all was. That had to be good enough for now.

And, who could complain about anything with a hot guy beside her?

Time to play, she thought. She pulled her hand from his, turned and headed for the water. At a run. Kicking up sand with every step.

"Last one in's a rotten egg!"

She almost beat him. Almost. She hit the wet, packed sand a moment before he did, but before she could dive, Neil scooped her up from behind. He lifted her into his arms, holding her tight against his chest, and strode into the water.

Cold Atlantic Ocean hit her backside, then covered her up to her shoulders, and still he did not release her.

"Let go—I'll be underwater if you don't let go soon."

"You know I won't let you drown, Chlo. Never."

Chlo. The only person who called her that.

Before he released her, he swept his lips over hers and whispered in her ear, "It's a good thing this water's cold because you make me sizzle. Sizzle, I tell you."

Chapter 3

Three hours later, the tone beneath the two faded striped beach umbrellas was less active than it had been when they arrived. The three S's—sun, sand and sea—had worn everyone to the point of drowsiness.

The picnic basket was empty except for a half bag of mostly crushed potato chips and three sticky snicker doodles. One can of Budweiser, Julia's crumpled, empty pack of Marlboros, and a bread bag filled with discarded wax paper squares leaned against the worn wicker. It had been a feast fit for kings, they'd declared when they devoured it. And, the best fuel for some serious body surfing and wave diving. They'd done both, except for Ted who supervised the more strenuous activities from his spot in the shade.

Chloe opened one eye. Neil was stretched out on the double-wide beach towel beside her. His eyes were open.

"You're supposed to be asleep, like everybody else." She kept her voice low. Her uncle snored from his chair. Reva's nose was still stuck in a law book. The other two women dozed, curled up on towels just a few feet away. "What are you doing watching me?"

"You're not asleep."

"That's not a good answer."

When he favored her with a slow smile—the Elvis smile, she called it in her mind—pulling the left edge of his upper lip high before the right edge moved, her stomach did that fluttery thing it did whenever he smiled that way.

"Didn't think you'd like real answer."

Uh oh. He was probably right but she was a sucker for that smile, so she plowed in to the surf when she should have stayed on the beach. Figuratively, that was. Truthfully, she was so sated, so full and lazy, she doubted she could doggy paddle let alone brave the surf.

"Try me." Two words that had gotten her into more trouble than she cared to recall.

"You sure?"

He gave her an out but she gave it a pass. "I am."

Neil rolled over onto his side and faced her. He leaned an elbow in the sand and put his head on his hand. The breeze sent tendrils of hair into his eyes; he brushed it back while he studied her face.

Instantly she regretted her bravado. They'd been dancing around the thing between them for years. In high school, they'd been the golden couple, the pair everyone thought would be married right after graduation. For a while, she'd thought the same thing.

They had gone to both proms together, slow danced in the gym despite Vietnam's claiming older brothers of their classmates as they swayed to Stairway to Heaven. They were homecoming king and queen, another day marked by sadness. Hard to remember that crisp fall day, when the military sedan delivered bad news yet again. Another family torn to shreds by the horror, and still they pretended it wasn't happening.

Graduation day and for once there was no turmoil in town. No bad news to mar the event—as long as no one turned on the Evening News.

But they'd made their own news that night. Long after the parties were over. Well past closing time at the local hangout. After everyone else had wandered home and turned in, they had made a memory of their own.

Right here on Quinn Beach. The spot where Chloe lost her virginity. The place where they stopped resisting the urges they'd fought for years and did what everyone else assumed they'd already done. The whole Woodstock era had hit even the Cove, and no one figured two kids weren't having fun after football practice.

But they'd had a secret. Kept a vow they'd made to each other, to not commit their bodies until they were adults. Consenting age. Neil had argued he was old enough to be drafted, but the argument did not fly. Chloe promised that if he were called to duty, she would break their vow, but that was the only exception.

She'd wanted to be wholly independent of the schoolgirl bit before she became a real woman. So, when she dropped her clothes at the water's edge and lay in the wet sand with him, it was no frenzied indiscretion. She knew exactly what she was doing.

And she knew what she was going to do when the experience was over.

For his part, Neil made her first time memorable. He caressed every inch of skin, then kissed her until she thought she would lose her mind. He fondled and teased, and showed self-control that she did not know he possessed. When he nudged her legs apart with a knee and covered her body with his, she was ready to meet his need with her own. They matched each other in love the way they had in life, and the consummation of their relationship seemed natural.

Until afterward, when everything went wrong and the shit hit the proverbial fan.

Now, she looked into his eyes and saw the truth they could not conceal. He loved her still, despite what she'd done to him.

But he didn't know the whole truth of that night. He had no idea what had happened later, after she'd broken his heart.

Better to leave the past in the past.

"I changed my mind." She saw the disappointment in his eyes but went on. After all, she was no stranger to letting the guy down. "Maybe we shouldn't go there..."

He glanced behind them. Everyone, except Reva, slept. And she was so involved in her studies the Russians could land on the beach, and until she was covered with borscht, she wouldn't even know it. They were on a crowded beach. Alone.

"In case you've forgotten, we've already been there."

"Don't..."

"You asked, remember? It was cool, acting brave, until the going gets real."

There were so many other things on her mind, weighing on her shoulders night and day, day after day, month after month, that one more bit of crap was sure to break her.

"I can't. Okay? Just give me some space. I-I— damn, you don't get it, do you?" She sat up and would have stood except he grabbed her wrist. She looked down, then met his gaze. "Let go."

Instantly Neil released her. She got up, grabbed her Foster Grants, and set off down the beach. As she adjusted the sunglasses on her nose, she tried to calm herself down.

Deep breath in. Slow exhale. Deep breath in. Slow, easy exhale.

It worked in childbirth, didn't it? Why, oh why, didn't it work any other time?

When she reached the rocks, she climbed. They were deserted, so she had the whole vantage point to herself. She folded her legs, sat on the sun-warmed surface, and stared out to sea.

Breathing couldn't help. Maybe looking at the horizon, wondering what happened when someone hit that point where sea meets sky, would calm her. It had always worked in the past, but the past was gone and the future seemed grim.

She hadn't told anyone, but the Bar Harbor First National had called in the loan she'd taken last year. The one to fix the leaky roof on the main house. She had no idea where she would get the money. First, to pay the bank. Then, to pay the roofer to return for the part of the roof that leaked now. How many Band-Aids would it take to keep the rain out of the old place? And, how long could she hold the waves of reality pounding at the doorstep at bay?

Chapter 4

A line of sweat trailed down her back, and it wasn't just because it was hot. And stiflingly airless. But working in a stuffy linen closet in the middle of summer wasn't as bad as hammering up concrete in the basement, which was also on her to-do list.

Chloe reminded herself to concentrate as she held the small rectangular metal box in two fingers. Wires wove in and out of the box. One had a tail of black tape dangling off it. The others she had already untwisted from each other.

Trying to keep them all from touching, she slid a screwdriver into a back pocket of her shorts and held out her hand.

"Can you hand me that needle-nose pliers?"

Julia reached into the dented red tool box in the center of the hall floor and rustled around. She held something up. "This?"

Chloe shook her head. "Nope. That's a wrench. Pliers. They open and close, like a scissor only not a scissor. I think they have a black handle. Rubber grips, should be, so I don't fry myself in this blasted furnace we're calling a closet."

"You said you turned the electricity off." More rummaging in the box, then she held up a second tool. "This?" Before Chloe could reply, she dropped it back into the box where it crashed against the other tools.

"No, you said black handle. That thing has blue, although how the hell I'm supposed to tell one color from another in the dark is beyond me."

"I unscrewed some fuses. Since the lights are out in the hall, I'm thinking I maybe got the right one for this switch, too. That's it—the black grips, sort of looks like a pointy-nosed thing."

Julia gave the pliers a two-second glare before she placed them in the waiting hand. "Silly looking things if you ask me."

"Agreed. But hopefully they'll let me wiggle these wires out of this little box so I can ditch the box."

She had no idea if what she had in her mind would work or not, but it was the cheapest fix for the problem. She hoped. This morning, she'd jogged to the library and read two pages in an electrician's manual. When she tried to check the book out, she'd been told it was reference material and could not leave the library. Since she couldn't bring the wonky wiring to the manual, she'd tried to memorize what it said about changing out switches.

Not that she wanted to do that. Replacing the switch meant buying a new one. Since the metal box had some singe marks on it, she was hoping to just change it. The metal box wouldn't cost a thing; she'd found three spares in the garage. Why would anyone leave spare metal boxes in a cardboard box in the garage was beyond her, but she didn't care. They were free, and if one could make the switch stop being so damn temperamental—without her having to lay out a thin dime—one of the items on the never-ending list would get a big black line through it.

Chloe freed the first wire. She nudged it away from

the others with a fingertip, then turned the box sideways a little to work another one out. Too late, she realized a Polaroid snapshot would help her remember which hole each wire went back into when it came time for that, but to wait while Julia went to get the camera meant she'd have to stand in the hot closet still longer. Screw it, she thought. Besides, she was pretty sure the camera didn't have any film in it. That peel-off, instant-picture stuff didn't come free, and while it was groovy to see an image materialize like magic, it wasn't worth breaking the bank over.

"You sure you know what you're doing?" Julia's breath was hot against her shoulder. She was so close the smell of her last Marlboro seemed to fill the space.

"No, I don't. Not one damn bit. But if I don't at least try to fix this thing, it's going to flicker forever. Maybe burn this place down while we're sleeping."

Her hair was pulled up into a loose ponytail, but one strand near her right temple had escaped the elastic and hung across her eye. She blew at it, sending it out of her sight, but it fell back. She blew again, but the lock was stubborn. The other woman reached out and tucked it behind her ear.

"Thanks."

"How can you see to do what you don't have a damn clue how to do when you're blinded by your own hair? Not cool." Julia's knack for cutting to the chase was one of the qualities Chloe, and the others, admired most about her. They'd told her that much, many times over during their late-night wine-and-cheese-and-gossip sessions. But sometimes others saw what the person wasn't ready—or willing—to see. It was too bad Julia couldn't straighten her own life out as well as she helped others with theirs.

"Halfway there." She rested for a moment. The box was so small, just a bit longer than the palm of her hand, that it didn't seem possible it could be the cause of so much annoyance. And the wires, they looked harmless enough.

Julia leaned closer and inspected the box; it was still attached to the wall.

"Hard to believe, isn't it?"

She found a lot of things hard to believe. The one that topped today's hard-to-believe hit parade list was that she even had the brass tacks to mess around with something like this. All her life, she had taken the "don't put your finger near the socket—you'll be killed!" admonishment as commandment. Now she stood with wires dangling and a river of sweat snaking into the back waistband of her shorts.

She took a deep breath, then blew it out slowly. The yoga practice she'd been vigilant about helped steady her nerves. Amazing what a couple of internally-whispered *om's* could do for shaking hands.

"What's hard to believe?"

Julia pointed a finger to the wires coming from the plaster. "I just can't wrap my head around the fact that those spaghetti-looking things make light. How is that even possible? Far out, don't you think?"

"It'll be far out if we can get this to stop acting like it's stoned." She turned the box so the two wires still tucked into their respective openings faced up. "Okay, let's get this done. Then we can put it back together and get the hell out of here."

"Amen, sister." Julia picked the spare box up out of the tool box and held it out in her palm. "I've got the replacement. I'm all for sticking it in and scramming. This job gives me the willies—and I'm not the one holding the juice."

Chloe pushed the thought that she was the one in the danger zone out of her head. Too late to turn back now.

"Hey, thanks for helping me with this." She grabbed the wire that dangled black tape in the tiny jaws of the pliers. "You're a great assistant, and I mean that. I'm glad I don't have to do this alone."

"No worries. I've got your back." Julia tapped her on the shoulder, an encouraging gesture that went wild.

Chloe's hand, as sweat-slicked as her back, slipped. The pliers jerked against the wire.

Pop! Pop-pop-pop!

Sparks flew. Sizzling, smoky scents filled the air.

Julia screamed.

Chloe dropped the box when it started to spark. The surge that traveled through her fingertips and up her arm sent her backward. She fell into the other woman, and they both landed in a heap on the hard floorboards.

She scrambled backward into the hallway.

"Shit!" Her fingers had already begun to blister.

Julia stopped shrieking when the switch stopped hissing and crackling. She sniffed. "What the hell is that smell?" She leaned forward, placed her face near the burned fingers. "Oh my god, it's you. Damn, you're electrocuted!"

Wild laughter bubbled up from somewhere deep inside her. She didn't try to stop, as she hugged her hand to her chest. When she began to laugh, Julia gasped.

"Oh, shit. You're wacked out, aren't you? Hang in there, I'll get some help."

She started to rise, but Chloe grabbed her wrist with her good hand and held her tight. Shaking her head, she swallowed the new round of laughter and said, "No, I'm not electrocuted. I'm just—shit, I don't know. Surprised. Relieved. Damn, my fingers hurt!"

They both looked at the spot where she'd been shocked. It was angry looking, and the blisters were growing.

Tears welled in Julia's eyes. "When I said I had your back, I didn't mean to fry your front!"

Chapter 5

If she hit the local hardware store, it would be all over town before dinnertime that she had nearly killed herself. Like the kids' game, Clue, where everyone tried to decipher the murder, guessing who did what, where and with which weapon.

Chloe didn't intend to be the day's guessing game. She wasn't about to be held up alongside ill-fated Colonel Mustard, knocked off in the drawing room with a lead pipe. Besides, Chloe Monroe, in the linen closet with a bad switch was dull as dirt by comparison.

No, when she went out it should be more dramatic. Although frying had left its impression...

Bar Harbor, the nearest "big town", was just a short ride. And on a gorgeous day, riding the sweet Suzuki GS 750 was a pleasure trip. She'd have rather gone solo, but since the closet incident, Julia was stuck to her like Bazooka to a sneaker bottom.

All of the girls had ridden with her on the bike, a '77 she'd scored when a guy in town decided he needed something bigger, so they knew how to respond to basic maneuvers. When she turned into the Plaza parking lot, Julia leaned into the turn behind her. They pulled in so smoothly her Harley-loving driving instructor would've been proud—if Hank been around to see the move. He, like so many others, hadn't made it home from 'Nam alive.

Damn ridiculous way to die had been her thought when she heard the news. But when the initial wave of disbelief passed, she had realized Hank, a hard-riding, mean-looking pussycat in disguise, would've loved the way he checked out. The chopper had gone down in a blaze, killing every Marine unlucky enough to be over the godforsaken rice paddy that bright morning. Accounts from the chopper behind theirs indicated a burst of white light as the missile struck the bird, then a red fireball as they fell to earth. All against a clear, brilliant blue sky.

Red, white and blue. It was a fitting way for Hank to head to heaven.

That is, if there actually was a heaven. Which side of the fence she was on about the whole heaven thing was yet to be determined. It was right up there with a God who would allow anything like the Vietnam conflict, Napalm, and Ho Chi Minh City's atrocities to exist.

A VW Bug, covered with flower decals, backed out of the space in front of the hardware store, so she slipped in. Kicking the stand down and angling the bike's front wheel a bit—another of Hank's tips to always hang to the left, which of course he said with a straight face even though the sexual implication made his brown eyes gleam—she shut the bike down.

Silence after the roar and vibration, a letdown every time.

"Go ahead." Making sure the bike didn't tip, she waited for Julia to get off before she swung her own leg over. Julia was already unbuckling the helmet she wore, so she added, "Just put it on the seat. We'll be in and out so fast, no one's going to lift it."

Julia followed directions, but when she shook her hair out of the knot she'd made to keep it inside the helmet, she said, "You need another one of those. No one has ever accused me of being Miss Prim and Proper, but even I know everyone on a motorcycle should be protected."

"Candyass."

"You did not just say that. To me? Me?"

They stepped onto the sidewalk running in front of the row of stores. There were the usual assortment of shops, most intended to cater more to locals than tourists. No glitzy t-shirts in store windows or tacky, seashell-crusted doodads plastered with red sale stickers here. No, just the ordinary. Aside from the hardware store, there was a pet store, pizzeria, and ice cream shop. Down at the far end, The Quick Set. As far as Chloe could tell, no one who came out of the beauty parlor looked any different from anyone else who walked out its doors. Same style, no matter who sat in one of its faded red vinyl chairs. She hadn't been in the place since before junior prom, and didn't figure she'd ever go back in. At least the long, free style she had always worn required very little maintenance. Every month or so, she snipped the ends with an embroidery scissor, the way she trimmed the floss off her designs when she finished sewing.

They paused in the shade. The bike afforded a breeze when in motion, but the sun still beat mercilessly on its riders.

"Yes, you." She wiped the back of a forearm across her forehead. No sense touching more with the fingers than she had to. They'd washed and bandaged them, but they still hurt like hell. Two Bayer aspirin hadn't put a dent in the pain. "Moaning and groaning about helmets—where's your sense of adventure?"

"I lost it in the linen closet."

"Damn shame, that."

"And you know I'm right. Everyone who rides that thing should wear a helmet. It's got nothing to do with being a candyass—which I'm not, by the way. Reva, maybe. She's candyass material, but me? Never."

Chloe was glad Julia lived in the house. She had some hard edges, and there were mornings when she wasn't altogether pleasant, but she had a good heart.

"All right, I take it back." She pulled open the heavy door and let the other woman pass. Following on Julia's heels, she added, "And you're right about the helmet. It's just that a second one costs bread. And that is something we both know is in short supply right now."

Her part-time job, three shifts a week counseling abused women at an agency on the other side of Bar Harbor, paid for necessities and her share of the household expenses but not much more. It was enough that she stayed ahead of her college loan payments. Knowing that the contents of her head were technically on loan unsettled her. That debt couldn't be paid off quickly enough to suit her.

"How about if I loan you the cash? You can pay it back whenever you want, no sweat."

Hard around the edges, but soft-hearted, flashed though Chloe's mind.

"Sweet of you to offer, but no, thanks. I'll put up a sign on the board at the grocery. Maybe somebody's got one they want to get rid of."

The hardware store was empty, except for two guys

sitting behind the counter. They both held guitars and did not stop playing. Chloe and Julia paused, listening to the melody while the men waited for their approval.

Julia did not let them hang. She flashed a thumbs up. "Groovy."

Both nodded, and grinned. They had near-matching long, bushy handlebar moustaches. Brothers, if Chloe's guess was right.

"Carlos himself would approve of the way you're playing *Oye Como Va*. I hear he gave a wicked rendition at Woodstock." Santana albums were an indulgence, but one that was worth sacrificing in another area for. The man could play the guitar like no one else alive.

"Were you in Bethel? Did you hear him?" The guy closest to the door stopped playing, laying his elbows on the guitar and giving each of them a thorough once-over. The up-down-back up look men gave women, the one that usually lingered on the breast area before finding its way to the female face. He was a pro at it, and swept them over in a heartbeat. When he met their gazes, first one, then the other, he asked again, "Were you?"

Julia surprised her when she admitted she had been there.

"Really?" Chloe wracked her brain, knowing full well that if a piece of information that cool had been shared, she would remember. "You never told me you were at Woodstock."

A fast shrug. "You never asked."

The guy chuckled, strumming again. "You must've been just a kid. What? Six, seven, tops?"

Julia raised an eyebrow. "Twelve. And I was with

my parents, who were there mostly to hear the music. It was fun. Dirty, but fun."

The other hardware store musician looked up. "I hear they're going to have another Woodstock, kind of a Woodstock Two, you know? That's what people say, anyway."

Rumors had swirled for years, but until someone began selling tickets to an event at the old farm, she wasn't loading a backpack. "I'll believe it when it happens."

"Well, sure…but it would be worth the trip if it does happen. That's all I'm saying." He paused, then asked, "What can I do you for? Just come in to talk about music, or do you need something?"

"The music was a bonus. We need one of these." Chloe held up the blackened fuse. "Actually, we need seven."

"Whoa! That's something we don't see every day." The men exchanged amused grins. "Which one of you chicks tried to blow the house up?"

"She did." Julia pointed at the bandaged hand. "And it was a pretty big show, too."

"I'll bet it was." A long, low whistle from the man who had checked them out so well. "I noticed that but, ah…let's just say I noticed other things more."

The telltale sign of an impending headache, the steady throbbing in her temples, made her words sharper than she intended. "Right, my boobs trump my roasted fingers. I get it. Now, where are the fuses?"

Five minutes later, they were getting back on the Suzuki. As she buckled the helmet in place, Julia wrinkled her brow. "Hey, are you okay?"

"Just tired, I guess."

She straddled the bike, pulling it upright. When the other woman sat behind her, she handed over the paper bag containing the box of fuses. "Hold this, please. I sure don't want to lose them and have to go back in there with the tit inspectors again."

"Aw, they're harmless. Men just being men, is all." She tucked the bag down the front of her middy top. "There. That'll give 'em something to look at, won't it?"

"You're something else. Men have treated you like crap, yet you don't get rattled when they look at you like you're tonight's dinner and they're starving cannibals. I'm not that nice, Julia. Not by a long shot. I see too much shit at work to find those guys amusing."

She started the engine and let it idle a minute before she backed up. A Buick waited, ready to slide into the parking space as she had done to the car that occupied it before them. The plaza was getting crowded with vehicles, people dashing in on their way home from work.

When she stopped at the exit, putting both feet on the ground and waiting for traffic to show an opening so she could pull out, Julia leaned forward. She spoke loudly, her mouth just inches from Chloe's left ear.

"I learned a long time ago to let things roll off my back. Men think they rule the world. We know they don't. Why should we care what they think? When they act like cavemen, they're just making fools of themselves. Don't take it to heart. It's not worth it."

"You're right. Again." She pulled out into traffic. The road back to Lobster Cove was winding, and with this many cars headed that way, she'd have to talk less and pay attention more.

When they came to a four-way stop, she pulled behind an open-top Jeep. Three teenage boys, two with cans of Pabst in their hands, waved at them. She nodded, taking their appreciative cheers at the sight of females on a motorcycle in stride.

"See? Men are all boys at heart. Isn't it easier to just smile at their ridiculousness, instead of letting them under your skin?"

Before she could answer, the guys hollered a warning. When they pointed, dropping their beer and screaming, she glanced in the rear view mirror attached to the handlebars. She caught movement, big and red, coming fast.

And then, she heard her screams meld with Julia's as the bike flew out from under them and they skidded across the pavement.

Chapter 6

The emergency department at Bar Harbor's small hospital was nearly empty.

Across the hallway, a young mother in the early stages of labor. They listened to her lovey-dovey murmurs stuck between contractions and all-out how-could-you-do-this-to-me screams directed at a bearded man who looked as if he might never, ever do anything to produce this result again. Ever. He left the room when she unceremoniously—and colorfully—threw him out and slunk back in when summoned. He paced a line in front of the door, staring at the floor and shaking his head.

In the next cubicle, there was a man who had fallen off a ladder cleaning the gutters on his house. The white curtain could not muffle his wife's harangue. Clearly annoyed she'd missed her mahjong game for what she called "this childish stunt" but which the orthopedic surgeon termed a high tibia fracture claimed everyone's attention. The nurse who took vitals from Chloe and Julia just shrugged when the wife called the man a jackass.

She tugged at the collar of the baby-blue hospital Johnny. Julia had tied it so tightly in the back that she felt nearly strangled by the ugly thing every time she moved. Which, granted, she wasn't doing a lot of. Her left side had been cleaned and disinfected, but until the doctor took a look and gave his opinion, it could not be bandaged. So, not much movement, because between the choking neckline, blistered fingertips, and road rash along her side, she was not at her best.

If anyone had to take the brunt of the accident, she was glad it was her and not Julia. Other than a burn from the exhaust pipe she'd landed on when the bike fell—and she fell on top of it—Julia was unscathed. To her credit, she wasn't even too shaken up. Maybe the five Marlboros she'd smoked while they waited for the police to arrive had calmed her down.

Chloe would've been wired for sound if she'd puffed her way through a quarter-pack of cigs but she was sensitive to tobacco. Sometimes even a smoky restaurant made her head spin.

Different strokes for different folks, she guessed.

"Are you having any pain?" The nurse folded the blood pressure cuff and stuck it into her pocket. The starched white uniform had massive pockets, one on each hip. From the other, she pulled a Bic and clicked it. She made a note on the clipboard lying across Chloe's thighs. "Miss?"

A man, dressed in a white physician's coat over a pair of faded blue jeans and blue button-down shirt, appeared in the doorway. Initially she thought he was going for the fallen man, but he merely peeked into that cubicle, assuring its occupants the specialist was on his way. Then, he stood at the foot of her bed, crossed his arms, and smiled.

And she could not tell anyone, not even if her life depended on it, what the nurse asked. The question had been struck from her mind the instant she got a glimpse at the handsome doc's pearly whites.

"Miss?" The nurse clicked the Bic several times. "Any pain?"

Oh, right. Pain.

Chloe shook her head. In the distance, sounding very far away, she heard Julia snicker.

"Okey dokey, then." The nurse handed the chart to the doctor. When she brushed past him, she said, "Doctor, the patient is ready for you. Real ready."

He did not respond to the woman's sarcasm. There was no doubt that she gave him an intentional jab, followed by a withering smirk, but that didn't faze him, either.

A quick look at the metal folder chart, then to Julia. Back at the chart, which he closed with a snap, before he smiled and locked gazes with Chloe.

"You must be the lovely Chloe. I'm Doctor Brown, and I'll be treating you today." He held out a hand, so she put hers in his. His skin was warm, and he slid a lazy thumb across the crest of her palm before he released her.

"Uh…ah, hi. I'm—well, you know, I'm Chloe." Even to her own ears, she sounded like a blithering fool so she shut her mouth.

"Chloe Monroe, right?" He didn't wait for an answer before looking down at her left hand. Running a fingertip over her bare finger, he said, "Mrs. Monroe? Or Miss? Or do you prefer Ms.?"

She swallowed. Hard. Tingles shot up her hand, and they had absolutely nothing to do with the bandaged tips of her burned fingers.

"Not Mrs." It came out as a near-whisper, so she cleared her throat. "Not Miss or Ms., either. Chloe— just Chloe. That'll do."

When he smiled she could not look away. "Such a pretty name." He became more businesslike when the man in the next cubicle began shouting for the nurse. "Now, I hear you had a pretty unfortunate meeting with the pavement. A motorcycle accident?"

"Yeah. It wasn't good."

She glanced at Julia, who was sitting in a pea-green vinyl chair in the corner. The wall behind her was a ghastly shade of pink, so between the blue Johnny, green chair, and horrid wall, it was like being in a Crayola nightmare.

"Not good at all." Julia agreed. Somewhere she'd found gum and snapped it now. Chloe realized her own mouth, and by default her breath, probably could do with a little Trident, but she couldn't very well ask, and her friend wasn't offering.

"The way I see it, it could have been worse, ladies. You could both be downstairs in the morgue, but instead you're here. Guests in my ED."

"Ed?" Chloe was not up on hospital lingo.

"Still have your tonsils?"

"Ah, yeah. They're exactly where they were the day I was born." She hoped they were, anyway. "What's that got to do with the accident?"

"Not a damn thing." He went to the sink beside the bed, turned the water on, and palmed his hand over an industrial-sized bar of soap. While he lathered, rinsed, and dried off, he said, "You see, most kids end up here when they've got appendicitis. Or a broken foot. Or tonsillitis. So, if you'd had an attack of the pus-filled, agony-inducing tonsils, you'd have been in a unit like this and would know ED stands for Emergency Department."

Duh. Heat warmed her cheeks, so she grinned. "How'd you know I never had appendicitis? Or a broken foot?"

"I read your chart. You were questioned about past issues. Appendicitis? Heart failure? High blood pressure? Broken bones? No, no, no and no." He lowered his voice conspiratorially and leaned close. "Currently pregnant? No."

So those questions hadn't been just a pain in the ass formality.

"I guess you ask all that stuff for a reason." She raised an eyebrow and kept her tone light. "Now I know there's no Ed hanging around the place."

"Nope. No Ed. Just me." He lifted the edge of the hospital gown, exposing her side but preserving her modesty. A bit of side boob showed, but his gaze remained lower. "You've got a helluva rash there, but it's been cleaned out well enough that it should heal without too much trouble. I'm going to write a script for an antibiotic cream. Apply morning and night. Keep it clean. Dry. You can shower, just don't take a bath until it's fully closed. And, any questions, call your family physician."

Pulling her gown back into place, he folded his hands near his waist and smiled.

"Okay, thanks. Any idea how long it'll take before it heals enough to go in the water? Not in the tub, but at the beach? I…well, I live in Lobster Cove, and every day is beach day in the Cove. You understand."

"I do understand. It's not that far between here and there, believe me. So, the beach? Well, I'd give it time to scab over. You don't want any sand in there, so a good, solid week. Any other questions?"

"No, you've covered everything."

"The nurse will come back in and bandage your side. I'll have her send you home with some samples for tonight, the ointment as well as some extra bandages. That way you're set until tomorrow. If I recall, the little pharmacy on Main Street in the Cove might be closed by the time you get there. And I want the ointment on first thing in the morning. So...are you sure you don't have any questions for me?"

"I'm sure."

He flipped open her chart and scrawled something on the last sheet of paper. Tossing the chart onto the foot of the bed, he gave her a sun-dimming smile.

"Well, that takes care of that." He put his thumbs in his jean pockets. Rolled back onto the heels of the worn Frye boots on his feet. "Now we can get to the important stuff."

"Excuse me?"

He didn't bat an eye. Grinning like a cat in the only ray of porch sunshine, he said, "The important stuff. You see, I just signed my name on your file. So I've officially released you from my care. That means, no doctor-patient relationship breach when I ask you out."

Chloe was vaguely aware that Julia slipped from the room when he launched into the small speech.

She blinked. Once. Twice. Hard to believe this gorgeous man was flirting with her, especially when she must look like—and probably smell like—crap.

Chapter 7

No one really knew how old the oak tree was. Everyone who saw it guessed at its age, but anyone who had been around when the massive tree was small was long gone. There wasn't anyone in the Cove who could recall a time the tree hadn't been there, probably because in all of their lifetimes, it always had been.

Six thin slate markers, slightly tilted and very worn, stood beneath it. Two said Sweet and on a third the "wee" was discernible, so assuming it had at one time said Sweet made sense. The rest were marked Fisher. On two there were anchor carvings in the upper corner, so they were probably seafaring men.

The small graveyard beneath the tree wasn't the only such spot in the village. Before the Lobster Cove Cemetery existed, families buried their loved ones in their backyards. Some homeowners had had the cemetery association disinter the remains from their properties and reinter them among the oldest headstones on the west side of the cemetery. Others never bothered, so scattered in with patios, sandboxes and flower beds stood grave markers.

"I'm not sure we should be sitting under this old tree." Reva had, for once, left her textbook inside. She put her head back and stared upward. "Does everyone see how the trunk is cracked? Up about twenty feet, near the big branch? Looks like it could snap any minute."

"They're all big branches, silly." Julia squinted, following the line Reva's pointed finger made. "I see it now. It looks like the tree was hit by lightning, doesn't it?"

"You're right, it does. Gabby, do you see that? I think the tree was hit in a storm."

Gabby peered up into the branches. She shrugged. "Honestly? Doesn't matter a bit to me, just as long as it doesn't keel over while I'm under it."

Julia raised an eyebrow. "Every woman for herself, huh?"

"That's right. If you hear it crack, run like hell, all of you." The emery board she held stilled as she looked at each of them in turn. "You'll know which way to go—just follow me. I've got better things to do than get squashed by a tree, I'll tell you that much."

Reva nodded, as if the tree issue was solved. "Lightning. Has to be."

The radio was tuned to the local station. Set on the coast, the reception wasn't great, so aside from Bar Harbor's news station or their classical music broadcast, WLOB was the only choice. Thankfully, they played popular hits.

She took a sip of wine, watching her uncle over the rim of the glass.

His lips twitched so hard he put a hand over his mouth. They were seated in a loose circle in the motley assortment of lawn chairs they pulled from the shed every spring. Most, like everything else in the place, had seen better days, but they were still comfortable enough. Besides, they were better than the alternative, sitting on the ground.

"What?" She loved seeing him smile. He hadn't been happy when she and Julia walked in, bandaged and dirty. Carrying the replacement fuses hadn't helped, either, because he insisted he had known all along the power company wasn't responsible for the house having no electricity. When he asked what happened, neither she nor Julia gave up either story— power or motorcycle accident. The other two women had made dinner while they showered. Uncle Ted insisted on replacing the fuses himself, so to keep him from scolding her further Chloe had let him.

With full bellies, everyone seemed mellower. And, with the air cooling down, attitudes were slightly adjusted.

She was glad he'd stopped glowering at her. The smile was a vast improvement.

"What, what?" He grinned fully now, pulling her into the game they'd played since she was a child. She rose to the bait.

"Oh, you know what, all right," she replied. "I know you know what—and I'm going to wait until I know what, too."

"Okay, we'll both wait!" The first time she could recall that they had shared the absurd exchange, she had been about eight. The nonsense had brought giggles instead of tears, and she'd been able to relay the tale of being bullied on the playground by a boy named Bill Hunt. He'd screamed at her, spittle flying from his mouth to her face after he'd cut in line at the swingset. It had been awful, and she'd been upset but unwilling to talk about it at first. That is, until the silly game.

Uncle Ted had accompanied her to school the next morning. And Bill Hunt apologized in front of the entire class. He never bullied her again, and she was pretty sure he didn't bother anyone else, either. His family moved out west the following year, but the What game, as it came to be known, stayed.

Uncle Ted shrugged. One leg crossed over the other knee, a casual pose that left the hem of his bell bottoms dangling so his ankle was exposed. A summer tan, with white feet where his sneakers hit.

She supposed she could have let the grin pass, but she was curious. He looked good—strong, fit and happy. Her heart soared. He was all she had left in the world, and she wanted to keep him as long as she could. Forever, if possible.

"Come on, what gives? I caught you laughing."

"Okay, you win. I was laughing." He flashed her a peace sign, two fingers of his right hand in the v shape, as he smiled from behind them.

"And you're still laughing." Julia pointed out.

Dappled sunlight cut the shade, dancing on Ted's hair as he looked at each of them in turn.

"I don't want to sound like an old sap or anything, but I'm content. I'm glad to be here, with all of you. It's not a drag, living with you ladies." He smoothed his moustache, weighing his words. "I don't know where I'd be if you all weren't here with me. I was the old fart who almost couldn't go to 'Nam. Squeaked in under the wire, almost had to stay home, right? Well, who would guess I'd just about come back in a bag."

"But you didn't." Reva smiled.

"And we're glad you didn't." Julia rubbed the back of a hand over her nose. "Very glad."

"What's in your head, Uncle?" Chloe considered getting up to hug him, but he'd gone from smiling to serious. No telling how emotional he felt; embarrassing him could make the conversation take a turn.

"It's just that I'm feeling very blessed right now, that's all. We're here, under this majestic tree, sharing some songs and spending some time. What more could a man want?"

"Not a damn thing." Julia giggled. "Except maybe some pot. That, I wouldn't say no to. Not after the day we had."

"Well, there goes that sweet moment..." Reva shook her head. Turning to the man a few feet away, she added, "I wouldn't want to be anywhere but here right now. Thanks for having me in your home."

He grinned. "*Mi gato es su gato.*"

"You did that on purpose. Your Spanish is better than mine." Gabby inspected a nail, giving it a final swipe with the emery board. "But if I had a cat, I'd share him with you, too. Those two look like cats with canaries in their mouths." She jabbed the newly filed finger.

The idea made Chloe chuckle.

"We do not." She turned and met Julia's gaze. "Do we?"

"I'm afraid we do, sister."

"Why don't you tell us what happened today? The no-light zone, the fingers all bandaged up, Julia's burned leg, and whatever it was that made you two late for dinner." Reva ticked items off on her fingers.

"Nothing to tell." She patted her side. She'd worn a baggy t-shirt to conceal the bandage.

"What about the scrape on the bike's gas tank?" Her uncle's tone had turned serious again. He wasn't sharing houses or cats now. The joking moment had passed.

"Nothing to tell." Looking for backup, she hit Julia with a stare. "Is there?"

She could see she was going to be ratted out a second before Julia opened her mouth. The gleam in the eyes gave it away.

"Oh, hell yes, there's something to tell. And, if you're not going to cough up the details, I will."

"But—"

"But nothing, sugar. That man is hot, and you're keeping it all to yourself."

The other women sat forward. It galled her that they were so shocked she had anything to do with a man—especially a sexy one. They could at least act like it wasn't such a big deal.

"Am I sure I want to hear about this?" Her uncle acted scandalized but she saw through it.

"Woo hoo, you've been keeping the good stuff from us!" Gabby leaned over so far her breasts practically fell from the low-neck shirt she wore.

"Uh, Gab, you're about to pop out." Reva pointed. Turning to Julia while Gabby adjusted her assets, she asked, "Where did she find this sexy man? Don't keep us waiting—this is better than wondering if the stupid tree's going to fall on us."

"The where of it isn't what matters." Julia winked at Chloe, then faced the others. "The important thing is—you're all going to see Mr. Hot Pants when he comes to pick her up for their date tomorrow night."

Chapter 8

"Is it too much to ask, to have enough hot water to rinse my hair?" She squinted at the tarnished shower head, where water trickled in a quickly cooling spray. Shampoo made her right eye sting, so she closed it and gave a frustrated scream.

There were no locks on the old doors, so Reva entered. "Are you okay? Not doing a Janet Leigh thing in there, are you?"

Last week the local theatre had rerun the old Alfred Hitchcock film, *Psycho*. The pivotal scene, where the beautiful actress gets murdered in the shower by the deranged hotel owner had them all peeking behind the shower curtain before turning the water on. Surprisingly, the one most affected was the brilliant law student. Apparently even a logical mind is susceptible to having her wits frightened out of her.

"No such luck." She knuckled her eye, rubbing and blinking until the sting subsided. "I've got shampoo in my hair—and in one eye, which is probably beet red by now—and the hot water—which was never hot to begin with, only warm-ish—is giving out."

Reva's hair was nearly waist length, and thick. "So not cool. That happened to me two days ago. I stood in the shower—waiting for the Bates guy to come with his knife—for fifteen minutes with the water turned off. I figured that if I waited, more would heat up."

"Smart move, but I don't have time to wait." She angled her head beneath the cool water, scrubbing her scalp to rid the tangles of as much Gee Your Hair Smells Terrific as possible. The water grew cold too fast for her liking, so she turned the faucet off and grabbed the towel hanging over the chrome shower curtain rod.

The pipes clanged in protest. Two rapid bumps, then a bigger bang.

"That doesn't sound good." Reva moved aside a small step and leaned further over the sink when Chloe stepped out of the shower. The fluorescent light fixture shone down on her, so she lifted her face to it and plucked her eyebrows with a tiny pair of tweezers.

"It's not good." She patted herself dry, taking care not to be too rough with her side. The road rash was already healing, so she had discontinued keeping it bandaged. The air, she thought, would do it some good. And her fingers were better, too. The blisters had subsided, and it wasn't horrible to pick things up anymore. "I don't know what the banging noises are, just that they can't be any good for the system. Neil says it's probably air in the lines, and he could come over and maybe do something about it, but I passed."

"What? Why not take the help?" She scrunched her nose up and targeted a hair between her brows.

"What's up with that tweezer? It's so little—how can you even grab anything with that thing?"

Reva looked from her reflection to the instrument in her hand. "I know, it's not good for much of anything. I had a better pair, but I lost them last week at the pier. I went down with a book to read and got a splinter in my foot. So I pulled it out with the tweezer I had in my backpack—and promptly dropped the stupid thing. The tweezer, not the splinter. It slipped between the dock boards on the pier—right into the water."

"Ugh, that stinks." She opened her cosmetic bag and took out her own tweezer. "Here. Use mine—just not on the dock."

Reva heaved a sigh of relief. "Thanks. These are my back-up pair, but I see now they're pretty useless."

She tossed them into the wicker wastebasket. "Am I in your way?"

"Nope. Just going to dry off, comb out this mess, and slap some mascara on."

Ted had his own bathroom on the first floor, so the others were used to sharing the facilities. It was almost like being in the college dorm again. Everyone shared pretty much everything, but no one abused the share-and-share-alike atmosphere. When the Tampax was getting empty, whoever was using them picked up another of the all-important blue boxes. Same thing for shampoo, cream rinse, and even everyone's favorite, "touchably soft" Rave hairspray. They had two blow dryers, a basket filled with curling irons, and Gabby's hair diffuser. The round thing fit on the nozzle of an ordinary hair dryer, and almost magically created a headful of waves—or in Gabby's case, lush curls.

Chloe's hair fell naturally into the Farrah-inspired cut she'd been wearing recently. As long as she brushed the wings into place and didn't do anything that required a lot of hair flipping while it dried, she was ready to go. And the occasional embroidery scissor trim kept her tidy. Now, she parted her hair in the middle, standing behind Reva and using the same mirror. She combed the layers into place, smoothing a bit of

Dippity-Do along the roots to give it some lift and called it good.

"I wish mine would do that." Reva met her gaze in the mirror. "So pretty, the way it curls around your face. And the color—honey with streaks of gold—I don't think you realize how stunning you are."

Chloe had always figured she was on the ordinary side. Average, not unfortunate looking but not drop-dead gorgeous, either. She'd had her share of male attention, but she'd never really considered herself anything spectacular. Certainly not stunning.

"You're sweet, but I don't agree." She gave herself a critical assessment. Hair was good, Reva was right about that. Eyes, a pretty shade of hazel. She would have preferred brown, or blue, but hazel worked. One was redder than the other right now, courtesy of the bad water heater and flowery shampoo. She shrugged. "I see someone who could fade into a crowd. I'm nothing special. But you, our dear brain child, are another matter entirely. What I wouldn't give for that gorgeous, straight, black-as-night hair."

Reva's Asian ancestry gifted her with flawless alabaster skin, wide brown eyes, and hair that fell to her waist in a gleaming black drape. She was petite, exotic, and definitely more stunning than anyone else in the house.

"No, not wise. If I tried to do the Farrah Fawcett look with this unending black mess? Oh, it would be a droop-in-my-face disaster. No curl. No wave. Just straight—and no color. Black is not a color, you realize that, don't you?" Reva pulled a face at herself in the mirror. Then, she smiled. "Never going to be one of Charlie's Angels this way, am I?"

"That makes two of us. And who wants to be an angel, anyway? I'd rather be a little devil any day of the week."

Gabby showed up just then, pushing open the door that had been only half closed. She looked from one to the other. "What's so funny?"

Reva waved the tweezer in the air. "Just deciding it's more fun to be devilish than angelic. I bet the good doctor will think that's groovy tonight, having Ms. Wild Thing on his hands instead of Miss Prim and Proper."

"Stop. I haven't been a wild thing in a long time." She twisted the cap off her Maybelline mascara and began to work on her lashes. "And I'm not going to be wild tonight, either…I don't think…"

"Ha! I love it—you're considering playing doctor with the doctor." Gabby crossed the small space, reached onto the wicker shelf above the toilet, and retrieved her cosmetic bag. It was considerably larger than Chloe's bag. "Well, sit over there. That's right, put the lid down and park yourself on the throne. We're not going to let you get out of here with just a bit of mascara and a spritz of Charlie, are we, Reva?"

Accepting she had no option, Chloe did as she was told, even surrendering her mascara into Reva's outstretched hand. The two women peered intently at her face, and for a long, silent minute she knew how an insect under a microscope must feel.

"Eyes?" Reva asked.

"Smoky, don't you think?" Gabby pulled out an assortment of eye shadows. An eyeliner brush and cake of liner followed. She put the items on the toilet tank. Zipped her bag closed, put it back on the shelf, and brushed a finger along Chloe's brows. "Good, they're fine the way they are. Nice arch, by the way."

"Thanks. Don't make me look too funky, okay? I don't want to scare the guy."

"Relax. We're going to bring out the sexy in you, in such a big way the doc is going to need CPR."

Reva nodded her agreement. "That's right. CPR—and you're going to give it to him. Oh! Lips?"

"Close your eyes." Gabby began to apply shadow, using soft, feathery strokes. She relaxed under the competent touch. She hadn't wanted to seem overly eager to impress her date, but he had already seen her in a hospital gown so making a decent impression wouldn't hurt.

"I'm thinking red." She heard the sound of a cap sliding off a tube. "What do you think? This is my favorite—I keep it for special occasions."

"Hot damn, that's fabulous! What's it called? I want one of those." Gabby began to work on the second eye.

"'Moonlight Madness'—but it's discontinued. A Revlon shade that was replaced by something more sedate, I think."

"Probably because it set the shelves on fire."

When she tried to open her eyes to see the fiery lipstick, Gabby said, "Keep 'em closed, sister. We've got you on this one. And you're going to be so hot by the time we're done, Doctor Hunk is going to need more than CPR. He's going to need a fire extinguisher—for his pants. You're going to set that man aflame with desire tonight—and we're going to want a full report in the morning."

"That's right." Reva giggled. "A full report—and

don't leave out the juicy bits, either. We've got them coming, don't we, Gabby?"

"We do."

"That's right, we do. After all, it's not every day I share my Moonlight Madness!"

Chapter 9

She had to hand it to him. The doctor was slick. He'd pulled up to the house in a vintage red Mustang. On time. Wearing gray slacks, black loafers, and a brightly-patterned shirt that looked both silky and expensive. He carried a huge cluster of white-and-pink peonies that smelled like heaven—and handed them to her when she opened the door. A quick peck on the cheek was enough to let her know that he not only looked hot, but smelled delicious.

When he'd suggested they head to the Mingo Grill, halfway between Lobster Cove and Bar Harbor, she'd agreed. Chloe had wanted to see the inside of the place for a long time. It was, as were so many other things, more than her wallet could afford.

The way a man handles a car is a good indication of how he loves a woman. She'd been watching him drive, taking the curves in the coast-hugging road with confidence and control. Most of the time he just used his left hand, resting the right either on his thigh or the shift stick.

"Did you really grow those flowers?" The first lull in conversation; it gave her too much time to consider how the man "drove" in bed, so she said the first decent thing that popped into her head.

A low chuckle. "You sound surprised."

"I am. A little bit. I mean, it's not every day you

meet a guy who knows his way around a garden."

There was a small vegetable patch at the house, in the only corner the huge oak didn't shadow. It produced enough tomatoes, lettuce, and cucumbers for salads in the summer. And, an occasional watermelon. But she'd always been the one to tend it. Uncle Ted kept far from it; his only comment had been that he'd help with it when she grew something he could smoke. So far, that hadn't happened.

"Ah, so it's the old flower power stereotype, is it? You think I'm a girly man for stopping to smell the roses?"

Teasing felt natural, so she gave it right back.

"I should've known."

"Okay, I'll bite. Should've known what?"

"That you have a thing for roses, too." A long, dramatic sigh. "That's it. I'm out. Now that I know there're roses to be competed against, I'm pitching the white towel in."

Kyle slowed. Ahead, traffic had come to a near-crawl.

"Ah, so that's the way you work, is it? A non-competition clause?"

"Pretty much."

He glanced over and his smile made her mouth water; she was so hungry to feel his lips on hers. A current buzzed in the air between them, similar to the jolt she'd gotten from the house wiring but without the blistering and pain.

"Explain, please." He took his hand off the wheel and waved it toward the line of cars ahead of them. "Doesn't look like we're going anywhere fast."

"It's just that a woman wonders when—and if—a

guy will make that big show—flower-wise. Roses? They're the big guns of flowers. Everyone knows that."

He had been staring at the cars in front of them. They'd reached another bend in the road, so seeing past the four cars directly ahead wasn't an option. There was no telling how long the line stretched, or why they were idling.

"Yeah, we guys get that. Roses mean something, and the colors make the meaning even more intense. So what does that have to do with my having flowers in my garden? Or being a joker who cuts his own flowers to take to a pretty woman on their first of what he hopes to be many dates?"

Hopes to be many. Wow, the guy didn't let any grass grow under his feet.

"Not a joker. You misunderstand entirely." She grinned when he turned and met her gaze.

"Make me understand, please. I'm not sure I would've confessed to the peonies being homegrown if I knew it would've unsettled you. The last thing I want to do is…" His gaze dropped and lingered on her lips, before he met her eyes again. "Unsettle you, Chloe."

"It's not that big a deal. I was teasing you, is all." Her hands had been folded on her lap, but she lifted the left one and held it palm up. Kyle caught it. Gently pulled it down until it rested on the shift beneath his. He did not crush her healing fingertips, but his touch warmed her and sent a fresh wave of tingles along her nerve endings.

"And I'm teasing you right back." He gave her hand a tiny squeeze. "But I'm still curious about the flower thing. Help a guy out. That way I don't step in something and embarrass myself."

She doubted he knew how to embarrass himself. The other men she'd dated, and there had been a good number of them, were amateurs by comparison. Granted, the evening had just barely begun, but if it continued in this vein, it was sure to be one of those once-in-a-lifetime, unforgettable nights.

"It's just that we wonder if a guy will bring roses. Make the big decision to go buy them, choose a color, show up at the door. It's not an everyday bouquet of carnations or daisies. Are you with me so far?"

He nodded, a small smile playing around the corners of his oh, so-tempting lips. She ignored the urge to kiss him and went on.

"So if a man has a flower garden at his disposal, he can conceivably bring roses any time. No thought. No intention. Nothing. Nada. Zip. Zero. Zilch. He might just want to impress, maybe make it the home-run night, if you get my drift."

He raised an eyebrow, sending it hiding beneath the wave that fell onto his forehead.

"I get your drift, all right."

"So, you see…a guy with flowers in his back pocket, so to speak? Awful hard to figure out. Get it?"

He looked through the windshield, so she checked as well. The cars ahead had not budged. The guy in front of them had shut his engine off.

He turned toward her with a puzzled expression in his eyes.

"This traffic…anyhow, I do get it. But in my defense, I chose peonies because they are one of my favorite flowers. They smell like what I imagine heaven must smell like, and they remind me of you…all ruffled, wavy, sexy layers that make a man want to lean in close and inhale their beauty."

He paused, gave her hand another tender squeeze. Chloe was at an absolute loss for words, so she kept her mouth shut. Better, sometimes, to keep a lid on it rather than make a fool of oneself, which was surely what she'd do now, given that no man had ever spoken to her so sweetly before. Never.

"I bought the house with its gardens already there. All I have to do is keep them up, and I admit I have a bit of help with that. But I promise, I won't bring roses—any color roses—until we're at the rose-bearing stage." He shook his head. "And I'm not the kind of guy who plies a woman with flowers to score a 'home run'—damn, are there really men who do things like that? If I become intimate with a woman, it's because we both want to share something special, not because I've won her over with roses. Or anything else, for that matter."

He was sexy before the flower speech. Now, he sent her hormones into overdrive. And, he tugged her heartstrings.

A shout came through the rolled-down windows. They looked up as a man rounded the curve, running on the yellow center line. He called to every car he passed.

"A doctor! Anyone a doctor? Please—we need a doctor!"

Kyle opened his door and stepped out. "I'm a doctor."

The man grabbed his arm. "Please—you gotta come. There's a kid—he's hurt real bad!"

Without looking back, her date sprinted down the street.

Chloe followed, not even considering they'd left

the keys in the Mustang, her handbag on the passenger side floorboards, and the doors wide open.

Chapter 10

A cluster partially obscured the figure on the pavement in the right lane. A blue Ford pick-up truck pointed nose-down into the ditch at the side of the road. Beyond it, a guard wire separating macadam from rocky shoreline.

"Outta the way—we've got a doctor here!"

The shouts of the guy who'd found them got people's attention, and the crowd opened up. Kyle went right through the bodies as if they weren't there, and when he reached the victim, he fell to his knees.

Chloe kept tight on his heels, but when she saw the child lying on the street, she froze. Her hand, the one still warm from Kyle's touch, rose to cover her mouth.

The boy couldn't be more than eleven. Twelve, tops. He wore a striped t-shirt, jeans and black Converse sneakers. A baseball cap lay in the gravel. Further on, a green bicycle, its front tire mangled.

If she didn't know better, she'd think he slept. With one leg twisted at a horrible angle beneath him, the boy was completely motionless. Two women knelt beside him. One had tears streaming down her cheeks. A man stood near the kid's bike, his face buried in his hands. The sound of his anguish made gooseflesh appear on Chloe's arms.

Kyle took the boy's wrist in his hand. Then, he put his fingers on the slender neck. Covering the center of the t-shirt with one hand, he looked at the woman nearest him.

"Has he moved at all?"

She shook her head. "No. And, I don't think he's breathing. I can't-it isn't-there's no—"

The crying man wailed louder. "I didn't see him! Oh, God—I didn't mean to hit the kid. He slid—shit, he slid on the damn gravel—one minute he was on the side—then, oh God—"

Kyle looked around. When he spotted her, he motioned her forward with a nod. He was already reaching into his pants pocket when she knelt beside him.

"I need a lighter. And a pen. A Bic, one of the ones with the hard plastic on the outside."

He pulled out a pocketknife and flipped it open. His gaze held hers, forcing her to forget the child beside them. "Fast, Chloe. His life depends on it."

She stood, and turned to the crowd.

"A pen. Anyone, a pen? And I need a lighter. Who smokes?"

He spoke loudly. "Someone find a phone. Call 911."

Voices from the crowd. "A lady ran to that house—across the street. She called."

"Yeah, a lady called. Should be someone coming any minute now."

"Kid gonna be okay?"

"Doc, what do you think?"

Kyle ignored the crowd as they peppered him with questions.

A man with a cigarette hanging out of his mouth dug in his pocket and pulled out a yellow Bic lighter.

He handed it to her. "Keep it. I got more."

"Thanks." She looked to the others. "A pen? Anyone?"

Two ballpoints were offered, but she held out for what he wanted.

Finally, after what felt like twenty minutes but was really less than two, a woman held one up. She'd dumped her purse onto the pavement and had scattered its contents in the mad scramble to find the pen. Keys, tampons, a pack of Newport Lights, a wallet, and the other detritus hidden in a big purse surrounded her feet, but she smiled as she waved the pen.

"Here! Its cap is missing—does that matter?"

Chloe grabbed it. "I don't think so—thanks!"

She knelt beside Kyle and held out the items.

The boy had not moved, not that she could see, except that his head had been tilted back. Her date had a hand on the smooth forehead, and held the child in position.

He spoke quickly. "Take the guts out of the pen."

She stuck a fingernail under the blue cap at the top of the transparent tube and flicked it. The rest slid out when she gave it a good yank. Tossing the ink cartridge onto the ground beside her, she held it out to him.

He shook his head. "No, hold it for now. I'll tell you when I need it." He held up the pocket knife. "The lighter."

She lit it with her thumb. He held the blade in the flame, shooting her a look.

"You okay?"

Chloe swallowed. She wanted to scream but nodded instead. "You're not really going to do this, are you?"

He took the knife out of the flame, wiped it on his trouser leg, and gave her a quick grin. "We're going to do this."

It happened so fast she didn't have time to think. He stuck the point into the boy's throat, opening his windpipe. He dropped the knife, stuck his finger into the slit, and reached a bloody hand toward her.

"Pen."

She handed it to him, and seconds later, he'd inserted it into the child's body. Almost instantly, the boy began to move. Kyle held the pen barrel in place, leaning close to the patient's face. He made eye contact with the boy.

"Hey, it's okay. I'm a doctor, and you're doing great. Hey, my name is Kyle. We're going to go to the hospital now. I'm going to ride with you—you'll never be alone. I'm here, and you're going to be just fine. No, don't try to move."

They heard sirens. Around them, people began to back up, making room for the help that was finally coming.

He never looked away from the boy, who had begun to moan.

"Chloe? You okay to drive?"

She nodded.

"Chloe?"

It was a struggle to find her voice, but she did. "Yes."

"Good. You did great, honey. Now, if you wouldn't mind following us to the hospital. I'll meet you there, after I get my friend here settled. Think you can do that?"

A cop pushed the crowd back even further as an

ambulance rolled to a stop beside them. The back door opened, and two uniformed men alighted, dragging a gurney.

"Yes."

She started to rise, but his voice stilled her. A glance, just a quick, single-heartbeat look from the child into her eyes, but it was enough.

"Thank you, honey. You were wonderful."

Chapter 11

Honey. He'd called her honey—not once, but twice. And, she hadn't realized it until the hum of the car's engine was the only sound—aside from her pounding heart, that is.

When the ambulance pulled out, the crowd returned to their cars. Onlookers, their attention taken from the Nightly News or dinner tables, filtered back into their homes. A stretch of cottages dotted the far side of the road overlooking the ocean. Summer people, mostly with children in tow, returned to their rentals. All had a story to tell, and most shook their heads as a policeman retrieved the boy's Schwinn and stowed it in the trunk of his patrol car.

Chloe had waited until the ambulance doors slapped shut before hurrying back to the car. She'd wanted to sit for a few minutes, catch her breath, and let her hands stop shaking, but traffic behind her didn't allow that luxury. So she put the car in gear and began to drive, following the bumper ahead of her with mindless precision.

Brake lights flashed, but it took almost too long to react. Her foot came down hard on the brakes, and she avoided ramming the chrome with just inches to spare.

"Danger, danger Will Robinson," she muttered. When the car ahead moved forward, she followed but as soon as an opening on the shoulder came up, she pulled off. She cut the engine, took a deep breath, and just sat still.

When she was a kid, she and Uncle Ted watched *Lost in Space*, a television show about the Robinson family who were stranded on a distant planet. They used their wits to combat every obstacle that came their way, and with the help of their trusty robot always managed to stay alive.

The robot's most important duty was to warn of impending danger. Usually the little boy in the family, Will, was with him whenever something was about to go drastically wrong.

It was the robot's voice she heard in her head as she nearly collided with the other car.

"Get a grip." She inhaled as deeply as her too-tight bra allowed, held the breath, then let it escape past her lips in a slow, steady stream. "So he called me honey. He probably didn't even realize he did it—shit, he was saving a little boy's life at the time."

A vision of the child, lying on the hard road, filled her mind.

"Oh, my God." Chloe crossed her arms, placed them on the steering wheel, and put her head down. The lump in her throat felt big enough to choke her. Then, she recalled seeing Kyle thrust a knife blade into the tender skin at the base of that boy's throat, and the tears started to fall. "Oh my God." She wondered if the parents had been called yet. Wondered how awful it must be to send your child out into the world perfectly fine—probably smiling, even—to have him busted up by the grill on a truck.

She said a quick prayer, not just for the kid but for his parents, as well. It didn't come without a struggle, the so-called word with the higher power, but at least she tried. For that broken boy, she would do almost anything. Even talk with God.

Part of her work at the center involved trying to persuade women their children would benefit from their mother's leaving an abusive relationship. So often, the battered women she counseled claimed to stay for their children's sakes. They could not—or would not—concede that a single parent family trumped one where the innocent watched their mother being abused.

Almost before the ink on her diploma dried, she realized that a mother's love is limitless. Some women would do anything for their children, including being tossed around by the man who fathered those children.

A few—so very few—were willing to put themselves first, expecting the family dynamic would eventually benefit from a more peaceful environment.

No mother she'd met had been willing to give up a child in favor of a man. That, the strength of a mother's love, was what kept her going. Helping the women she met was a small way of making up for the mothers who weren't loving enough to do what was best for their children.

The boy's mother—and hopefully he had a father in the picture—would be at the hospital by now. Kyle would still be busy with his patient so lingering until the wobbliness left her limbs wasn't a bad idea.

I might have been a good mother, she thought. One day, I might have made the right decisions for me—and for a child.

Dwelling on would have, could have, or should haves was futile. Chloe hitched a breath and sniffed.

A sharp rapping on the door frame startled her into

lifting her head. The window was rolled down, so the face peering into the car was less than a foot away.

"Miss? Are you okay?"

The man was old enough to be her grandfather, with more wrinkles than an elephant's ankle, and dressed in dusty overalls paired with a washed-out navy blue t-shirt. Wiry white hair covered tanned forearms. When he leaned an arm on the door, she caught a whiff of fish.

Cod, most likely. That's what was running this week. Last week, too.

She met his gaze. "I'm fine, thanks."

His cornflower-blue eyes were kind. "Now, I'm no rocket scientist, but a pretty young lady, dressed to kill and driving a fancy car wouldn't be sitting on the side of the road crying if she was fine. Fine is what people who mostly aren't fine say."

She sniffed, wishing for a Kleenex. Not worth looking in her purse, because she never carried tissues. Why bother? She hated crying and wasn't a big sneezer, so any time she stuck one in her purse it ended up shredded and covered with bits of Life Savers.

Knuckling the tears from beneath her eyes, she attempted a smile. "Really, I'm okay. Just a little bit…" She shrugged. "Shaky, I guess." Pointing a thumb to the roadway behind the car, she added, "There was an accident about a mile back."

He nodded. "I know. I was stuck in the traffic. Heard it was a kid, on a bike. I sure hope he's okay."

"My—" Her what? Boyfriend status didn't come with the first date, especially when the date hadn't even technically taken place. "I, ah, saw the boy. He was pretty banged up."

"Oh, man, that's not cool. I was afraid it was something bad." He pulled a pack of Marlboros from the pocket of his overalls, shook one up, and offered it to her. She declined, so he took it for himself and lit it. Blowing a long, thin stream of smoke over his left shoulder, he asked, "Think the little fella's gonna make it? Or was he crushed too badly? You know, these things are heavy, and a kid? Well, meeting a car on a bike must feel as shitty as a bug smashing a windshield. Man, what a bummer…"

"I—well, I hear you but I think—I hope, anyway—he's going to make it. My date is a doctor, and he ran to help." She swallowed hard, trying to push the squishy noise the boy's throat made when Kyle opened it with a knife from her head. "This is his car. My date, not the kid's, obviously. That would be silly, saying the kid was in a car because damn it, if he had been in a car we wouldn't be talking, would we?"

The man lifted one bushy white eyebrow when she began to babble. And, knowing she was jabbering didn't mean she could just instantly stop. The urge to laugh bubbled up inside her—but she pushed it down. Too bad she didn't smoke cigarettes. It would give her something besides the boy to think about.

"So, you're taking your date's car where?"

She cleared her throat and tried to keep her voice steady. "The hospital. He went in the ambulance with the boy, so I'm bringing his car."

"Not much of a date, is it?" A lop-sided grin as he flicked the butt to the ground.

"No, it isn't. And, it's our first date." She didn't know why she added that, but now it was out.

"Quite a memory-maker, as first dates go. Me and

the missus? We had corned beef and cabbage at her aunt's place, just a couple of miles from here, in Lobster Cove. Our first date, as it was. Not near as memorable as yours, but I hope it works out as well for you and your doctor as it has for me and the missus."

"You got married?"

"Three months after that first date, I asked her to be my wife. The rest, as they say, is history." He raised the eyebrow again. "In school, I always slept through history. Dull as dirt, that old stuff."

He looked so serious she kept a straight face. But when he wiggled his brows, she knew he was waiting for a reaction so she smiled. "Been married long?"

"Thirty-five years next November. Planning a trip down to Florida, a kind of surprise for the lady who's put up with my guff all these years." He scratched his cheek, giving a speculative gaze that she did not try to avoid. "So, think you're okay to drive now?"

"I'm fine." When he opened his mouth, she held up a hand. It was steady. "Really, this time I'm telling the truth. I was just a little shook up before. You know, feeling like I'd seen an accident or something. I'm okay now. Really."

He nodded. "Good enough. So, you're headed to Bar Harbor, then?"

"I am." She took another deep breath. "That's the plan, anyway."

"Well, seeing as I'm headed there myself, I'll follow you up the coast. If you feel like you can't drive, put your flashers on and pull over. I've got your back—oh, I guess we haven't been introduced, have we?" Sticking a hand in through the open window, he said, "Carl Titchell. Born and bred in the Cove, and at your service."

They shook. His hand was calloused but the touch was gentle.

"Chloe Monroe. The Cove isn't very big, why haven't we met before?" When he released her, she put her hand on the ignition key. It was hard to tell how much time had passed since Kyle left for the hospital. She didn't want him thinking she'd taken his car on a joyride.

"Hard to say. We have a place just to the south of the village. I guess if you aren't looking to buy fish, our paths wouldn't cross."

"Well, I'm glad you came up on me now." She flashed a smile as she turned the key. The car roared to life, so she pressed the gas once for the heck of it. It was just a thrill to hear the big Super Cobra Jet V8 engine—a real change from the Suzuki she was used to. "Thank you."

"Hey, no problem. We take care of our own here. I'm just glad you're okay." He pointed to the brown truck parked behind her. "Remember, I'm right there. Take it slow and easy, and we'll get you to the doc. No speeding in this Fastback baby—not tonight. You've had quite a shock and probably haven't had dinner yet, so it's no wonder you need an escort."

"Again, thank you."

"Again, no problem." He winked, then turned to walk back to his truck. "It was a pleasure meeting you, miss. When you see the doctor, please tell him a fellow traveler thanks him for taking such good care of humanity. Good karma, that."

Chloe waited until she saw him get into his vehicle. He started it, then flashed his headlights. She checked her side mirror, then pulled back onto the road.

Good karma. The old what-goes-around-comes-around vibe.

If Kyle was going to be repaid for the deed he did tonight—and all the other good deeds he'd probably done in his career—he was going to benefit greatly.

Not me, she thought. She clutched the wheel and followed the road, glad there was no one ahead of her. When karma finds me, I'm shit out of luck.

Chapter 12

This time, Chloe knew where the Emergency Department was located. She pushed through the huge glass swinging doors and into the lobby, her gaze sweeping the noisy room.

In one corner, a young woman wearing an apron over her outfit, holding a child whose cheeks were too rosy by far. She cradled the cranky-looking toddler against her breasts, her hand on his forehead as she worried her bottom lip with her teeth.

A row of green plastic chairs set against the tinted windows held a motley assortment. Bikers, all in black leather, filling the air above them with a cloud of gray cigarette smoke. She caught snippets of their conversation, which wasn't library-quiet by any means.

"Damn, but did you see the guy?" A leather strip held the man's ponytail but could not keep it from whipping across his broad back as he shook his head.

Another guy slapped a thigh, his palm making a loud smack when it hit the leather chaps covering his Levis. "The cat was airborne."

The only woman in the group, also covered from toe to shoulder in black leather, put a hand over her face. "Flying. He was freaking flying, man!"

"If I live to be a hundred—no, a freaking thousand—I'll never forget the way he sailed through the sky."

"Sailed."

"Through the damn sky."

"Like a bird."

The chorus of wonder echoed, then broke out in laughter which gained a disapproving glare from the charge nurse seated behind the high counter.

"A dodo bird, man!"

"Hell, yeah—a dodo bird is right!"

The woman peeked out from between her fingers. She wore leather gloves that fit her like a second skin. "More like dodo bird splat—did you see how he landed? How can you assholes be laughing? He cracked his helmet, man."

They instantly sobered. Shuffled their feet, the heavy boots scraping over the worn linoleum.

"She's right."

"Good thing he didn't crack his skull—"

"Maybe he did."

"My little brother, man—don't say shit like that…"

Chloe looked away when one of the men began to cry. His sobbing was worse than their joking had been, stopping nearly all conversation in the crowded space.

The mother held her child tighter to her chest.

A man with a bloody handkerchief tied around his hand looked over at the bikers, then down at the floor. Even the charge nurse stopped giving the group disapproving glances, suddenly busy with the papers in front of her.

When the nurse looked up, Chloe gave her a small smile.

"Can I help you?" All professional, pushing aside paperwork and holding a pen poised over a clipboard. "You can sign in here—then I'll need your insurance and personal information on some forms."

"No, it's not necessary." She dangled the car keys from her index finger and moved closer to the desk.

"Miss, even if you drove yourself here—which it looks like you did—I still need the forms filled out. Ambulance or walk-in, it's all the same in the ED." The nurse snapped the gum in her mouth, pushed the clipboard and pen across the Formica, and shot Chloe an I'm-in-charge look.

"I just need to see the doctor."

Another gum snap. "Look, you fill out the forms, then you see a doctor. Same rules for everybody."

This was not working. And now that her knees were no longer shaky she realized she was hungry. As if the message went straight from her brain to the rest of her, Chloe's tummy rumbled. Loudly.

The nurse sat back against her chair.

"You a teacher?"

"No—"

"Got one of those icky stomach bugs that's been going around?"

"No, I—"

"Maybe it's just starting then. Fill out the forms, and I'll get you a bucket."

"I don't need a bucket."

"Listen, sweetie, eventually you're gonna need a bucket. Believe me, I've seen more puke this week than I've seen in years." The nurse called over her shoulder to a candy striper who walked past. "Carla? A puke bucket from the closet, please. We've got another gut rumbler here."

Being long on patience had never been high on her list of positive character traits. Roller coasters had never been a favorite, either. Now, her patience for continuing the ride that the evening had become was gone. Not a shred remained.

"I don't need a puke bucket!"

The room fell into stunned silence. The candy striper stopped dead in her tracks. The charge nurse stared, wide-eyed and mouth agape. No one behind her uttered a word, although she did hear a snicker. Maybe two.

A voice, silky smooth, beside her shoulder made her turn.

"That's good to hear."

The nice shirt he'd been wearing was gone. It had been blood-spattered when he'd gotten into the ambulance, so it was probably trash. A damn shame, that. Kyle wore a white medical coat, with a black t-shirt beneath.

She was glad to see him. Again, a calm presence in a maelstrom of crazy.

"Hey." Not the brightest thing to say, but it gave her a chance to take a deep breath. She waved a hand to the nurse, who had had the good sense to shut her mouth so she didn't look like a startled carp anymore. "She thinks I've got some kind of…I don't know…stomach virus or something. I tried to tell her I'm not—well, I'm not sick."

He chuckled and reached a hand out. Placing it on her shoulder, he began to massage, sending tiny, hot sparks of fire dancing from her tight muscles to her center.

"Is that what's going on, then?"

She tried to ignore the heat pooling low in her gut. Hunger, perhaps. More likely, desire—something that stole her breath for an instant.

It was hard to concentrate when his fingers were touching her. Magic fingers, and a magic touch—

He interrupted her daydream with another low, sexy chuckle. "You sure you're okay?"

She shook her head. Her hair fell across his hand. He twined his fingers in the curls, stroking them so softly she wanted to melt.

"I'm fine. It's just some confusion." She pushed the clipboard across the counter and gave the nurse a tight smile. "I said I wanted to see a doctor, and I guess that meant I was on the verge of being sick."

"I'm not sure that's a good thing, being sick when you're looking for me." He put his hands on his hips, which pulled the white coat tight across his chest. She noticed his name tag was not clipped to the pocket, the way it had been the last time she'd been here.

"Stop—you know what I mean."

He turned to the nurse, gave her a wink, and asked, "Did she say I have that effect on her? That she wanted to see me so she could puke, Barbara?"

Barbara put her hands up. "I don't know a thing about how you affect her, Doc. All I know is she said she was here to see a doctor. I figured she was sick, is all."

Chloe met the nurse's gaze. They smiled across the counter now. "Right. I wanted to see a doctor, not be sick."

"Listen, sweetie. You asked for a doctor—you never said nothing about wanting to see Doctor Dreamy here. That's a whole different story." She rose, grabbed a clipboard, and walked toward an open doorway behind the desk. Motioning to the candy striper, she said, "C'mon, let's give the doctor here some breathing room."

Chloe raised an eyebrow and shot him a grin. "Doctor Dreamy?"

He colored. Shrugged. "Hey, don't believe the hospital scuttlebutt. By tomorrow the gossipers will have me married and us expecting twins. Triplets, maybe. That's the way it is around this place." He paused. Raked a hand through his hair. "Do you mind?"

There were worse things than being romantically associated with a hunk, even if the gossip was pure fairytale.

She shook her head. "Nope. My uncle says that when people are busy talking about him, they're not gossiping about someone else. So, let 'em talk; it doesn't make any difference to me. I mean, I'm not the one who has to work here."

Kyle took one step closer, which brought them so close his breath mingled with hers. Again, he smelled wonderfully masculine. The spicy aftershave he wore hadn't diminished, so she inhaled deeply.

"Your uncle is a smart man." His voice lowered. "And you're right, I do have to work here, in Peyton Place of Bar Harbor."

The television series had always been held up as the most gossip-minded show on the air.

When he put his arm around her shoulder and pulled her close, she was too stunned to resist. Not that she would have resisted, anyhow.

The instant before his lips touched hers, he murmured, "I say we give them something to talk about."

Chapter 13

She'd been worried for her life. That's why she'd run. But now seated in a hard plastic chair beside Chloe's desk, "Hope" had turned stubbornly silent.

Chloe pretended to look for something—anything—in a desk drawer. The cold gray steel number was so industrial looking that even the flower power and peace sign stickers she'd plastered on the side nearest the visitors' chair couldn't soften it up. A sparse philodendron trailed over the edge, but it looked as neglected as most, if not all, of the women she counseled.

Her fingers closed around a plastic pencil sharpener. She pulled it, and a blue-leaded drawing pencil, from the drawer. With what she hoped was a voice to inspire confidences, she asked, "Do you draw?"

The young blonde shook her head. When she did, the hair she'd kept draped across her left cheek moved. The bruise was ugly, with swelling that made her face lopsided.

It must hurt like hell. A surge of anger invaded her usual calm. Anger that any man would touch a woman the way this one had been touched. Anger, too, that even with what must be the world's worst headache brewing, the animal was being protected by the one he hurt.

Sometimes the world sucked so bad it made her want to excuse herself from it. Not that she ever would, but that didn't mean she wasn't affected by the brutality she came in contact with. College had given her the facts, and tools for dealing with cases like this one, but there wasn't a book around that could prepare someone for witnessing the suffering one human could inflict upon another.

The blue pencil wasn't in need of sharpening, so she gave it a fast twist before opening the drawer again and tossing it inside. When she glanced at the other woman, she realized she'd sparked some interest, so she dug around and got another pencil. Green.

Chloe took her time sharpening the green pencil. A twist, then a fingertip across the colored point. Another twist. Another fingertip.

"I do." She met the other's gaze and offered a friendly smile. It was imperative she establish some connection. Otherwise, helping someone who wouldn't even share her real name would be nearly impossible. "I guess I fell in love with drawing in kindergarten. One of those kids who carried around the Crayolas everywhere she went." The green pencil joined the blue one in the drawer. The next one out was magenta. She held it up. "My favorite color."

The only sound was the rasp of wood against steel as she shaved the pencil point. When it was nearly perfect, she stopped. Held it up. Blew the bits of shavings off. Then, she put the sharpener and nearly-sharpened pencil in the drawer. Closed it with a gentle push.

A furrow appeared across her visitor's brow. "Aren't you going to finish that one?"

She had left the pencil far from pointy. The lead was still rounded when she returned it.

"Nope."

When the other woman didn't follow up the line of questioning—which was typical of a battered woman, to not ask a question because often the innocent inquiry resulted in being thrown about—she went on.

"I'm leaving that one the way it is because it's my favorite. I use it all the time." She tipped her head toward the framed drawings above her desk. Two scenes. Both Quinn Beach. One showed sunrise. The other, sunset. Both were peppered with magenta streaks in the blue sky.

"You drew them?"

"I did. I know they're not great, but they make me happy. I live in Lobster Cove, so I spend a lot of time on that beach. So many good memories..."

"I think they're pretty neat. I could never do anything like that." A small sigh escaped. It sounded so defeated, Chloe's heart clenched. "Never..."

The moment to break through presented itself, so she pushed the door that had just opened a crack, praying it would open wider.

"You're wrong about that. I think you can do whatever you set your mind to doing." She leaned toward the woman, and when she saw the struggle on the pretty, albeit beaten face, she placed a hand over her nearest knee. The long, flowing tie-dyed skirt hid a slender form. She was careful not to place her hand roughly. Often the worst bruises were concealed from view. "You've got your whole life ahead of you. Yes, you're in a bad spot now, but that doesn't mean it's going to stay that way."

Another sigh. Looking down at her hands, clenched tightly in her lap, she said, "My life is shit. Total shit."

"That can change. I promise, I can help you."

Immediately the victim began to shake her head, the denial coming so quickly it coincided with the last words from Chloe's mouth.

"Nobody can." A tear rolled down the bruised cheek.

"You're wrong. I can—and I will. But, you have to let me. Why don't we start over? I'm Chloe. You are?"

The gaze that met hers was heartbreaking. Emotions scudded across the watery blue eyes like clouds against a stormy sky. Fear—so strong she could almost smell it—came from the pretty woman.

"I told you my name." It was a whisper.

"No, you didn't." She rubbed a comforting fingertip across the knee. "We both know your name isn't Hope Partridge. Good try, though."

A small smile, just an ever-so slight twitch of the lips. "You think?"

"First thing that came to mind, eh?"

She nodded. "Yeah. I guess I didn't think that one out, did I?"

"Well, it looks as if you've been dealing with some pretty heavy shit."

"Yeah." A nod, which uncovered the bruised cheek again. "That's for sure."

Time to seal the deal, Chloe thought. She leaned still closer, so their faces were just a few inches apart.

"I can help you. But first, I need to know your name. No one else will know but me. I give you my word about that—to anyone who asks, you'll be Hope Partridge."

"He'll kill me if he finds me." Spoken so low, had Chloe not heard the words uttered by other women she might have misunderstood. But she saw the truth in the pretty blue eyes.

"I know." She swallowed hard and hoped she could keep the promise she was about to make. "I won't let him do that. I promise."

A long moment of silence, when she wondered if she'd been earnest enough to inspire confidence.

"Jackie." She cleared her throat. "My name is Jackie."

Chapter 14

The sky was dark, the moon bright when Chloe closed the door to the short-lease apartment behind her. She waited until she heard the bolt slide into place on the other side before she walked down the hallway. It was dismal, the kind of place one imagined but never really thought to see. The hall reeked of stale urine, sweat, and underlying all the rest, despair. Trash, mostly cigarette butts and the occasional Hershey's chocolate wrapper, spotted the dirty linoleum.

She inhaled deeply when she exited the building and stood on its small front stoop. It was just one of a row of houses, nondescript and on one of the worst streets in Bar Harbor. Past the year-round residential neighborhoods and further still from the tourist spots, it was definitely on the wrong side of the tracks—if there had been any tracks, that is. It was just a sad street where no one looked too closely at anyone else's life because most were too busy scrambling to eke out an existence in one of the wealthiest burgs on the east coast.

An example of the haves and have-nots, Bar Harbor style.

The rental suited the social workers' needs. The last woman to occupy apartment 2C had vacated barely twenty-four hours ago. Thankfully she had been considerate enough to give the three miniscule rooms a cleaning. The threadbare sheets, laundered and folded with near-military precision, sat stacked on the foot of the lumpy, stained mattress in the bedroom.

Before leaving, Chloe had helped make the bed. Tucked a bottle of milk, a jar of instant coffee, a dozen eggs, a loaf of Wonder bread and some Peter Pan peanut butter in the kitchen cupboards and noisy fridge. She'd rounded on the windows, checking to be sure each was locked and the roller shades were pulled.

Only after she'd done all she could do—for now—did she leave.

After being in the stuffy apartment, breathing hot, humid fresh air was heavenly.

She had driven her bike, and Jackie had followed in her car. It was a rusty Dodge, but it was more than a lot of women had when they left abusive situations. They had parked it in the rickety, leaning garage behind the apartment building. Better to keep it—and Jackie—out of sight in case the man who thought she was his property came looking for her.

Before leaving the office, Chloe had changed into jeans and Keds. Her skirt was stuffed into her backpack, which she shrugged into as she walked over to the curb. She put the helmet on her head and tucked in as much hair as she could fit before fastening the buckle beneath her chin.

Climbing on the bike, she wished things could be different. Wished she didn't have to drive away, back to her normal life where the only thing that went crash in the night was a tile falling from the leaky roof or the pipes as they made steam. Wished she didn't have to leave behind yet another scared, maltreated woman who felt as if she'd never be happy. Valued. Loved.

Damn, but the world could be cruel.

Chloe looked up at the single light burning in what she knew was the apartment's bedroom window. She hoped Jackie would have a restful sleep and begin to heal. They had a long, difficult road ahead, but she had no intention of letting her new friend down. Tonight was the first step forward; and as long as Jackie wanted to go forward, she would stand beside her.

She pulled out, taking the road slow so as not to cause a disturbance. It was, after all, nearly nine o'clock. If anyone had small children behind the sad-looking doors, they should be getting ready for bed.

When she hit the winding, two-lane main drag that led out of town, she gunned it. The roar gave her satisfaction that all the day's paperwork, phone calls and financial wrangling had not been able to provide. For two or three miles, she enjoyed the kiss of warm breezes on her cheeks and the freedom riding brought.

Just before she reached the spot where the boy had been hit on his bike was a mom-and-pop roadside burger joint. She pulled in and parked near the big neon sign that flashed Burgers—Fries—Rings.

Business was brisk inside the small building. She skirted the crowd and headed for the back hallway. A pay phone hung on the wall between the two restrooms. She picked up the slightly greasy black handset, fished a dime from her pocket, dropped the coin into the slot, and dialed. The clicking noise as the big plastic dial rotated from number to number sounded loud in the hallway.

She hoped the person who'd used the telephone before her had washed their hands if they'd come from the bathroom. The thought that they might have head lice flashed through her mind, but she did what she did every time she used a public phone. She pretended it was in the house in Lobster Cove, not attached to a wall beside two stinky bathrooms.

Three rings. Five. After the seventh ring, she shifted from foot to foot and tightened her grip on the receiver.

"Hello?"

Uncle Ted's voice was loud, as usual.

"I thought you weren't going to answer. What took so long?"

"In the back, playing some music for the girls."

The girls. They were such a help, keeping an eye out when she had to work. And all three had taken a course at the Bar Harbor YMCA on resuscitation. If he suddenly keeled over, they would know what to do, and that put Chloe's mind at ease in an enormous way. Of course, he had no idea such a course even existed, and they all planned to keep him in the dark.

"Reva's nose in a book?"

A major exam was on the horizon, so it didn't seem likely her nose would be anywhere else. Nearly crunch time, although with Reva, it was always crunch time.

"Nope. She's got her harmonica. Man, that girl can play!"

She smiled. So, he'd charmed even the Bookworm into having some fun.

"Love it. Hey, have you all eaten? I'm at The Grill—want me to bring anything home?"

"Hmm…"

God, she knew him well. "Onion rings, it is. One order or two?"

"Got enough bread for two?"

Payday was still days away, but she had the trusty Emergency Stash in the side pocket of her wallet. The ten-spot currently folded and stored had been there for over a month. Time to break into the hobo bag's Fort Knox and live a little.

"I have plenty." She rushed to add, "Listen, my dime is almost up. Anything else I can bring home?"

"Nope, that'll do. Thanks, sweet pea. Drive safely—we'll be in the back when you get here. Just follow your ears, and your feet will find the way."

They hung up just as the operator came on to inform her that she needed to insert more coins into the slot if she wanted to continue speaking.

The day had had so many ups and downs she was mentally exhausted. Time for a celebration. She dug the folded bill out. Dropping the wallet into her bag, she calculated how much it would cost to get everyone their own order of onion rings. A feast by the fire pit, certain to lift spirits and bring smiles. She had some change in the bottom of her bag; surely it would be enough to cover five orders of rings.

Chloe headed for the end of the line waiting at the counter. She had one hand in her bag, her fingertips searching for coins, and her gaze on the chalkboard that listed the food prices. Fortunately, the price of onions held steady. She closed a fist around the coins in the corner of her bag, then pulled her hand out.

"Oof!"

The solid wall of spicy-scented muscle she collided with sent the air from her lungs and, embarrassingly, the change from her hand. It scattered at her feet as she looked up into the face of the man she'd just run smack-dab into.

"Oh!" Her gaze met familiar sultry eyes. She blinked. "It's you!"

"Yes, it's me. I'm sorry to nearly run you down this way." Kyle smoothed a hand across her shoulder, sending a ripple of something hot and electric along her nerve endings. "Are you okay?"

Okay was hardly the word for the heat pooling inside her but she nodded. "Fine, thanks."

"Good. I don't think either of us was paying attention to where we were going." He smiled at a little girl who handed him the change that had flown from Chloe's hand. "Thank you, honey. Here, why don't you keep this? Maybe your mom will say yes to an ice cream cone?"

He shot a smile at the woman who accompanied the child. "I'm a doctor; it's a hot night, so ice cream could be a nice way to cool off. Here, I think this should cover a cone for you, too."

He pressed two singles into the child's hand, tugged on one curly ponytail, and raised a questioning brow. "Sound good?"

The woman looked ready to kiss him, but she glanced at Chloe, then the now-jumping-for-joy child. "Thank you...Doctor."

Chloe looked around. There didn't seem to be a man with the two. There was a definite similarity in facial features, so she figured they must be mother and daughter. A fast peek at the twenty-something's hand showed no wedding ring. Other rings, and a ton of bangle bracelets, but no gold band.

She smiled. Leaned close to the child and said, "Doctor Dreamy—that's what he's called. Enjoy your ice cream, ladies!"

Chapter 15

They walked around the side of the house and into the back yard without anyone noticing and stood in the shadows for a minute, listening to the quartet around the fire. Reva made the harmonica sound like an angel's song. Gabby strummed a guitar. In his spare time, Ted had been giving her lessons. They were paying off. She followed his lead smoothly, amplifying the notes and giving dimension to the tune. Julia's fingers tapped a conga drum held between her knees. The rhythm was steady, like a heartbeat, with an occasional five-finger tapping spin to jazz it up.

"Minute by minute by minute, I'll be holding on…"

They weren't the Doobie Brothers but there was heart to the song. Reva, with the harmonica to her lips, was the only one who didn't sing. The others harmonized beautifully.

When the last notes faded and the fireside group looked up, Chloe tipped her head to Kyle.

"Come on, meet the crew." She led, holding the white food bags away from her stomach. She'd driven her bike, and he'd brought the food in his car. It was still hot, and the grease from the onion rings seeped through the white paper. "They're not the Partridge Family, but I love 'em anyway."

The Partridge Family was still on her mind after

the day's events. She wondered how Jackie was doing, but forced herself to push the thought aside.

Concentrate on the moment.

"Hey, hey, look who's here." Uncle Ted propped his guitar against the side of the wooden folding chair he occupied. He stood, holding out a hand. "And I see you've brought a friend."

"Uncle Ted, this is Kyle. Kyle, this is my uncle."

The men shook hands.

"And these pretty ladies are my friends. You already know Julia. This is Reva and Gabby; this is my friend Kyle. Remember, I told you guys about him?"

Reva smiled. "You're the doctor who saved a little boy, aren't you?"

He gave a modest shrug. "I'm the guy who was in the right place at the right time, that's all. Hey, you sounded great. I love music, especially when it's from the heart, the way yours is. Mind if I sit in?"

"Of course we don't mind." Gabby pointed to a wooden glider built for two. "Have a seat."

"We come bearing food, courtesy of the kind man here." Chloe handed each person a bag. They were identical; onion rings and grilled ear of corn in its husk, with an apple turnover for dessert. "We, ah…"

She looked over at him and shook her head. When he grinned, she smiled back.

He held two bags. One he handed to Reva. The other he placed on the table beside Gabby's chair. She was busy putting her guitar back in its case but smiled when he put the bag down.

"We ran into each other. I stopped for dinner on the way home from my shift, and we just—bang!—ran into each other." He waited until she handed him a bag, then motioned to the glider. When they sat, her thigh grazing his, he turned to her and asked, "Or was it more of a whack—not a bang—the collision?"

She tried not to giggle, but it was hard. Reaching a hand into the bag, she pulled out an onion ring. They were just the way she loved them; crispy and browned, and with just a hint of sweetness.

She took a bite. Chewed. Beside her, he did the same. And while the others had begun to eat, she sensed their attention was on them.

"Mmm, I think it was more a kablammy." She looked sideways and saw his focus was on her. And, a grin played around the edges of his mouth as he chewed. She nodded. "Yes, it was definitely a kablammy."

Gabby snorted. "Sounds painful."

Ever the peacemaker, Uncle Ted said, "Well, I'm glad you two ran into each other. It's nice to have an extra for harmony. We've got some Three Dog Night planned, and maybe some Chicago if we can talk Gabby into it."

"Too mellow, Chicago." Gabby took a bite of her apple turnover and groaned. "But after all of this yummy food, I just might need mellow. And a nap."

"Oh, I'm not here for the singing. I can't carry a tune."

It was the first thing that he balked at. The protest over not singing had a hint of desperation to it.

"Don't be silly, Doc. Everyone can carry a tune." Reva gave him a long, quiet look. "You should know that. It's as easy as talking. If you can talk, you can sing."

"Don't try to wiggle out of it." Gabby polished off

the turnover, then focused her attention on the onion rings. She took one from the bag and shook it at him. "We need harmony for Three Dog Night. And, if you can save a kid's life with a twig and a soda can tab, you can sing."

He nearly choked on the food in his mouth. Uncle Ted had handed them each a beer from the cooler beside his chair before they sat down, so he took a long slug of Pabst.

The Blue Ribbon must've sent the food in the right direction, because Kyle cleared his throat as he waved a hand in the air. "It wasn't anything so drastic—or exciting. It was an ordinary pen casing, and a pocketknife. And don't forget Chloe's part in it. I couldn't have asked for a better—or more level-headed—assistant. Without her, I would've been up the creek."

"It's sweet of you to say that, but I didn't do anything. You're the one who saved that kid, not me. I just followed orders and tried to be helpful."

He'd stopped eating. When she met his gaze she forgot she'd been famished just a half-hour ago. The way he looked at her made her heart skip a beat.

"It might not have turned out as well if you weren't there." His tone was soft and tender, his gaze gentle. "Don't sell yourself short; I'm certainly not going to. You were amazing, and I'm very grateful for all you did. The boy's parents are, too. I told them..."

"You told them what?"

He smiled, looking a tad sheepish. "Well..."

"Well...?"

He raised the beer can to his lips and took a slug. "Well, I told them we were on our way to dinner when we found their son."

"That's true. We were."

"Right." He took another pull at the can. "I told them I was taking my girlfriend to dinner when we found their son. And, uh, without your help, I'm not sure what would have happened."

Chapter 16

Chloe leaned the wooden ladder against the wall of the house, toeing the peonies aside so the legs sank down into the soil. She placed a foot on the bottom rung, lifted herself up, and gave a test hop. The ladder settled a bit more, so she climbed the second rung and shook it. No movement, so the old, paint-splattered thing was as steady as it was going to get.

Gabby's guitar lay in the sunshine on a tie-dyed blanket spread across the grass. Its owner stared down at it, chewing her lower lip and frowning. She was still wearing sea foam green baby doll pajamas and had her hands on her hips and feet spread wide.

What a shitty way to start a day. The rain at midnight had sounded so soft and made falling asleep as easy as slipping into the ocean. Her dreams were filled with visions of blue sea, ripe coconuts and pink butterflies flying low over a sun-kissed, sandy beach. When she came down to the kitchen, she was well rested, with a smile in her heart.

Until she saw the gloom on the faces that waited her arrival.

Reva's big, heavy tome, *Jurisprudence in the Modern Age*, suffered the indignity of blow drying, a la Lady Clairol. Julia's wedge sandals were no longer a light beige. The soaking they'd received turned the soft leather a darker shade of brown. A chair and, of course, the rug on the sunroom floor took a hit. But the heartbreaker was Gabby's guitar. Thankfully, it had been in its case, which gave it some protection. The case was shot all to hell, already warping so badly it would never latch properly again.

Uncle Ted had gone for an early tai chi session on the beach, along with some of his cronies, so he had no idea the roof leaked so bad. They would keep it from him if they could, although he had a way of figuring things out even when they tried to hide the truth.

Chloe put her arm around Gabby's shoulders. They trembled beneath her hand.

"God, but this sucks. I'm so sorry, Gabby."

"I feel like a jerk, but I'm kind of attached to that silly guitar."

"It's not silly." A tear slid down her friend's cheek, sending Chloe's spirits sinking further into the depths of despair. It was one thing to be in a leaky boat when the boat was hers, but to pull so many others into the sinking ship was wrong. For an instant she considered asking the girls to leave. But if she did, surely they would lose the house. And it would break Uncle Ted's heart.

She still hadn't figured out how to make the big payment to the bank. No amount of pleading could make them back down, although they did budge a touch on the money's due date. Six months wasn't a long time, but it was a reprieve. Maybe she could figure something out by then. If not, they'd all be looking for new places to live.

A sniff. Gabby knelt and turned the instrument, placing it so the sun warmed the spot on the side that still glistened wetly.

"I don't even know what to say to make this better."

"There's nothing to say, sister." Gabby looked at the house and pointed to the roof. "It's not your fault this happened. No one knew the roof was going to leak."

Chloe stared at the corner, at the spot where most of the deluge had entered. With the big oak spreading wide and throwing so much shade, a slick of moss covered the old shingles. No way to tell what was going on until she got a good look.

"I still feel terrible. Listen, I want you to know, I understand if you decide to move. Really, if you book it out of here, I won't hold it against you. No hard feelings." She couldn't meet the other woman's gaze. Concentrating on the point where her sneakered toe met grass, she added, "The other girls, too. You can tell them, if you want."

Gabby stood and put a hand back on her hip. With the other, she reached for Chloe's arm. Gave a squeeze—so tight that she had to look up.

"Hey—that hurts."

"It was supposed to." Gabby released her but her eyes were stormy when she spoke. "I am not leaving because the stupid roof leaks. That is an idiotic thing to suggest—and I'm not telling the others you even said something like that."

She sighed, waving toward the house. "The place is falling down around us. Damn it, I try so hard, but it's like being a one-armed juggler. No matter how high or hard I throw one ball, the next smacks me on the head before I can catch it. I don't know what I'm going to do. Really, I don't."

Gabby pointed to the guitar. "See that? It's drying. And by tonight, it's going to sound as good as ever. Things take a beating, but they bounce back. And you? You'll bounce, too. This is a little setback, that's all. Keep juggling; you're doing a great job."

"You're sweet for saying that, but I'm not so sure my juggling skills are all that." She took a deep breath as she reached up and pulled her hair into a high ponytail. The scrunchie on her wrist went twice around. She pulled sunglasses down off her forehead and onto her nose. "Well, it's not going to fix itself. I don't want you-know-who to know we're taking on water, so I have to get this done before he gets home."

"Good idea." Gabby headed across the lawn. She paused beside an enormous lilac bush, so big it nearly obscured the back steps. "Hey?"

She was busy shoving tools into her jeans pockets. She grabbed a hammer from the toolbox, then looked up. "What?"

"Your uncle—have you noticed?"

She straightened, giving the question some thought. There had been subtle changes in the man, but she had thought it was wishful thinking on her part. Or, an over-active imagination.

"What do you mean?"

"It's just that he seems stronger lately. Doesn't sleep as much in the afternoons, that sort of thing. The other girls—especially Reva—noticed, too. He just seems…well, better somehow."

Some of the heaviness that invaded her soul since finding the flood lifted. People mattered, things—even houses—less so. The roof would get sorted out, one way or another. Uncle Ted sorting himself out? More headline-worthy.

When she smiled, it came from her heart. "I love it that you've all noticed, too. I…I really thought I imagined it, you know? I just want it so desperately that I…well, damn, I'm glad it's something real."

"It's real. We've been waiting for a sign that he's improving, and I think this might be it. He's changing, and it's all good. Now, we'll just take a note from your uncle." She put a hand on the back screen door and pulled it wide. "He's like a Timex, sister. We've got to do the same."

A giggle, pure relief after the past tense hour. She swung the hammer, testing its weight in her hand. "That's right. He takes a licking—"

Gabby finished the tag line with her. "And keeps on ticking!"

Chapter 17

The roof wasn't as bad as she feared. Where the sunroom, which had been added on a few decades earlier, met the main house there were spots with shingles worn thin. After she'd poked a finger through one, she began pulling them off. It was hot, sticky, dirty work, and she quickly became covered with slime from the moss, but the shingles lifted without too much trouble.

Getting the bad stuff off was one thing. Figuring out how to replace the valley between the roof and siding, and shingle the bare spots, was another entirely. Some of the nails in the asphalt strips were rusted clear through, which made it hard to tell just how the whole thing had been constructed originally, but as near as she could tell, there were three or four nails in each strip of shingles.

Just put it back the way you found it, she told herself. No big deal.

A pile of shredded shingles beside where she squatted had grown enough that it was sliding sideways across the mossy gunk. She grabbed a handful and tossed them over the edge of the roof. When she heard them smack against the ground, a second, bigger, handful followed.

"Hey!"

The voice was as familiar as the beating of her

heart.

"Neil? What are you doing here?"

Shit. Just when she was beginning to get past the leaky fiasco and let her mind wander back to last night, when the hunky doctor had kissed her goodnight. The last thing she needed—and wanted—was this flash from the past. Not when the future looked—finally—rosier than it had in longer than she could remember.

Neil's upper body appeared at the edge of the roof. He smiled at her, then his gaze traveled along the work area.

A long, low whistle. "You've got a mess here."

"No shit, Sherlock." She heaved a bunch of ripped black paper over the edge. The look on his face made her instantly contrite, so she picked up another handful of paper and shrugged before throwing it. "I don't know what this stuff is called but it was under the shingles. It's all torn, so I'm just peeling it up."

He swung a leg over the edge and climbed onto the roof. Nudging her over with his hip so he could kneel beside her, he said, "It's called roofing paper, and yeah, it needs to be replaced. Why didn't you call me? I would've come over anytime and taken care of this."

When she moved sideways, scuttling like a crab along the beach, she slipped. The moss was slimy everywhere, but more so in spots still wet with dew. Chloe's heart lurched, but she caught herself before she went too far.

He reached for her, but she waved him away. "Careful—you'll fall off this damn roof and hit your head."

"Think that hasn't crossed my mind already?" She crawled, ever-so carefully, along the slope until she was back near the top. "The last thing I need is to fall on my head."

"The last thing the concrete needs is for you to crack it with that hard head of yours."

"Did you come up here to make jokes at my expense?"

He shook his head. She noticed he wore his favorite blue shirt tucked into low-riding hip hugger jeans. On his feet, beige suede chukka boots. Not his old ones, either. These were new, which told her he'd come by in the hopes of taking her out.

After practically a lifetime of knowing each other, he'd become too predictable by far.

"No, as a matter of fact, I didn't." He pressed his thumb to the wood she'd exposed. It gave under the pressure, sending small cracks along the board's surface.

"Look, don't wreck it any more than necessary, okay?" She tossed the hammer onto the roof, and it hit near the new cracks. A spider web of smaller lines spread from the dent it created. "Damn it."

Neil didn't say anything for a while, and she was content to just rest. She passed her forearm over her forehead, wiping away a film of perspiration. The mold made her eyes itchy, and she'd been sneezing the whole time she'd been working. Now, she sneezed again, catching the outburst with the back of the arm she'd raised.

He looked at her. "Allergies?"

"I guess."

"*Hmmph.*"

"What's that supposed to mean?"

He gave her a sideways glance. "Thought I knew

everything there was to know about you. Did not know you have allergies. That's something new."

"I didn't know, either. Not until this morning." She paused, sneezed again. "But I doubt you know everything about me."

He met her gaze. "How can you say that? We've known each other forever, remember?"

As if she could ever forget.

"Almost forever." She grinned, hoping to lighten the mood. His eyes were serious, and she was in no mood for one of their "talks"—in fact, she would have preferred root canal to another of the let's-get-serious-about-the-future discussions he sprung on her every few weeks.

"Chloe—"

She cut him off before he could utter another syllable.

"Not now, please." She plowed her fingers through her hair, then realized she'd pulled it up. Untwisting the fabric-covered elastic that held it, she looked down at the roof. "I have a big enough mess in my life right now. I don't think I can handle much more. Really, I don't."

His voice took on an edge, one she'd heard many times in the past. "So now I'm nothing more than another 'mess' in your life?"

"I didn't say that." She stood, leaning on her left leg to compensate for the angle of the roof. "And if you came over here to pick a fight, then mission accomplished."

Neil shook his head, frustration showing plainly in the tanned features. He was a great guy, a great-looking guy, but there was no getting past it. He wasn't "the guy" for her—regardless of how hot and steamy they could get in the back seat of the black Charger he drove when not using the pickup truck.

He stood and took a step, closing the distance between them. His tone was softer when he spoke.

"Listen, I didn't come to argue. Damn, I came to ask you to take a ride along the coast with me. I thought we could grab some lunch, maybe a matinee at the movie theater in Bar Harbor. I know you've got to work tonight; I just figured…"

She waved a slow hand at the debris at their feet.

"You figured I would be polishing my nails or doing something mindless, like weeding the garden, right?"

He nodded. "Kind of."

"I get it, Neil. Really, I do." She pushed the curls back off her face. The humidity made them grow, and with the sun rising higher in the sky she felt entirely too warm. "I didn't expect to be doing this. Believe me, I'd much rather be putting a coat of Maybelline on my fingernails."

"I could've fixed this already. Why didn't you call me?"

She sighed. The answer was obvious—to her—but not so much to him, or else he wouldn't be asking.

"Two reasons: First, it just started leaking last night. I knew it looked kind of shitty up here, but the sunroom was dry until this morning."

"Fair enough. Reason number two?"

Time for the truth. Again. They'd touched on it more than once, but it never seemed to become a part of their lives, this reality of theirs.

"Reason number two? I'm not your problem to

take care of. It's nice of you to offer, but the truth is, we're not going out. We've been over for so long…we both know we just tease each other a bit, just because we can. We're not going anywhere—together, I mean. So why would I call you? My problems are nothing you need to be involved with. Nothing."

He looked as if she'd slapped him across the face. Shaking his head in denial, he took a step closer and tried to put his palm on her cheek. She wanted to pull back but it seemed too cruel, so she let him touch her.

"I want more, and you know that. Damn it, Chloe—I've been waiting for you to come around for years! We were teenagers, for God's sake—you're my one and only, don't you get it? I want more—I don't want to push you but hell, how much can a man take? How long can a guy wait for someone to love him the way he loves her?"

Neil leaned down, but she couldn't do it. She couldn't let him kiss her—not now, and maybe not ever again.

"No, don't—"

Instinct made her step back, out of his reach. Rotten boards sent her crashing through the roof.

"Chloe! No!"

Neil lunged for her, but her foot was already through. She scrabbled for a handhold, but the moss slicked beneath her palms as she fell.

He grabbed her by the arm, nearly yanking it from its socket as gravity pulled her into the hole. Throwing his body down, he laid on his stomach and grabbed her in a bear hug, his arms wrapping around her just beneath her armpits.

When she stopped falling, both legs dangled in

midair somewhere below her. They heard Gabby, Reva, and Julia screaming, but their cries seemed distant.

Chloe felt his breath against her cheek. Her heart thudded so hard it felt as if it were trying to escape her body. She was afraid to move, afraid she'd pull them both into the hole and into a pile of twisted limbs and broken bones.

Slowly, she met his gaze. Gave him a shaky smile.

Licking her lips so she could speak, she whispered, "I guess you got more than you bargained for, didn't you?"

Chapter 18

Quinn Beach was nearly deserted. A group of surfers braved the waves near the rocks.

Chloe and Reva crested the path on the dune that led to the sand. They stopped, placed hands above their eyes to shade the sun, and watched the wave riders. Two men sat on boards, legs dangling in the water, cheering on the two who were upright and, it seemed, racing for shore.

"I never tire of seeing that," Reva said. "It defies logic, watching people stand on water."

"Like magic. They walk—no, run—over the ocean. Too cool for words, really."

The wave beneath the racers dropped off, forcing them to swerve and fall. Each surfaced, grabbed the board attached to their leg, and waved fists in the air with their free hands. Even from the path, they could hear the good-natured exchanges the men threw back and forth.

"Good thing the mommies are home with their little darlings." Reva snorted. "I guess the beach has its own schedule: mornings, for the old folks who get their exercise while smoking their Camels, midday for the tourists, mothers and kiddies, late afternoon and evening for guys like that, who want to have fun without offending anyone, and nighttime…"

"Nighttime…" She touched her side with gentle

fingers, then ran a hand along the outside of her left thigh. "Not quite sure I'm up to any nighttime fun on the beach, to tell the truth. In my mind? Hell, yeah. But this bruised body screams, 'no way!' so nights are off-limits."

"For now." They took their time with the downward slope of the sandy path.

"Yeah, for now." Chloe squeezed the cooling sand between her toes. There was such a grounded feeling that came with being on the beach. It soothed her soul every time she dug her toes into the point where ocean met land. "What about you? Any nighttime fun I should know about?"

Their resident scholar had been involved with another law student for about a year. Everyone—including Reva—thought the match was perfect, but it ended on a sour note. The guy decided dating a law student "cramped" his style, that he needed someone more lively who could take his mind off precedents, procedures, and protocol. She had been crushed, and they tried their best to lift her spirits and show her she was worthy of a better specimen of manhood than any jerk who dumped her like that, but friends could only do so much. Time was the great healer, so six months later, it was possible someone else—and hopefully less of a jackass—had caught her attention.

"No, none of that for me." Reva turned to the horizon with a resolute stare.

She looked ready to walk on water—without a surfboard. If determination had a face, it was the one beside her, Chloe thought.

"Hey, let's cop a squat." She brushed the biggest seashells from the area at their feet with a toe, then folded her legs and sat on the sand. Her friend did the same, pulling her billowing, ankle-length broomstick skirt up around her thighs.

"Not a lot of sun left, but I'm in the library so much that every little bit on these white legs helps." She waved a hand over the legs she kept straight out in front of her. They were alabaster, a tone not seen much in a beach community. Reva leaned over, bumped her shoulder against Chloe's. "I bet your ass isn't as white as my legs are, sister."

Their future lawyer was generally so serious, statements like this were priceless.

She grinned, returning the shoulder bump. Now that they were sitting, it hurt less to move.

"I don't think *anyone's* ass is as white as those sticks of yours." She wasn't sure she should do it, but she plunged in anyway. "You know, it's okay for you to see a guy—or ten—if you want. Not everyone is as big a jerk as—"

Reva held up a hand. Her manicure was perfect, every nail filed to an oval and polished a bland barely-there pink.

"Don't even say that loser's name. Please, I solicit you, don't say it."

"Fine. But you've got to remember that he-who-can't-be-named is a jerk. Not every guy is like him."

"Right. I understand that. Statistically, it's impossible for every single man to be as big an asshole as The Dickhead. But, that doesn't mean I feel compelled to waste my time with any of them."

She gave it one last shot. "But what if you meet someone who's really nice, who respects you and your goals, treats you wonderfully, and makes you feel like a million bucks? What then?"

Reva turned, disbelief plain and accented by the single raised eyebrow. Which, of course, was as polished as every other part of the woman.

"You have just described a myth. A legend. An old wives' tale. That man? The one who you speak of so glibly? He does not exist. I'd be better off selling my law books, the little black pumps I plan to wear during my first trial case and even my goldfish, Pete, and heading up into the Canadian provinces."

"What? I don't get what you're saying—why sell everything and go to Canada?"

A shrug as she turned to face the ocean again. And, in a voice that did not allow for dispute or cross-examination, said, "Because a woman has a better chance of finding Sasquatch than that mythological man you insist exists."

There was no point arguing with a genius, so Chloe accepted the defeat.

They sat in silence for a long while. She was content to let her mind wander, and wonder if her companion was doing the same—or if that brilliant mind even had the capacity to wander.

Finally, a question.

"How do you feel?"

"Well, considering I've been shocked in a closet, slid along the road with my bike, and fallen through a roof, I think I'm doing pretty damn good. Bruised here and there, but I'm still standing, so I think that's an encouraging sign."

Reva shook her head, turned, and gave what the girls in the house called her are-you-crazy,-criminal? look. "I can't believe you think I'm asking how your broken fingernails and scratches are. They're going to heal—what I want to know is, how do you feel inside? I mean, you've got Doctor Dreamy sending loud and clear love signals while Mister Same Old, Same Old wants you to make him 'the happiest man on the face of the earth' and marry him."

The Lou Gehrig reference was one of Uncle Ted's favorites, so it got bandied around a lot in the house. A real lot.

It cut the sting of feeling foolish. She should have realized her bumps and lumps weren't cause enough to take time from studying to head to the beach with her. Now it was clear; this was an information-gathering excursion, when all she'd wanted was a tiny morsel of the peaceful pie.

She jokingly held up the peace sign. "It's all good, sister. My body is healing, my mind is spinning, but it's fine. What's the song say? A good rain is gonna come…?"

"Don't quote Bob Dylan to me."

"Hey, you started with the Gehrig bit."

Reva held up her own fingers in the familiar v shape. "Listen, I hardly realize I even say that anymore. I don't think any of us do."

"I hear you. Uncle Ted has been saying it for so long I don't even remember the first time I heard it."

A young woman, about their age, probably, walked toward them. By her side, a little girl who looked to be about six or seven years old. The kid was cute, with honey-colored curls hanging down her back. She wore purple shorts and a midriff-baring top that had crazy pink daisies on it. She skipped, so that with each step her curls bounced.

"Probably when you were about that age. So, your whole life, practically."

The woman nodded as she passed, but the child stopped. Holding up the two fingers on her left hand, she giggled. "Peace!"

They both turned their hands toward the girl, smiled and in near unison said, "Peace!"

Her smile froze when Chloe saw the child up close.

The face smiling back at her was her own...from twenty years earlier.

Chapter 19

The child's face was haunting. It had to be a coincidence, seeing someone with such a strong resemblance. She tried to tell herself it couldn't be anything else, but that smile, dimples, and eyes were a picture she couldn't get her mind to forget.

If Reva had any thoughts on the matter, she kept them to herself. If she discussed what happened with the others when Chloe wasn't around, well, that was something that couldn't be helped. It felt silly to ask that the incident—if exchanging peace signs on a beach with a stranger's kid could be called that—be hushed up, so she didn't.

Besides, when they got back to the house, she barely had enough time to change into her work clothes, reassure her uncle she was well enough to go to the office, and speed up to Bar Harbor. It was good the fuzz weren't hiding anywhere in ambush, because she put the bike through its paces.

There was always a social worker on duty at the agency. Twenty-four hours a day, seven days a week, they were available to any woman who required their services. It was tough to cover like that, given they really did operate on a shoestring budget and bare-bones staff, but somehow they managed it.

Taking turns on the overnights was part of the job, so they rotated duty. It screwed with a girl's social life, but as long as women were being battered and abused, there was no other way. Until society stepped up to put an end to the barbarism, Chloe and the rest of the social workers knew their obligation to women in the community could not be shirked.

She'd hoped to stop in and visit Jackie before manning the phone, but her timing had been lousy. Falling through the roof, and the subsequent arrangements, explanations and even the foray to the beach had robbed her of a minute to spare.

Ree Bolivar, the oldest member of the team, waited at the door. Her clogs, so often stuck under her desk, were on her feet and the long, flowery shawl she favored was pulled around her shoulders. Somehow, despite being shaped like a barrel, she always looked polished. And, the waist-length, snow-white braid she wore did not ever seem to have a stray hair threatening to come lose. Chloe figured the hairs on the mature woman's head knew better than to give her any trouble.

"I'm sorry—I know I'm late." She dashed into the office without bothering to take her helmet off first. She unbuckled it, freed her hair with a fast shake and apologized again. "Really, I'm sorry."

The other woman waved a hand, sending points of light dancing off the ceiling. Every finger on her right hand wore a ring, including her thumb. "No sweat, chickadee. And if I didn't have a date, I wouldn't be standing here at all." She looked down and scowled at her feet. "Damn shoes—why can't a man take me to a place where shoes are optional?"

There was no good answer for that, and Ree probably didn't expect one, anyway, so Chloe dumped her backpack and the helmet on her desk.

"You've got another date? Same guy as last time?"

"Different gentleman."

"What does that make this week? Two? Three?"

Ree examined her fingernails with a critical eye. They were fluorescent pink, with blue swirls at the tips. She blew on one, then looked over and smiled.

"Four, actually."

She put the helmet beneath the desk, pushed the backpack to the far side, and plopped down into her chair. It squeaked, but she was so used to hearing its oil-thirsty protest she didn't flinch.

"Four? Wow—a man for every night. How do you do that? Spill your secrets, please! I keep reading Cosmo and still can't rack 'em up the way you do."

Ree scanned the street, obviously waiting for Man Number Four to show up. She squinted out the glass panel in the door. A small smile twitched her lips upward.

"That's him. Nice car, too." She looked over and winked. "Listen, they're men, not mysteries. There's no secret to it—smile when they look at you, act like you're listening even if you're not when they go on interminably about whatever it is that makes their boat float, unless they ask for something really, you know, kinky, accommodate them. That's about it, sugar. Follow those suggestions and you'll never have to buy your own dinner again."

She had her hand on the bar across the center of the door and was about to push it open, but Chloe stopped her with a question.

"What about Women's Lib? All the women who burned their bras for us, all the gals who fight for more pay for women and even those suffragettes who marched so we could have the right to vote? Do you think they'd want us to sit by and grin at men just so we don't have to be alone?"

Her colleague gave a little wave to the guy idling at the curb. She smiled at him, then looked toward the desk. The smile still on her face didn't reach her eyes.

"Listen, I didn't ask anyone to burn their underwear for me. And the whole equal pay thing? Between us, I don't think that'll ever happen. More likely men will live in a, I don't know, floating space station, than women get compensated for the work we do. And, as far as those suffragettes? Hell, I think we should kick them in the pants—or those ridiculous long dresses they wore. If it wasn't for them, no one could ever say a woman had anything to do with electing Richard Milhous Nixon to the White House. President Watergate, my ass! I might be old-fashioned, but the tried-and-true ways of a woman getting what she wants are good enough for me. It's a man's world, honey— don't you forget that. Now, lock this door when I leave. And try to have a good night."

Leaving a cloud of Patchouli in her wake, Ree swept out the door. Chloe hoped the man of the evening made her co-worker happy, but personally, she'd much rather buy her own dinner than agree to anything— kinky or not—with random men.

The free love, Woodstock bit had come and gone. She'd done her share of hooking up in college. Now, she wanted more. Even if she didn't know for certain just what she wanted, she knew it was more than what the other woman was doing.

After she locked the door, she shuffled through the day's paperwork. Nothing out of the ordinary to catch her attention. Six women had called and been given appropriate referrals to agencies that catered to their situations. One school nurse touched base, just an assurance that one of the kids belonging to a mother they'd helped find a home two months ago was doing well in his new classroom. They loved hearing stuff like that. Ree had put a big heart around that number on the daily tally. And the food bank had surplus feminine hygiene items it was willing to bring over so they could directly distribute them as needed. Most people never thought of tampons and sanitary pads but a woman fleeing her home had very little room to carry those things. Often she had no means to purchase them, so they did their best to help out on that front.

When she finished reading the day's notes, she went into the small staff kitchen. It was not much bigger than a closet, but it served its purpose. She poured herself a cup of coffee from the pot. It had been freshly brewed, one of the kindnesses Ree bestowed upon whomever followed her shift. She stirred a spoonful of sugar into the hot liquid, rinsed the spoon off, and dropped it into the blue plastic dish drainer beside the sink. She flipped the light switch when she went out.

She sat at her desk, kicked off her shoes, and pulled her feet up under her. The spots beneath her armpits where Neil caught her were sorer, even, than her legs where they'd crashed through the rotten wood. It was still hard to believe it had happened, and only this morning.

Avoiding thinking hard about something—or someone—or in her case, a couple of someones—didn't solve anything, but she sure as hell wasn't going to think about Neil or the little girl now. Not about the house, its decay, or the bills she had no idea how she was going to pay. None of it.

Better to focus on other issues than mine, she thought. The desk phone was old, industrial-looking and often persnickety when it came to making connections. She picked up the handset, looked at the scrap of paper she'd pulled from her pocket, and dialed. The clicks, longer for higher numbers and shorter for lower ones, sounded like they were going through so maybe, just maybe, her luck was on the upswing.

She waited while it rang. She'd told Jackie she could expect a call, but that didn't mean the other woman might not be intimidated by the ringing phone. In her spot, a once-upon-a-time social call could now be a discovered-by-her-assaulter signal. Chloe said a little prayer when the seventh ring still hadn't been answered.

It was possible something happened to Jackie, but she pushed the notion from her mind. In the business, that was always a factor to consider. Unfortunately, bad things happened to good people—which necessitated the existence of social workers like herself.

"Shit, girl, where are you?" She bit her thumbnail as the phone rang for the tenth time.

"Hello?" The voice was flat. Low. Frightened.

Infusing as much warmth as possible into her own tone, she hoped to ease the tension she heard in the single word.

"Hey, sister, it's Chloe. Just calling to see how you're doing, is all."

A sigh of relief, audible over the phone. Then, a nervous giggle. "Oh, thank God, it's you! I—um, I, ah, well…"

"You thought it was him." Heartache that a woman could be so frightened of someone she'd trusted tore through her. It made the job of gaining any remaining trust hard. "Hey, didn't I promise you no one has this number? Really, it's safe. He can't find it."

"I hope you're right. It's just…"

"Hard. I get it. Even though I have no way of knowing how you feel because I've never personally been abused the way you have, I still understand how awful these past months have been for you. And, I know it's tough to leave the past behind."

"The past? If I could I'd burn it—and him, too—to the ground. I'm so over him, over the way he treated me, over the helpless feeling of having no way out of the shittiest situation in the world. Believe me, I want to leave the past."

The outburst showed that Jackie was stronger than she looked and willing to battle her way into a new life. Sometimes it was nearly impossible to instill a sense of anger in a battered woman. This was a very good sign.

"Excellent news. And that's just what we're going to make sure happens for you, that you get a fresh start somewhere else. Somewhere safe. You deserve that."

She took a swallow of her coffee, running through the location possibilities in her mind. There were only so many places a woman could hide in Maine. Most weren't willing to leave the state. If she could talk Jackie into moving to New Hampshire or Vermont, which were both pretty similar to Maine so she'd feel somewhat at home in either place, the odds of eluding the man who thought her his property were far greater than if she stubbornly refused to change states.

"You can't always get what you want." Jackie's voice sounded soft and wistful.

"But if we try, you might get all you need to begin a new life."

She hoped Jackie would get what she needed—and what every woman deserved: freedom.

Chapter 20

As she waited for Pam to show up and relieve her, Chloe ruminated on the night. It had been quiet, so she'd had a lot of time to think. Too much time.

She put her feet up on her desk, which had been cleared and was ready for her next shift. It made sense, having an orderly workplace, when those who came for help so often ran from chaos and were in the worst time of their lives. Living in the tornado. That was the term applied in sociology classes to the point when a life is turned upside down, its contents and people are swirled around and those living the life waited to be spit out of the funnel cloud, wondering if they'd survive. And if there would be any pieces left to pick up after the tornado passed.

So, a tidy desk. Big potted plants arranged around the rooms. Soft music playing in the background. A place to instill confidence.

Except now, the only one in the space had a bad case of the early-morning jitters.

Too much caffeine, not enough sleep, she thought as she drained her coffee mug.

The phone rang. She glanced at the big wall clock. 7:50.

Great. Ten minutes later, and the call would be Pam's. Now, she'd have to deal with it.

"Good morning. Anchor Women's Services, Chloe

speaking."

"Just who I was hoping to find." The voice was smooth, sexy, and not female—and she recognized it instantly.

The tired, cranky funk she'd been cultivating for the past hour was blown right out the open window.

"Well, this is a surprise."

"I called the house. Gabby gave me this number—I hope it's okay I call you at work."

"Of course it's okay. That's what I do; answer phone calls and help out when I can. Except the voice on the other end of the line usually belongs to a woman."

"Hmm…I hope you're not disappointed." A low chuckle. Even over the phone he had the power to make her body warm. "I could pretend to be female, if that's any help…"

"Don't be silly! I'm glad you called. Honestly, I've been sitting here staring at the wall for an hour. Drinking too much coffee. Waiting to go home. This is a nice surprise."

"I'm glad. But your day is ending, while mine is just beginning. I've been at the hospital for maybe an hour. My ED is pretty quiet now, but I know it's going to begin to hop well before lunchtime. So, this is the perfect time to touch base with you. How are you doing? I heard you fell through a roof—are you injured?"

She sighed. Leave it to Gabby to spread the news. "Only my pride. Apparently I'm not the Ms. Fix-It I thought I was."

"Gabby said the sunroom roof is shot—is that where you fell?"

"It is. And it is."

"Hey, I'm not bad with a hammer, if you need someone to repair the thing. I have this weekend free. I'll be happy to take care of it for you."

All her life she'd waited to meet someone who cared enough to step up and support her, just for the sake of putting someone else's—namely hers—needs before their own. Oh, sure, Neil made it clear he would help, but his motives were also clear.

She and the good doctor had only just met, yet he volunteered to work on her rotten roof?

"You're a saint, offering to help."

He laughed. In her mind, she could see the way his eyes twinkled when he was so amused. "Hardly. Just a guy looking to help out, that's all. So, do we have a date to fix your roof? Saturday morning? I'll bring the hammer; you make the coffee?"

How she wished she could say yes.

"Ugh, I hate this, but no, we don't have a hammer-and-coffee date. The roof—well, it's already being fixed by a, ah, guy."

A short silence. "Okay, then. A roofing guy should do a fine job for you. Just stay off it until it's fixed, if you would. I don't want to see you in my ED again."

"So…we're off for Saturday morning?"

Chloe prayed she hadn't pushed too hard. She wanted to see him again, and soon. And, without his hammer.

"Well, I kind of hoped to see you before Saturday. I—ah, hang on…" A beeper sounded, followed by a sigh. "I hate to cut this short, but I've got a multiple vehicle accident on its way in. Listen, if you're not doing anything tonight—dinner? There's a place in

Lobster Cove; I'm sure you're familiar with it. Replaced the burger joint that burned down a few years ago—The Shack, I think it was. The one that burned down. Now, it's a place called The Dockside. Anyhow, they make some great seafood dinners. Burgers, too. And vegetarian, if that's your thing. So…whaddaya say? Dinner? Tonight?"

She heard another beeper go off, and the rushed tone told her the phone call was ending.

"I'd love that. Six?"

A female voice, calling to him. It sounded urgent.

"I'll be right there," he said, presumably to the nurse summoning him. "Um, how about seven?"

"That works. See you then."

"Great. And Chloe? Don't take the shore road home to the Cove. Go around, through the fishing lanes. Longer, but less messy. See you later."

With that, the line went dead in her hand. She looked at the heavy black mouthpiece, wondering what had happened on the road, until the silence was broken by beeping and the operator's voice.

Beep-beep-beep. "Please hang up." *Beep-beep-beep.* "Please hang up." *Beep*—

Chloe hung up just as Pam unlocked the front door and sailed in. It was ten minutes after the hour, and for once she wasn't put out that her replacement had a rotten sense of punctuality.

Chapter 21

The sound of a hammer woke her. Chloe looked at the alarm clock on her bedside table. Three o'clock. She'd gotten a solid five hours of sleep. It wasn't enough to make her feel like bounding from bed, but it would have to do.

She stretched, testing the way her muscles felt when tried. I must be a good healer, she thought, pressing a hand across her ribcage. The motorcycle rash was healed. And the points where she'd hit the roof as well as the places Neil grabbed when he saved her were all much better. Unless she twisted hard to the left, she was pretty close to feeling absolutely normal.

A pair of denim cut-offs hung on the chair beside the bed, so she stepped into them and pulled them over her hips. They were loose again. It was a constant battle to remember to eat, so she lost weight without effort and when she didn't really want to lose it. She had so much else to consider that eating fell to the bottom of her to-do list. It showed, now, in the saggy shorts.

Forgoing a bra, she pulled a baggy t-shirt with the words What's Gnu? printed above a caricature of the big animal over her head. It fell nearly to her hips, effectively concealing the shorts.

As she went downstairs, she prayed Neil would not try to continue their doomed conversation. When would he learn that their so-called love story had ended years ago? He needed to move on. Let go. Live and let live. Someone should tell him that, she decided as she hit the first floor. Someone—as long as it didn't have to be her.

The kitchen was empty. She opened the ancient refrigerator and peered inside. An assortment of items, none of which particularly appealed to her. Not eating was not an option, so she grabbed the milk and let the door slam as she got a bowl from the cupboard.

It was like stepping into a time capsule sometimes, living in a house that had stood for over two hundred years. Rotting beams, faulty wiring, and overgrown trees aside, the place was filled with odds and ends left behind by previous owners. The appliances, including the round-top, forties-era refrigerator, were still being used. The red Fiestaware bowl, chipped on the edge, that held her cereal. There was talk that the red Fiesta was radioactive, but somehow a few pieces avoided being buried in people's backyards. Chloe grabbed a silver spoon from the drainer on the counter. It, too, was a basement find. One of three or four pieces of flatware with the initial S pressed into the handles, it could probably tell stories if it could speak.

Now, it scooped Cap'n Crunch from bowl to mouth.

She went through the kitchen into the sunroom. A blue tarp had been nailed to the ceiling to keep the sky from the space. The hammering was loud here.

Neil was on the roof. She could hide inside or act like a grown-up and go out and say hello. Compliment him on the progress he was hopefully making.

Sometimes it was hell being an adult. Pushing open the door with her hip, she stepped out onto the stoop, avoided being hit in the face by the overgrown lilac growing beside the door and made her way onto the lawn.

She walked to the shade of the oak. Then, she turned and looked up. Neil had already seen her; he stood on the roof, one hand holding a hammer and the other on his hip.

"Hi." It wasn't Shakespeare, but it was the best she had at the moment. She crunched the cereal and surveyed his work. Now instead of one hole, there were two—and they were considerably bigger than the one she'd made falling through.

"Chloe."

Shit. The tone was one he reserved for times when he was really pissed. Really, really pissed.

She smiled. They'd known each other too long for her to be cowed by his attitude. It was hard to fight with someone grinning at you. The maneuver had worked in the past. Maybe it would work now, too.

"Got yourself quite a mess up there." She pointed with her spoon, which splashed milk onto the front of her gnu. Wiping it with the tip of her finger, she added, "Looks worse now than it did yesterday."

Neil threw the hammer off the roof. It landed with a dull thud on the ground beside the bottom rung of the ladder. A look of pure annoyance turned his handsome features hard when he stomped across the roof and took the ladder lightning fast.

So the smile-when-he's-cranky ploy wasn't going to work this time. Rather than wait for him to stalk across the lawn and get in her face—which was what he evidently had in mind to do—she turned and chose a chair near the fire pit. She sat, crossed one leg over the other and acted as if she hadn't seen a meal in a week.

He stood in front of her, hands on hips and scowl on face.

"Yes?" she asked in the sweetest voice she had.

"I just don't understand you. I'm up there busting my ass to fix your roof, and all you can say is it's worse now than it was before."

"Just an observation." She chewed the cereal in her mouth. Swallowed. "I know nothing about what you're doing. It's probably part of the plan, to make it worse before fixing it. I was just trying to make conversation, that's all. So shoot me."

He huffed his annoyance. It was another of the irritating habits he had, huffing like a bear rather than saying whatever was on his mind.

She was in no mood to let his bad attitude affect her, but the huff couldn't go unnoticed.

"Stop with that, all right? Just cool it."

"Excuse me?"

Acting as if the bowl hid the Holy Grail, she did not look up. "The huffing. It was cute when we were kids. Now? It's just annoying, actually."

Neil started to do it again—but caught himself. She struggled not to grin when she heard him nearly choke on the sound he swallowed.

"I-I—shit, Chloe!"

She looked up, meeting his thundery gaze with what she hoped was utter calmness. "You know where the powder room is. Feel free to use it if you feel the, ah, need."

He raked his fingers through his hair, sending the thick locks into a tangled mess. Despite the wacky hair, he was handsome. She never wondered how she'd fallen for the guy. It was, though, something of a mystery deciphering the exact moment when she'd fallen out of love with him. She'd spent countless hours wondering but had never been able to pinpoint that event. Maybe she wasn't meant to know the hows and whys, only that it was a fact of her life.

She'd accepted it. Poor Neil, he steadfastly refused.

"Damn it—what the hell are we doing?"

"I'm eating breakfast. You're yelling at me. I think that about sums it up, don't you?"

"You know what I mean." His tone softened, and to her utter horror he dropped to one knee beside the chair. "Chloe, my honeybee…"

"Don't." The high school endearment sent the Cap'n Crunch flip-flopping in her belly. She met his gaze. "Please, don't."

He shook his head, bewilderment stamped plainly on his face. His eyes tore at her; they were so filled with hurt she could hardly stand to look at him.

"We were good once." He swallowed. "Can't we be that way again?"

She leaned over and placed the bowl on the grass beside the chair. Her appetite had vanished.

"It was a long time ago. We were different people then."

"Not so different. I'm still me. You're still you. Come on, can't we give it another go?"

She searched for the words—the right words—to make him see how she felt. They'd had similar conversations in the past, many of them, but he still didn't get it. How to show a man your love for him was long faded without hurting him unnecessarily?

When Neil placed a hand over hers on the wide

arm of the Adirondack chair, she did not pull away. But she did not hold his hand, either.

"I don't think that's a good idea." Her voice was soft, and she hoped her words did not sting. She ignored the expression in his eyes. "We have changed; don't you see that? We want different things out of life, I think." When he opened his mouth to protest, she hurried on, "I get it—you think you can give me what I want and still be happy, but that's not happiness. We can force it, but that doesn't mean it's meant to be forced. Please, let this die. I can't stand the way we keep hurting each other."

He didn't say a word before he stood up, turned, and walked away.

Chapter 22

Everyone was on the front porch when she went outside. It was a smallish porch, and the floorboards were so warped in one corner that anyone who sat in the chair in that spot tilted forward. Gabby sat there now, with her bare feet propped against the wooden railing for support.

Last summer, Chloe contemplated repairing the porch, or tearing it off the old house altogether. But as usual, the checkbook wouldn't accommodate either option, so the shaky spot stayed put. Even a tear down meant hiring someone with a truck to haul away debris, so there was no free fix.

"Woo hoo, look at my girl!" Uncle Ted whistled when she came through the screen door. It slapped shut behind her, and she gave a small curtsey.

Dinner would be casual, so her pegged jeans, tucked into her favorite brown suede boots, and lavender peasant blouse were perfectly suited to The Dockside. After their disastrous dinner date, she couldn't have cared less if he wanted to grab sandwiches from the deli and eat on the beach. She just wanted to get to know him, no dinner reservation required.

Uncle Ted was not done complimenting her. He attempted a howl, Wolfman Jack style, but it went south real quick. He began to cough, a horrible sound that stole his breath and made his lungs spasm. Thanks to Agent Orange, the once strong man stared at them with tears streaming down his cheeks as he fought to pull air into his body.

They'd all seen it before, but it was still alarming.

She went to him, dropped to a knee in front of his rocker, and put a hand on his shoulder. He was wracked with a fresh fit of coughing, so strong it sent shock waves from his body to hers. The helpless feeling that consumed her whenever this happened never grew easier to bear.

Gabby was through the door like a shot and back in an instant with a glass of water. There was no way to hand it to him, though. He could not hold it, and trying to give him sips of anything would likely choke him.

Reva and Julia stood nearby. Uncle Ted's gaze passed over each of them, then settled on Chloe. She held him with her eyes, praying the hacking would abate.

"Hang on, it's going to be okay. I promise, it's going to be okay." She soothed with her mouth as her mind spun. How much could one man take before his body gave out? That damn Vietnam conflict—not even a war, not even a defensive move for the States!—had ruined so many lives. Shattered hopes and dreams. Left so many struggling to survive, even now, years later. Damn it but the world was so uncool sometimes. "That's right, it's going to stop. Just hang in there, honey. Please, stay calm."

She heard him before she felt him beside her. His footsteps, hard on the steps and rapid across the floorboards.

"Looks like my timing is excellent." Kyle knelt

beside her, so close his body pressed against hers. She moved just a bit, giving him room as he put a hand on her uncle's wrist and checked his pulse. His question, in a low voice, directed at her, "'Nam?"

"Yeah. Fucking Agent Orange." She spoke from the heart.

"Thought as much." He looked up into the other man's eyes, which were now bloodshot. She noted her uncle's lips were tinged blue. "Stay with me, okay? We're going to help you, just stay with me."

He nodded. The big coughing had subsided, leaving a wheeze which grew fainter with every passing minute.

Kyle spoke to the others over his shoulder. "I need a towel—a big one, a bath towel. And someone go ahead of us and open the freezer door. You know, to the refrigerator. Fast—we don't want to waste a minute."

He glanced over at her as he stood. "I'm going to help him inside. Make sure there's nothing in our path—we're coming through pretty fast."

She nodded, stood, and turned for the door. Reva held it open. The other two were gone.

"I'm going to get you up. We're going inside. Just another minute, and you'll feel lots better. Don't try to help me, just let me carry you." He reached down, put an arm around Ted's back, and pulled him to his feet. The doctor took the limp left arm, draped it across his shoulders, and began to walk.

Chloe saw her uncle try to move his own feet, but his power was gone. They dragged along the floor, and tears slipped from her eyes as she met his gaze. His lips were full blue now and he'd stopped struggling to breathe. The wheeze was fainter.

Running ahead, pushing a chair out of the way and slamming the open bathroom door closed, she cleared the path.

In the kitchen, the freezer door hung wide open, and Gabby held a big blue bath towel.

Kyle went straight to the open freezer door and put their faces into the cold fog rolling from the compartment. "The towel. Drape it over our heads. Make a canopy, a tent. We're going to let the cold air shrink the bronchial tubes. A minute, that's all we need. The towel—fast!"

She did as she was told, holding it over their heads. Julia grabbed one edge from her, and together they held it tight against the cold metal frame. They heard Kyle speaking slowly, in a low, reassuring tone.

It felt like an hour, but was barely a minute before they heard a gasp. Then, a fit of coughing, but not as horrible as the first round had been. They heard him gulp for air, with Kyle coaxing him to breathe slowly and normally.

The tears streaming down her face couldn't muffle the sob that escaped her throat. Reva put an arm around her and pulled her close as Gabby took the edge of the towel and held it in place. Chloe let herself be led outside, past the roof construction, overgrown lilac and charcoal grill.

When her back found the trunk of the enormous oak tree, she slid to the ground, put her face in her hands, and wept. Her friend didn't say a word but simply sat beside her and rubbed a comforting hand between her shoulder blades.

Hitching a breath, she finally managed to stem the tide. Rubbing her hands over her face, wiping off the slick evidence of her outburst, she sighed.

"I hate the war." Her voice was so shaky it was near impossible to get even four words out.

"We all hate the war. Nothing but a poor excuse for a pissing contest. Dropping bombs, killing babies…just a way for The Man to show the rest of the world who's in control." Reva patted her shoulder, then folded her hands in her lap. Had she been fatter, and bald, and a man, she would have resembled Buddha. Now, she looked philosophically at the branches hanging low above their heads. "No one's in control. It's a damn illusion, but we're all too chicken shit to admit it."

Chapter 23

The dinner crowd had come and gone, so there were plenty of empty tables inside the restaurant.

Millie, the white-haired waitress, waved a hand at the space behind her when they stepped through the door. Lobster Cove attracted characters of all kinds. Millie was a local celebrity almost, having gained notoriety during an annual Founder's Day parade years ago. She'd been the now-infamous mermaid who had lost her clamshell bra to the snapping scissor claws of a slightly inebriated crab who rode the same float. If gossip were to be believed, she'd given Andy the Handy Crab a taste of his own hijinks a few months afterward, dosing his Christmas ale with a generous dollop of liquid laxative.

Peace between mermaids and crustaceans had never been breached again, and the village appreciated a woman who could tame a wild man. Millie and Andy had been married for nearly a decade, and to everyone's knowledge he'd kept his pincers off his wife's undergarments.

"Seat yourselves. Anywhere's fine." She whizzed by wearing high-top sneakers on bare feet. It was a dubious fashion statement coupled with the wait staff's black shorts and white shirt ensemble. "Take a load off—be right with you."

Kyle pointed to a table beside one of the big, wide

windows overlooking the water. "Over there okay?"

"My favorite place. That part hangs off the pier."

"I know. It's my favorite spot, too."

They walked between tables and around chairs. When they reached the table, he pulled out her chair and waited until she was seated. Then, he sat across from her.

A candle dripped yellow wax down the side of an already-wax-coated Mateus wine bottle in the center of the table. He pointed to it and shrugged.

"I wanted to take you someplace a little fancier than this for our first date."

She poked a drop of wax with a fingernail and teased, "Oh, so my visiting you in the ED wasn't a date, then?"

He shook his head. By candlelight, he was handsomer than ever. The shadows sculpted his features, and his eyes were such a dark brown they seemed nearly black. When he smiled, his teeth looked brilliantly white.

"That most definitely was not a date."

"No? What was it then?"

He accepted the menu Millie handed him with a smile. When the waitress walked away, he said, "A lesson, I hope. Wearing a helmet on that pretty head is a must if you're going to be a motorcycle mama."

She opened her menu, laughing at the description.

"Hardly a motorcycle mama, thanks! I always picture a big—I mean really big and wide—woman when someone says that."

"I do, too. I just couldn't think of another bike-riding description that doesn't allude to Harley Davidson, and you ride a Suzuki."

"Ah, that explains it. So, no first date in the hospital?"

"Nope. And no first date in the hospital when you delivered my car, either."

She waited while Millie took their drink orders. When he suggested a bottle of pinot noir, she agreed. After the pre-dinner excitement, a glass of wine sounded excellent.

"So that wasn't a date, either. I agree; seeing that little boy on the road—well, that isn't something I want to remember as part of a date." She paused, wiggled an eyebrow across the table at him and saw he knew what was on her mind by the look in his eyes. "But you did kiss me, remember?"

Millie returned with the bottle, which he thanked her for opening. She poured, he tasted, then nodded, so she poured both glasses full. When she suggested the special, grilled vegetables with salmon croquettes, they both agreed to try it, although Chloe requested her salmon be served to someone else.

The waitress walked away, muttering about a double order of vegetables and saying she'd eat the croquettes herself.

He took a swallow of his wine. "That moment? When I kissed you? Not something I'm likely to forget. Believe me, a man does not forget a kiss like that."

Heat rose from her chest as something began to simmer inside her. He made her feel like one of those molten lava cakes, all sweet and sticky on the outside, hot and melty where it didn't show.

"Is that so?"

He broke a piece of bread off the loaf in the basket between them. Taking his time buttering it, he said,

"Oh, yes. It's so." He bit into the bread and began to chew.

Had he been someone else, she might have felt strange staring at him. But they'd already been through some tense moments, and there was a level of comfort she felt with the man. If she read him right—and she hoped she did—he felt the same way.

Better to change the subject before too much more of her grew hot. If he had any idea she was smoldering beneath his gaze, he did not let on.

"Um, my uncle?"

The look turned serious. No more winking or flirting; Kyle was all business.

He put the bread on his bread plate, brushed his hands together and cleared his throat.

"Your uncle is unfortunately a casualty of war— that is, he would be had it been a war. I'm sorry his body was so damaged by the chemicals. Has he been like this since returning home?"

"Yes. But when he first came home, he was much worse. Now, it only happens when he exerts himself. When he tries to do something he shouldn't."

"When he tries to do something his body is no longer capable of doing." Their dinners came, but neither touched their plate. "He is being seen by a doctor, I assume?"

"At the VA hospital near Bangor."

"Quite a distance."

"It is, but his treatment is all covered. He can't…I can't…we can't—"

"It's okay, I understand. Medical bills can be astronomical. Let Uncle Sam pay for whatever he'll pay for. God knows, if it hadn't been for the ridiculous government position on world issues, there'd be no need for your uncle to have any treatment. But does he have a doctor closer to home, as well?"

She picked up her knife and fork. "Eat, before your dinner gets cold. You must be hungry."

He cut into the salmon, speared a piece and put it in his mouth. A look of satisfaction crossed his face.

She began on the mound of grilled vegetables Millie had brought. It was enough food for two, maybe three, meals. When she tasted the broccoli, she moaned softly. It was wonderful, grilled to perfection.

They ate in silence for a few minutes.

Kyle finished his wine, poured a new glass and topped hers off.

"So does he? Have another doctor aside from the ones in Bangor?"

"He does. Right here in Lobster Cove. But I don't understand why no one told me to stick him in the freezer before." She placed her fork on the edge of her plate. Wiping her lips on the brown plaid napkin, she added, "I've never seen him come out of a fit that quickly. It was like magic."

He put his fork down and took a long swallow of the wine. Then he steepled his fingers and gave her a serious look. "First of all, don't stick him in the freezer. Just put his face in the cold air, the way I did tonight. It opens up the passages, shrinks the tissues, so the air can get into his lungs. I don't know why no one told you to do that; all I can think is it's a pretty unconventional way of dealing with a very serious medical emergency. And make no mistake, when he stops breathing like that, it's an emergency. A grave emergency."

"I've seen him turn blue. I know it's a life-or-death

moment." A lump formed in her throat. "He's all I've got—the only person in the world I call family. I can't lose him. Don't you understand? I can't lose him."

Kyle once again topped off the level of wine in her glass. He poured the small amount left in the bottle into his own glass. He drank it down before he answered.

She wiped away the tear that had fallen from one eye with her napkin. A nod toward her wine glass, and a small, kind smile from the man was enough to coax her to lift her glass. Drain the wine.

"Listen, Chloe, I can't promise you won't lose him. We all lose people we love. It's a sad fact of life. But I can tell you that if we can manage to keep the episodes where he's taxed to the limit, like the one he had tonight, to a minimum, there's a chance his body will heal itself. He'll never be able to do crazy things like chase blondes down the beach, but he should be able to live a happy, normal life."

"Can you tell me what to do?"

"Of course. Mostly, it's keeping him from doing anything to trigger an episode. And, if he's overcome with coughing, get him to breathe the cold air. You saw how it works almost immediately. Over time, he should heal, and the episodes will diminish."

"You're pretty amazing. You must know that—that you're an amazing man." The wine had loosened her tongue.

He leaned in over the table, lowered his voice and said, "What I know is that I'm finally sitting with a beautiful, sexy woman, and I can only think of one thing. One thing, that's it."

It was a shame the table was between them. Chloe leaned close, mindful of the flickering candle. All she needed was to set her hair on fire, and the romance would be over. They'd already had too much excitement, and this was still, technically, their first date.

She licked her lower lip, hungry for something that was not on the dinner plate.

"What's that? The one thing you're thinking of?" She waited for his answer, watching his gaze slip from her eyes to her mouth and back to her eyes again.

Kyle raised a hand, signaling for the check.

"Being alone with you."

He glanced at the scrap of paper Millie brought, then handed her a wad of cash. When she left, after thanking him profusely, he stood and came around the table. Leaning close—so close his breath swept across her cheek and turned her nipples to pebbles—he whispered in her ear.

"I hope it doesn't shock you, but I've been wondering how you would look without so many clothes on…wrapped around my body. And that, pretty lady, is what I can't get off my mind."

Chapter 24

Anyone who grew up in Lobster Cove knew the post-date make out spot was, of course, Quinn Beach. There was the dock, but although it was long on ambience, it was short on wooden benches, so the first-come, first-serve rule applied there. Also, it was much more public than the beach. A good option for young teens, getting-to-know-you dates and seniors trying to recapture a bit of their youth, but as far as serious lip-wrangling went, the beach was as good as it got.

They passed a pay phone on the way out of the restaurant.

"Mind if I give a call home?" In her heart, she felt her uncle was probably fine, but it never hurt to check.

He pulled some change from his pocket, held it out on the palm of his hand and said, "Here, I've got a dime."

"Thanks."

The dime she took was warm from being in his pocket. She rubbed a fingertip over it before she lifted the black receiver and dropped the coin in the slot at the top of the phone. She dialed. It only took two rings for someone to answer.

"Hello?" The television blared in the background.

"Gabby, it's me. How is he doing?"

Kyle stood close, his attention on the conversation.

"Perfectly fine. Watching The Rockford Files."

"No more trouble breathing? Did he eat dinner?"

She gave him a thumbs up sign. He looked very satisfied with her end of the conversation.

"Reva opened a can of chicken noodle soup, I made some grilled cheese sandwiches, and we had that apple pie Julia picked up at the farm stand yesterday. So yeah, he's fine. And no, no more trouble breathing." She lowered her voice a notch. "Although we may all need hearing aids by the time we're thirty. Damn, but I'm sure they can hear James Garner all the way in the MacDonnell house!"

The neighbors were probably watching the same show, so it didn't much matter if they got it in stereo. Lobster Cove was a spot on a windshield, size-wise, and didn't have a huge assortment of channels in their television lineup.

"Hey, you all don't mind keeping an eye on him for a bit longer, do you?" She pulled her bottom lip between her teeth. She didn't think anyone had a date; hopefully no one wanted to go to the movies. They really had all been so busy no one had had much of a chance to catch up with anyone else.

Her uncle was a grown man, and normally she wouldn't be so paranoid about his being on his own, but the near-death experience couldn't be dismissed from her mind. Not yet. Maybe not ever. She could still see the blue lips and pleading eyes.

Just as she decided to go home, Gabby answered. "Oh—sorry, I was handing the popcorn bowl to Reva. What? Do we mind? Are you kidding me? We're all in sweats and baggy t-shirts, eating popcorn and filing our nails."

"You're not feeding him popcorn, are you?"

A snort. "Yeah, and nuts, hard candy and peanut butter. Lots of stuff to make him choke and gag." She paused. Dropping the sarcasm, she said, "Of course we're not giving him popcorn. I'm having popcorn. Reva's got ice cream—Rocky Road, I think it is. And Julia and our favorite man are eating the rest of the apple pie. With whipped cream, no ice cream. No nuts. Nothing bad for him, I promise."

She should have known they'd take good care of him. With a nod to the phone, where the operator was due to break in any second, she said, "Thanks. I'll be home later on, okay?"

"Go have fun with that hunk—uh oh, there's the operator! Bye!"

Gabby disconnected, so Chloe hung up the phone.

"He's fine, right?"

"Thanks to you and your enchanted freezer trick." When he held out his elbow, she tucked her hand through his arm. He held the door open for her, so she passed into the night ahead of him.

"No trick." They walked slowly toward the car. The angled street parking near the dock was so full during the day cars circled, waiting for a place to pull in. Now, there were very few spots filled.

"Trick or no trick, you saved his life."

He opened the passenger door for her. "How do you feel about a drive to the beach?" He jutted his chin toward the velvety canopy above them. "The moon is full, the night is warm, and it feels kind of right to go walking on the sand with a beautiful woman. What do you say?"

It was a no-brainer.

"I say yes."

Chloe sat in the leather bucket seat, put her hands on her lap when he shut the door, and then waited for him to walk around the car. A thrill of excitement shot up her spine. The beach. The moon. The man who turned her knees weak and made her girl parts warm. The evening had started out horribly, but it was getting better with each passing minute.

The dome light came on when he climbed into the driver's seat. He shut the door, leaving them in darkness again. The key fit into the ignition and when he turned it the dash lights came on. Only then did he turn, look into her eyes and smile. "I hoped you'd agree to the beach. I've got to come clean; I've been thinking of taking you there ever since I met you."

"Tell me why."

People loved the beach for a million reasons. Kite flying. Surfing. Shell collecting. There was more to do on the sand than get hot and heavy. For all she knew he was a sand castle aficionado. There were enough of them around, and they looked quite ordinary until they began to salivate at the sight of buckets and shovels.

She watched the fabric on his shoulders stretch as he took a deep breath. The muscles beneath the shirt pulled the seams nearly to their limit, and not for the first time she had an urge to reach out and feel his biceps. Purely a physical reaction, she knew, but the sight of such strength turned her on.

The answer didn't come right away.

He turned to her, moved close and gave her a small kiss on the lips. It was a tease, a sweet, sensual tease, one that left her wanting much more.

"To do that. And hold your hand. And hear your voice. And make you laugh. Then, kiss you some more."

She just stared at him, wondering if her dinner had been laced with something psychedelic. Surely this couldn't be happening.

"What do you say? Now that you know why I want to take you to the beach, do you still want to go?" A devilish grin turned sexy and sophisticated to hotter than hell in a heartbeat. He wiggled one eyebrow.

She managed to nod. "I do."

Kyle backed out of the space with a shake of his head.

"The two most dangerous words in the English language."

Chapter 25

It was a perfect night for a stroll on the beach. The night air sultry and the moon couldn't have been more gorgeous if Norman Rockwell had painted it.

They'd left their footwear in the car, along with her purse. He'd even left the keys in the ignition. Lobster Cove was the kind of place where people slept with their doors unlocked and their Buicks in the driveway with the keys in the visor.

Luck was with them. Quinn Beach was deserted.

As they walked across the dune and down the path to the sand, he took her hand. His skin was warm, his touch gentle. Their fingers threaded together without conscious effort. Neither spoke until they were near the water's edge. Even then, they stood looking out into the distance for several minutes.

The night was pure enchantment. Moonlight skittered over the waves. Cocooned in the darkness, they could have been on a deserted island, the last two survivors on the planet. Nothing existed beyond the bubble around them.

Chloe sighed, without realizing it.

One strong arm around her shoulder pulled her against his side. She molded to his physique as if made to fit to him.

"What was that about?"

"Hmm?" Her mind had wandered—to a point that

featured him shirtless, so she wasn't about to divulge that information. "What was what about?"

He tightened his grip on her shoulder, bringing her still closer.

"Don't try to deny it. I know a sigh when I hear one. So the question is: What's a sexy lady like you have to sigh about? You're not still worried about your uncle, are you?"

She'd already seen his compassionate nature at work. He genuinely cared about people, and that was part of what made him an excellent doctor. He didn't just attend to the broken bones or scrapes of humanity; he concentrated on healing the whole person. And, as she'd seen by his continuing care for little Eddie, the kid they found on the road beside the busted bicycle, his attention didn't end when a patient was out of sight.

Chloe loved that about him, that he immersed himself in the lives he took under his care.

"Not at all. He's in good hands with the girls. We all watch out for each other, you know? A family of sorts."

"Hey, family is where you find it. Not all families are tied by blood. Believe me, I know."

Now, he sighed.

The question came without thought. "What do you mean?"

"I'm adopted. I have an amazing family—they live in New York, and I'd like you to meet them the next time they visit—but they're not my blood family. I love them, and we're family, but it's not because blood ties us together."

The bottom dropped out of her belly. At least, that's how it felt. She swallowed hard, searching for a response because she knew he waited for one. Funny, the question had come on its own. Now, words were elusive.

The important question, the one that hammered at the front of her head begging to be given voice, is where she settled. "Do you remember your birth mother?"

"Nah, not a bit. She had me and never even held me. That's what I was told, anyhow. Left me at the hospital, where a social worker came to get me and bring me to my parents' home." He paused. "I have always wondered why she didn't even hold me, although it really doesn't matter."

"Maybe she couldn't." The words came from a constricted throat.

"Maybe." He pulled her against his side tightly again, then said in a lighter tone of voice, "You still didn't tell me why you gave that great, big sigh a few minutes ago."

"Oh, that."

"Yes. That. What gives?"

She shook her heard. "Nothing. It just took my breath away, that's all. When I see the moon dancing on the water…it just makes me happy." She turned to him. Shrugged. "Silly, huh?"

His arms came around her and for a second she thought he was going to hug her, but he put one hand on the small of her back and took one of hers in his other. The hard-packed sand beneath their feet was a wonderful dance floor. He whirled her once. Twice. Then, he began to move and she followed easily.

The good doctor's singing voice was as pleasing as his dancing skills. He hadn't been serious when he claimed he wasn't able to carry a tune.

"Well it's a marvelous night for a moon dance…"

The words trailed off. Kyle's humming was music enough. He pulled her closer, so close they were intimately molded.

Her cheek rested on his shoulder. Being in his arms was peaceful. So much had happened recently, and all on top of the usual burdens, that she hadn't time to clear her mind. Not once had she managed to feel an ounce of contentment since accepting the weight of the house, her uncle's health concerns and everything else. There were times she thought she might drown beneath it all.

But now, her life and its issues were all so far removed, she felt as if she were floating.

Chloe lifted her cheek and looked up at him.

"You're a vision in the moonlight. An absolute goddess in my arms." His voice was husky, a low rumble against her chest.

Her head spun, as if she'd been drinking, but they hadn't consumed enough wine to get either of them drunk. But drunk? Yes, that's how she felt when he smiled down at her.

He lowered his mouth to hers, capturing her lips in a kiss that was nowhere near as sweet as the one in the car had been. This was pure passion, right from the first moment. He groaned, his tongue parting her lips and slipping into her mouth. She met his touch with her own, swirling her tongue past his lips. Tasting him. Intimate exploration that deepened their ardor.

Chloe bent her knees, letting him lower her to the sand. It was still warm from the sun, and soft beneath her back.

A hand found its way beneath her loose blouse.

She wore a lacy bra which he pushed aside. His hand cupped her breast, sending jolts of desire to distant points in her body. He ran a fingertip over her nipple, murmuring his delight when it pebbled against his skin. She arched her back, pressing her body against his.

He covered her with one leg, his arousal hard against her hip. Her hands caressed his back through his shirt, but she wanted more. She ached for more.

A moan when he broke their kiss. Her shirt bunched high on her chest, exposing her breasts to the moonlight. It did not occur to her to look around, to see if they were being observed. She did not care. All thought had flown from her mind, cast aside with the first touch of his lips on hers. He'd turned her into a red-hot bundle of desire.

Her left hand slid lower on his body, cupping his backside, but only for a moment. He chuckled, then touched his tongue to the nipple he'd fondled. Peppering her skin with tiny kisses, ratcheting the desire coursing through her to a fevered pitch, she ground herself against him and put a hand to her mouth.

Chloe bit down on her finger to keep herself from begging for more. She wanted it all—every inch of the man whose mouth suckled her breast. Her hand fisted in his dark curls, holding on tightly lest she be lost to the sensations flooding her.

It did not register immediately when Kyle released her. He held his body over hers, his elbows supporting most of his weight. Their gazes locked, their breathing ragged and their mouths wide.

"I can't." Regret tinged the two words.

His hard-on pressed hotly against her, insistent and tempting. She knew he could—and that he wanted to, as badly as she wanted it.

"I don't understand." She heard the shakiness in her voice. Swallowed hard and repeated herself. "Kyle, I don't understand."

He stared into her eyes, looking so filled with regret it nearly broke her heart. He wiped a thumb across her cheek, touched her lips and trailed it down her jawline.

"I just can't. Not this way. Not on the beach, where we'll forever remember that I took you to dinner, then to Quinn Beach and made love to you beneath the moon. Believe me, that's exactly what I want to do, but I can't."

No man had ever refused to have sex with her, and that was what this was—painfully, a refusal to get closer. It boggled her mind. So confusing, to feel his desire—so blatant and erotic—while he turned her down.

"I-I…" Hitching a deep breath and searching for something to say, she closed her eyes. Looking at him just made it worse, so she shut him out.

"Chloe, please."

Humiliation swept over her just as ardor had done just a short while ago. Hot and cold, found and lost—none of it made sense.

Her life did not make sense. Why should this be any different?

He tapped her nose with a tender finger. "Please, open your eyes. Look at me."

She wanted to crawl off into the dunes but since he was still on top of her she had few options. Opening her eyes, she avoided his gaze.

It felt like a cowardly move, but humiliation didn't

instill courage.

"Chloe…" He moved his head so she had no choice. Their gazes locked. He offered a slow smile. "You don't get it, do you?"

"I get it. Can we leave, please?"

He shook his head. Did not make a move to let her up. She wasn't at all afraid; he devoted his life to helping others. He would never hurt her.

"Not until you understand why I'm not…hell, I can't believe I've got the woman of my dreams half naked on the beach, and I'm putting a stop to something that would have been the most amazing experience of my whole life. Shit."

Kyle turned his head to the sky. Closed his eyes. Shook his head in apparent disbelief.

She watched in pure amazement.

He looked at her again, with eyes that were compassionate and gentle. And, regretful—but determined. So many emotions, and all shown clearly.

"I want to make love to you, Chloe. I want it so badly I won't be able to walk straight for hours."

She gave a little giggle. It wasn't planned, and she couldn't stop it. It brought a grin from the handsome man still leaning over her. And, he pressed his erection against her hip as she giggled again.

"Oh, so you think it's funny? Well, I can't say I blame you. I'm a fool, turning down what I'm turning down—and I deserve to be reminded that being a gentleman sometimes comes with a penalty of its own."

"A stiff penalty." She covered her mouth with her hand, afraid she'd laugh out loud when his eyebrows lifted so far on his forehead they disappeared beneath his curls.

"A smartass. I knew it—the lady's not only beautiful and smart, but she's a smartass as well. Just my luck, falling for a woman who pokes fun at a guy when he's…ah, in a delicate state."

"Who's poking who?" She couldn't help it. She laughed.

And he did, too.

He pulled her into a hug, and she wrapped her arms around his neck and hugged him back. The night wasn't going the way she thought it would, but that didn't matter. Being with Kyle was wonderful—even if she wasn't with him fully.

Yet.

Chapter 26

It was a good thing Chloe wasn't doing a solo shift in the office. Her body was there, but her mind certainly wasn't. She'd spent the morning at her desk, trying to look busy and not let on to Laila or Jade that she couldn't concentrate on anything. Not one thing. Oh, unless the previous night's dinner date and subsequent entertainment on Quinn Beach counted, because try as she might she could not pull her thoughts from Kyle and the fun they'd had. And, the fun they'd almost had.

Damn, but the man made her feel like ice cream on a July afternoon. Soft, warm, melting…it was exactly how she felt even in the mildly air-conditioned office when the touch of his hands and the feel of his body pressed against hers was just a memory.

Laila walked into the room, humming along with the radio. It played from the corner, near the unreliable air-conditioning unit stuck into the window. Mick Jagger knew how to wail, and her co-worker had no problem embellishing.

Fortunately, there were no clients in the place, because Laila began to gyrate, sending the multi-colored caftan she wore swirling around her hips. It was a sight, the two-hundred-plus-pound woman dancing as the bangle bracelets on her gorgeous, coffee-colored skin jangled in time to the beat. When she began to sing, Jade and Chloe both watched the performance.

Her voice put Jagger's to shame, it was so strong and sure. She hit every note, and nailed every nuance of the song, all while keeping time with her feet and arms.

Jade and Chloe got to their feet and joined the action. What they lacked in vocal ability was made up for by sheer volume as they sang along.

Jade pretended to hold a microphone in her hand. She was the total opposite of their lead singer, blonde, petite and wearing ass-hugging jeans tucked into high-heeled, black knee-high boots.

She held the imaginary mic in front of Chloe's face. Bending from the waist, she belted out, "No, no, no!"

Then, to their leader, who pantomimed grabbing the microphone and carried them home. When the song ended, and an advertisement for Muffler City in Bangor came on the radio, they all collapsed onto the tops of desks.

Laila pushed a stack of papers off the edge of her gray steel desk, hoisted her bottom onto its surface, and waved a hand in front of her face.

"Now if that don't make a woman warm, I don't know what will." She peered around Jade, who perched like a tiny bird on a rosebush and made her desk look twice as big as it actually was. "You sure that thing is on? It sure feels hot in here!"

As if on cue, the finicky appliance began to whine. "Oh, it's on all right. For how long, nobody knows." Jade shot it a disgusted look, then turned back to the conversation. "We could all be dancing in our skivvies by tomorrow, with the way that stupid thing carries on."

Laila shook her head. "Not me. Tomorrow's my day off, so I get to keep some of my dignity intact. This is one old hippie who keeps her business her business." She grinned, showing one gold tooth. It matched the gold beads threaded into the corn rows she wore tight on her head. "Besides, what makes you think I wear skivvies? Hell, beneath this—no one knows what's under mama's caftan except mama."

Theirs was a good working relationship. Every member of the team knew that any minute the day could turn from serene to terrible without warning. When women came to them, bleeding and battered and often with small children in tow, the fun stopped and they went into full-on work mode. Saving the world one woman at a time, they called it. The ultimate women's liberation, taking females from bondage in modern society. So when they had downtime, everyone made the most of it.

"And that's more than even Helen Gurley Brown wants to know. You've just given me a mental picture that might be hard to shake." Jade put the back of a wrist against her forehead, the picture of a 1940s femme fatal movie star about to faint. "I don't know if I can bear the thought of you—good Lord, that's taking bra burning to the extreme!"

"Hell, those Playtex babies cost too damn much to burn. These boobies aren't dime-store underwear models. It takes some heavy-duty elastic to keep this bosom in line. Believe me, I don't buy 'em to burn 'em. Leave that to the flat-chested sisters; they don't fork over the bread I do on unmentionables." The beads hanging from the braided ends of her hair clicked when she punctuated her remarks with a vigorous upper shimmy.

"Enough!" Chloe waved a hand through the air.

"You two are going to kill me with all this crazy talk. Aging hippie, my ass. Laila you could dance both of us under the table any day of the week. Barefoot, in stilettos like Jade's or even in platform heels. Any day, you've got us beat."

Chloe swung her feet. She did favor platforms for work, mostly for comfort but also because they gave her an extra couple of inches. She didn't aspire to be an Amazon woman, but it never hurt to be tall enough to not get lost in a crowd.

"Sister, you look as if you were doing some below-table dancing last night. Doesn't it?" Laila looked for back up from the other woman—and got it.

"Uh huh. I didn't want to embarrass you, but I think I saw some sand fall out of those pretty curls of yours this morning." Jade raised an eyebrow, then nodded when their coworker burst out laughing. "I'm not kidding—it was sand. Somebody was rolling around on the beach last night."

Chloe opened her mouth to protest but Laila cut her off.

"Hey, don't try to deny it. We've all been there, rolled in the sand a time or two. Or three or four—" She gave a wink. "Just as long as you tell us what happened, we'll pretend we didn't see the seashells falling at your feet, won't we?"

"Amen, sister. We'll sweep the shells under the table and keep our lips zipped."

She couldn't deny it. Besides, she didn't want to. She was an adult, and there was nothing wrong with having some fun at the beach with a sexy man. They all read Cosmopolitan, didn't they? Sex was healthy—encouraged, even—for single women as well as those with bands on their fingers.

"Give. Who is he?" Laila wasn't a woman anyone ignored.

She wanted to blurt out every racy detail but knew better. No matter how much someone promised to keep their lips zipped, it was human nature to share news.

A package had been on her desk when she arrived. It had been left at the front door, with a note from Jackie. Chocolate chip cookies, a thank-you gift for having helped her when she was at her lowest. The note contained a Vermont address, which Jackie said was her cousin's place. She planned to stay there for a while, get her act together, and figure out what to do with the rest of her life. Chloe was sorry she'd missed seeing her, but grateful she'd stepped back out into the light of the world. A woman shouldn't hide in a dingy apartment, closed off from everything, for too long.

Now, she held out the box of cookies. The women both shook their heads.

Leila patted her left thigh. "Thanks, but those would end up right here. No need to add any more jiggle to my wiggle, if you know what I mean."

With an impatient sigh, Jade put her hands on her hips. "So? The man? The sand?"

"I guess you don't want any cookies, either." She put them back on the desk, rubbed imaginary crumbs from her fingertips and ordered her thoughts.

Before she could begin, the copper bells hanging on the front door tinkled. They looked at each other for a fast second. Then, Leila slid off her desk. She pointed a finger at Chloe and said, "You are not saved by the bell. Don't start without me."

In a swirl of colorful fabric, she left the room. They

watched her go, then remained quiet, eavesdropping on the conversation in the outer office. When she heard her name, Chloe got up and went through the door.

The woman standing just inside the agency's front door looked familiar but she couldn't quite place her. She was young, with long, waist-length brown hair that hung like a waterfall down her back. Jeans, a tie-dyed shirt and sandals gave her a bohemian air. When she saw Chloe she smiled.

"Hi." She gave a small wave. "I was hoping you'd be here. I, ah, wonder if I can talk with you for a few minutes."

Leila looked at the large round clock on the wall. "It's nearly Chloe's quitting time. Might I be of service to you? I have no plans to leave anytime soon, so you can have more than a few minutes."

The woman couldn't have been more than twenty-five or so, but she carried herself with confidence that made her seem older.

Shaking her head, she said, "No, thank you. I'm sure you're wonderful but it's not about…well, I'm not here on a professional level. I don't need any help—I'm not a battered woman. Heck, I don't even have a man to batter me." The attempt at glibness fell flat.

Leila shot a sharp look. "Well, that's a very good thing, now isn't it?"

Clasping her hands in front of her, she turned to Chloe. "I just need to speak with you. I won't take too much time, I promise." She jabbed a thumb over her shoulder. "I saw a coffee shop across the street. I can buy you a cup of coffee. Or tea, if you'd prefer. It's important. Please?"

Leila put her hand on Chloe's shoulder. "Listen,

why don't you consider yourself off the clock. You've put in extra hours this week, settling Jackie and all, so just go. It's all good. This sister looks like she's ready to pop, she needs to chew your ear so hard. So go— besides, we can see that coffee shop from this window. And, until you come out, me and Jade? We'll be sitting right here."

Chapter 27

The coffee shop wasn't big, but there was enough room between the wooden tables set around the space to have a private conversation and not feel as if the whole place heard every word. Besides, it was nearly empty, with two tables in the back occupied by tourists with thick New York accents. They were so loud Chloe doubted they could hear each other, let alone anyone across the room.

They chose a table by the window. A clear plastic cloth kept spills in check, and a big dispenser filled with rectangular napkins sat in the center of the table. Chloe pushed the dispenser to the side, waved away the menu their server offered and smiled.

"Just coffee, thanks."

They had slipped into chairs opposite one another. With a nod, the other woman said, "Make that two. Thanks."

The waitress, a teenager who looked thoroughly bored, went to get their order. Chloe debated waiting until they were served before asking what this was about. It was a wasted internal debate; the other woman dove right in.

"So I bet you're wondering who I am, right? And why I insisted on speaking with you, right?" She drummed her fingertips on the tabletop. Chloe saw she wore five or six silver rings. None on her wedding finger. "Right?"

The waitress delivered two cups of coffee. Chloe splashed cream in hers. The other woman opened a packet of sugar substitute, poured it into the liquid and gave it a fast stir with the spoon that had arrived on her saucer.

"Well, yes." She offered a friendly smile, the way she would with a woman who came to see her on a professional level. Being in social work trained her to get people to share. "I won't beat around the bush. I'm curious about why you came to see me. You're sure you don't need any help? We have lots of options open to women these days. Women's lib really has opened some doors wide for us. If you need something, we can help you."

Troubled eyes peered over the edge of the white stoneware. Swallowing, she shook her head. "No. Yes. No—I mean, I do need help but not the kind you're thinking. And I don't need an agency—at least I hope it won't come to that. I need you—you're the only one who can help me." She squared her shoulders. "You've got to help me. It's a matter of life and death. How it comes out is all up to you. I hate to lay it all on your head, but hey, my options are—well, they're non-existent."

While she listened, she considered the possibility the woman might be on drugs. She didn't smell like weed, which had such a distinctive aroma that hung on hair and clothing it was hard to miss. Her irises were neither dilated nor pinpricks, so that let out the psychotropic fun rides. She wasn't slurring her words, and there was no reek of alcohol on her, so she wasn't drunk.

Aside from acting too jittery for the bright, sunny day and the fact that she had a hard time meeting Chloe's gaze, the woman seemed pretty normal. As far as normal went.

It hit her that time was passing. And she wanted to get home to check on her uncle. Make him an early dinner. Avoid Neil if she could. Then pamper herself a bit. Wash her hair and get all the residual sand out. Shave her legs. Polish her toenails. Fine-tooth-comb brow tweezing.

All preparation for the moment when Doctor Dreamy went full speed ahead. After last night, it was just a matter of time. And, just thinking about getting naked with that handsome guy slicked her in spots that hadn't slicked in a long, long time.

Chloe forced herself to focus on the present. She took a sip of the tepid coffee, put her cup on the heavy saucer and pulled out the professional demeanor.

"I don't even know your name."

"Right! I should have told you that when I came to your office. And, by the way, I'm sorry I did that— come to your work. I mean, I know it wasn't cool, but I couldn't think of anything else. A girl's gotta do what a girl's gotta do, right?"

"Right." She drew the word out. The other woman talked at warp speed, as if late for a bus. "So, your name?"

"Oh. Right. My name."

It hit her that she should begin counting how many times the word "right" was used in the conversation. The conversation to nowhere.

"Yes." She couldn't say the other word again. She just couldn't do it. "Your name?"

A small quirk of the lips which finally had stopped speeding. "My name is Debra Linker."

They were making progress.

"Nice to meet you, Debra."

A slight head tilt sent a cascade of brown silk over a shoulder. "I'm Patty Linker's sister." She waited a beat. "Patty Linker. She married Philip Pendergast. So, she was Patty Pendergast. Ring any bells?"

Suddenly the world tilted sideways. Ice ran in her veins. And a sick, sour taste rose from her gut. Bells? They were the least of her worries.

Clarity hit her like a train. The child on the beach. It couldn't be—but it was. She had no doubt, the little girl was hers.

Debra glanced out the window. Stared at the traffic on Main Street for a long minute. Her eyes glistened.

"She and Phil were killed a month ago. Drunk driving—damn him, but Phil never could hold his scotch." She scrubbed a hand over her eyes. Then she met Chloe's gaze again, steely determination in the troubled gray eyes. "Six years ago, they adopted a baby girl. Your daughter. Penny is my niece—and she has no parents now."

The world spun around her. For an awful moment, Chloe thought she might be sick.

She didn't realize she was crying until Debra reached across the table and wiped her tears with one of the paper napkins. She pressed the napkin into her hand.

"It's a helluva shock, I know, but it seems the best way to tell you about your daughter. I have to do it. You understand, right?"

Chapter 28

Driving a motorcycle without wearing a helmet or concentrating on the road was a recipe for disaster, but all the angels in heaven must have been watching over her, because Chloe made it to Lobster Cove in one piece. It was a miracle, because she did not remember a single mile of the drive.

She parked the bike in the cracked concrete driveway. It had been installed sometime in the 1940s, and, like everything else in the place, had seen better days. Weeds grew up between the cracks, and a clump of wild Shasta daisies thrived in a far corner.

Neil's shiny red truck was parked to one side. It stood out, a glittering star against a faded background. The chrome was buffed, the wax job made the paint shimmer and even the whitewall tires had a coat of something shiny on them. It was either evidence of an orderly man or a life so dull he had nothing better to do than toy with the vehicle.

It wasn't the time to contemplate the state of Neil's existence when her own had been turned upside down—yet again.

She'd avoided him since their last disastrous conversation, and she'd hoped to continue the trend. It wasn't her intention to be home this early but Debra's visit and shocking revelation had blown her schedule all to hell.

And it might be blowing her life in the same direction.

Eighteen hours, that's about all it had been between the last time Kyle kissed her and the instant Debra walked into the agency. So she'd had nearly a whole day of bliss. It had been great while it lasted, but nothing good hung around in her life.

She wanted to kick herself for believing she could find happiness with someone like the handsome doctor. It had been a pipe dream, and she hadn't even gotten to smoke the damn pipe.

As she rounded the corner of the house, she heard the hammering. Five bangs. A pause. Five bangs. Another pause. There was a rhythm to Neil's work, a steadiness. Just like his life, she thought.

Maybe that was the root cause for her refusing to settle down with him. She'd resisted, knowing he was content to stay in Lobster Cove, live on the same street he'd lived on his whole life, pass his days in quiet satisfaction and eventually end up in the village cemetery. There was nothing wrong with wanting those things but it wasn't the life for her.

Shading her eyes with one hand, she looked up—and caught him looking down.

"Hi." His voice was flat.

He lifted his hammer, holding a nail against the new plywood covering the repaired beams and struck it. The sharp metallic ping sounded louder back here. One. Two. Three. Four. Five slams, and he pulled a new nail into position. Her avoidance tactics had earned her his determination to ignore her.

"Neil?"

He paused, the hammer pulled back to his

shoulder. He did not look up from the work. "What?"

"Can we talk?"

She hadn't planned on discussing the situation with him at all. Then, when she saw his truck, her heart softened. He deserved to know the truth—finally.

"I think we said all we have to say the other night." He struck the nail, so she waited while he pounded it in.

"I really want to talk with you."

Scooting over twelve inches, he held a new nail in place. Before he raised the tool, he said, "So it's all about what you need, is it? Excuse me if I'm not falling all over myself to listen but if I recall, you've never been real big on hearing about me. What I want. What I need. How I feel, damn it!"

Neil hit the nail so hard it only took two smacks with the hammer to send it home.

"Please. It's important."

It occurred to her those very same words had gotten her to agree to go to the coffee shop.

He moved again, closer to the edge of the roof. She didn't need to look to know they had attracted attention. Out of the corner of her eye, she saw a curtain move on the second floor. Someone, she couldn't tell who, had already heard them.

Positioning another nail, he shook his head. The intensity of his anger surprised her. Through the years, she'd witnessed the normal moments of annoyance when things hadn't gone his way or when the football team lost a game but none of that had even been close to being this destructive.

Social working skills let her recognize he was very nearly beyond hearing reason. She gave him a moment, hoping the silence would let his hot head cool. He didn't hammer the nail in, and he didn't yell, either. Sitting back on his heels, he finally looked at her.

With a sneer, he said, "We've said it all. It's a bitch, but I'm beyond caring about what you want. You've made it clear you don't give a shit about what I want, so why shouldn't I give you a taste of that? Hmm?"

"I hear you, but I really do need to talk with you, Neil. Please, I'm begging you."

He raised one eyebrow. Instead of looking charming, he seemed incredulous.

It would have been easy to back down. Walk inside and tell herself she'd tried to do the right thing—if this was, in fact the right thing at all. But she couldn't do it. Couldn't leave without telling him the truth—even if he made her feel subhuman beneath his icy stare.

"Please? Really, I'm begging here."

He wiped a forearm across his chin, the hammer dangling from his hand. "Begging? Well, that's something new, isn't it? Fine. Call me St. Nick and pretend it's Christmas Eve. I'll give you this one—but I've got to warn you, I'm in no mood for more bullshit. Even Santa Claus has a bullshit limit."

"No bullshit, I promise."

"So, talk."

She waited for him to come down, but he didn't move.

Shouting across the space between them? Too awful to contemplate, so she shook her head. "Come down so we can talk. Please."

"I can hear you from up here."

"I'm still begging—come down so we don't have to screech across the yard. Our business doesn't need to be broadcast to the whole town. Please?"

When he sat resolutely on his heels, not budging even a whisker, she added, "I'll do anything if you'll just come down so we can talk."

Even if it meant going for dinner with him, or a walk on the beach so he could give her whatever piece of his mind he was chomping at the bit to give, it was worth it. Her news would reach the rest of Lobster Cove quickly enough; now was not the moment to divulge.

"You *are* desperate! Anything? Would you do anything, Chloe?"

In for a penny, in for a pound. The old-time saying had been carved into a lintel in the house by an early settler. She had no idea who'd left the message, but it was never far from her mind.

"Anything."

"Marry me."

Shit. She hadn't seen that coming.

He waited, holding her gaze with his in what felt like an optical wrestling match. Tossing the hammer onto the plywood, Neil stood and headed for the ladder. She watched, thankful he hadn't pressed on the marriage bit.

He covered the space between the house and where she stood in three strides.

"Fine. I'm down."

"Thank you."

"Talk fast—I swear, my patience is shot, and I haven't slept since you told me to piss off. I'm ready for a cold six-pack—or two. And, I don't want to argue with you anymore. I've spent my whole life waiting for a woman who doesn't want me—I feel like shit on a shingle and I'm at the end of my rope. So, make it fast. I'm not sure I can take much more."

Chapter 29

"I've never meant to hurt you, Neil. I'm sorry."

His gaze did not soften. A pulse beat at his temple and his jaw clenched. She had no doubt he meant what he said; she just had no idea how she was going to broach the difficult subject when he was so angry.

She inhaled deeply, catching a whiff of hard-working man, wood shavings and a hint of the spicy after shave he wore.

"I, ah—God, this is hard." She looked away, to the oak. It had withstood so many storms. She wished she were half as strong as the old tree. How to start a conversation she did not plan to ever have?

"Whatever it is, just say it. How much worse can my life get?"

Dismal words from a man who encouraged others to keep their sights set on the positive parts of life. He was a pro at finding the silver lining in all of life's clouds. This sarcastic man before her was someone she'd never met before.

"I just—I don't know how to say this." She hated the way her voice trembled, so she cleared her throat. It might not make a difference, but it couldn't hurt.

He raked a hand through his hair. The waves fell nearly to his shoulders.

"Just say it, okay? I'm too shot for guessing games."

She nodded.

"We have a daughter."

The world around them faded and time stood still. They stared at each other, neither flinching. Neither looked away. A flood of emotions passed through Neil's eyes. Some of them she'd seen before but there were an unidentifiable few.

They stood that way for what felt like forever. When she couldn't stand the hard stare boring into her heart, she lifted a shoulder. "Do you understand?" She kept her tone soft, as if trying to gentle a frightened animal.

"No. I don't understand—not one bit. What the hell is going on?"

She looked away and realized they must have attracted more attention when he ceased hammering and they stopped hollering across the lawn. A neighbor stood on tiptoe in the yard next door, craning his neck to see above the shrubbery. She looked at the house. A figure was in one of the windows.

"Can we go somewhere to talk?" She waved a hand to the house next door, then swept it to her home behind him. "We don't need an audience."

"Come on." He grabbed her hand and moved so quickly she practically had to run to keep up. When they reached his truck, he opened the passenger door, and she climbed in. It was as pristine inside as out.

The key dangled from the ignition. He turned it before his door closed, put the vehicle in reverse and backed out with less caution than he ordinarily exercised. Swinging wide, he headed down the street. They both knew where he was going.

Lobster Cove was so small that four minutes later

Neil nosed into a spot near the beginning of the beach path. Atlantic waves peeked between the dunes, but they didn't sit and gaze. He drummed a hand on the wheel.

"I have a million questions." His voice was as hard as his hand.

Whatever anger he had, and however he planned to express it, she couldn't evade. She owed it to him to accept whatever he dished out. They wouldn't be having this conversation if she had been honest with him.

"I know."

He snorted. "And that's the whole problem between us, isn't it? All these years, and you've known everything while I haven't known jack shit."

His voice grew louder with each word, until he practically yelled.

Somewhere between Bar Harbor and the Cove, some level of numbness had washed over her. Now, the impact of his anger didn't cut deep. It was there, and she was aware, but detachment insulated her.

Detached from my own life, she thought. Not a good thing.

She nearly said, "I know" but snapped her mouth shut before the words passed her lips.

"Damn it, Chloe. When are you going to be honest with me about anything?"

"That's not fair—"

"It's not? All these years, I thought you'd finally come around and love me the way I love you. But you never had any intention of doing that, did you? You led me on, and I was a chump who waited blindly."

"I never led you on. I just…"

"Led me the hell on."

She swallowed the tears she knew were close. The lump in her throat made it difficult to talk, so she shook her head and looked away.

The venom in his words was killing her.

"I don't suppose you'd like to tell me about your date the other night. You know, the one with some fancy pants guy you met?" He paused, drew a ragged breath. "No, I didn't figure you would. I'm an idiot—one who's wasted his life wanting someone who never loved him."

She turned, angry now that he tried to back her into a corner. Fair was fair—but this wasn't fair.

"You are not an idiot."

"Why don't you tell me about the date you had the other night? Hmm?"

His tone was so belligerent she wanted to slap him.

She balled her fists in her lap. "That's none of your business."

He let out a derisive whoop. "No? Listen, chickie, in the Cove, everything is everybody's business, remember? This place is too damn small for secrets."

They were getting nowhere. Fast.

Chloe opened the heavy door and jumped to the ground. She slammed the door closed, headed for the path, and did not look back. She was sick of talking with him, anyway.

It stung that he was right—to a point.

Neil followed. She tried to move faster, to put distance between them, but he had her by a mile with his long legs. He caught up to her, reached for her arm and swung her around to face him.

"You're the one who wanted to talk." His gaze

swept over her face and lingered on her mouth. For a crazy second she thought he might kiss her. "Now, talk."

Taking orders was not something she did with a smile on her face. And, he'd pushed her buttons hard enough already.

"I never lied about how I felt about you. We were young, Neil. We were in love. I was—I don't know!—confused. Young—did I say young yet? Damn it, just before we graduated I began to have doubts about things. About us."

"Which you didn't bother to share with me."

She jutted out her chin. "No, I didn't. I knew how you felt, and I didn't want to hurt you. Besides, I'd agreed to…you know…graduation night…"

"Say it." He spat the words.

She swallowed. Again, tears threatened. She felt tossed about, more confused now than when they were in high school. So much time had passed, but theirs was a wide and deep history. Getting mired in it took no doing at all.

"Say it, Chloe."

Her mouth was dry. "I kept my word to you."

"Not really. I thought we were making love, that we'd waited until we were adults, but all the while we were—" He swept his arms out. "We were here—right here!—we had two different ideas. I was making love to the woman I adored." A muscle worked in his jaw. He leaned close, so close his breath warmed her face. "And you? You were keeping an agreement—and screwing me."

She took a step back. He hadn't touched her, but she felt as if she'd been backhanded.

"I did not."

"Maybe I should've paid you. With cash, you know? I mean, it wasn't love, so it was just sex. And women who screw as part of a business arrangement? Well, they get paid for working, don't they?" When he reached into his pocket and pulled out his wallet, she snapped.

She had never hit anyone before but sheer fury took over. Her arm went back, her hand opened flat and without any conscious thought or effort, she sent her hand flying.

The slap was loud. The sting on her skin made her grimace. The look of astonishment on his face gave her some degree of satisfaction.

He raised a hand to his cheek. His eyes had gone so round they would have been comical if either of them had been in the mood to laugh.

Her voice was deadly calm when she spoke. It was a surprise to her, because her insides felt anything but.

"You are being hateful, and I don't deserve it. I loved you. I was young. I got confused about college, my feelings for you…about everything. But I never let you down. We vowed to lose our virginity together, here, the night we graduated. I never, ever considered letting you down on that point." She stopped, shook her hand to squelch the pain. "And up until a minute ago, I loved you. On some level, I loved you. I think I always would have…but right now you disgust me. I think you just cured me of loving you, Neil."

He could have passed for Lot's wife, turned to a pillar of salt. He barely moved at all, his breathing had gone so shallow. His gaze followed hers, though, so she knew he understood every word.

She took another step back. All she wanted was to get away from him, so she turned to walk down the beach. There was a path beyond the boulders that led back into the village. He had the truck, so would not follow if she left that way.

A few yards from where he stood, she turned. He watched her, immobile.

"Graduation night? We should have used a condom, because I got pregnant. I gave our daughter up for adoption. I found out today that she was recently orphaned." Tears began to slide down her cheeks but she did not try to stop them. They were, she knew, only the beginning of what would be a flood once she got off the beach. "So, I did lie to you, actually. A lie of omission. And for the record—it was the only time I lied to you. Ever."

Chapter 30

Chloe stretched, sending the sheet sliding off the bed into a puddle on the floor. She flexed her muscles. Arched her back. A slight twinge when she twisted from side to side, but it wasn't bad at all. Considering the abuse her body had endured recently, she felt pretty good.

Amazing what a date with Jack Daniels and Coke, with a couple of aspirin as a late-night snack, could do.

She rolled on her side and looked out the window. The glass was ancient, and the top pane was cracked in one corner. Last summer a crew of aluminum siding and window installers had cruised through the Cove. A lot of families had upgraded their houses, gotten rid of old wooden or shingle siding and outdated, drafty windows. They had not been able to afford the luxury, so the window was repaired with clear tape.

The place was held together by string and spit, but as long as it stayed that way, she had no intention of dumping cash she didn't have into repairs. It was bad enough the debt for the main roof was sucking her under. Six months were going to fly by, and unless she won the state lottery or an act of divine intervention presented itself, she was going to drown. She didn't play the lottery and didn't think she believed in religion, so it was going to get ugly.

But that was months away. Today, she had other

issues to deal with, things that wouldn't wait six months.

Like Neil. He must have taken a few days off from work, because it wasn't the weekend and unless someone else had the same five-count nail-bashing cadence, he was on the roof. There had been no discussion of payment for doing the job, and she doubted he planned to charge although after yesterday anything was possible. But she had seen the plywood leaning against the house, and two rolls of heavy black paper beside bundles of shingles. All of that had to be paid for.

What she needed was an *I Dream of Jeannie* moment. A genie to make wishes come true, sweep away the crap and make her life shine.

Clouds floated lazily in the soft blue morning shy. She watched, wishing she were on one and riding high, contemplating what her next genie wish might be. Daydreams were anything-goes moments, so the list she compiled in her head knew no boundaries.

Most importantly—and at the very top of the list— was restoring Uncle Ted to good health. After that, everything else seemed insignificant. She'd figure out how to deal with the daughter she didn't know, how to make the kid's life everything she thought it would be when she'd given her up. The girls? They'd all be set for life, doing whatever they wanted to get them closer to realizing their dreams. Even Neil—he'd get a genie wish. The man behaved like a jackass sometimes but he deserved to be happy—as long as she didn't have to marry him to make that happen.

The jagged line in the window cut a fluffy cloud in half. The house. Oh, yes, the house would get a ride on the magic carpet, too. She'd have the whole place done over. Make it sparkle so well it would be the prettiest place in town.

Then, with Uncle Ted healthy, everyone on the right track and the house done over she could finally make the dream of a lifetime come true. One of them, anyhow.

It would be within her reach to open a home for women displaced by neglect, violence or other unfortunate circumstances. A college professor had warned that anyone taking on social work as a profession had to have a heart for the downtrodden and a desire to impact the world for the better. If not, it was time to change career paths but that was unnecessary advice as far as she was concerned. There was nothing she wanted more than to help people—but unless that daydream genie showed up—and soon—the dream would remain just that.

There had only ever been two big *when-I-grow-up* dreams in her life. The first was the women's home. The second seemed even further away than the first.

Staring at the clouds wasn't going to change her life. And if she didn't change her circumstances, there was zero chance she could change anyone else's. She knew that. But, she rolled over onto her back again and gazed at the ceiling. A wall-to-wall crack cut across the painted plaster. She closed her eyes and tried to push her surroundings away, the way Beth down at the yoga center advised.

It was impossible to forget she lived in ramshackle central when people kept reminding her.

"Chloe? Are you awake?" Julia called up the stairs, in a voice so loud it carried over the hammering.

"I am now." Instantly contrite, she added, "I've been awake for a while. What's up?"

Julia appeared in the doorway. A hand on her hip and fire in her eyes, she didn't mince words. "You have today off, don't you?"

"I do. And tomorrow morning, too."

They'd discussed her schedule earlier in the week. Julia had a gallon of paint for the walls of her room and they'd planned a painting party. Gabby had agreed to take Uncle Ted to the beach, then out to lunch, so that by the time he returned the paint fumes would be out of the house.

The other woman already wore her painting clothes. The baggy t-shirt and ripped jeans looked entirely out of place on her.

Chloe sat up and swung her bare legs over the side of the bed. Grimy shorts, used mostly for gardening, topped the clean laundry pile so she reached for them.

"Give me a sec. I just need to grab some coffee and check on Uncle Ted."

She stood and began to pull on the shorts. Julia stepped into the room, closed the door and put her back against it. The house had settled so much in over two hundred years that most of the doors didn't latch—including the bedroom door.

"No, you don't." Julia folded her arms across her chest. "You can grab coffee somewhere else, and your uncle is fine. He and Gabby have a relaxing day planned, starting with breakfast at The Dockside. They're already gone."

She buttoned her shorts. "What gives?"

"I don't want to pry into your private life, but we all heard the argument you and Neil had yesterday. No, that's wrong. We heard banging and yelling, and then we watched you leave together. You came home alone and I'm sorry to say this, but you're not one of those women who can cry a river and still look gorgeous. Your eyes are bloodshot."

She ran her fingers through her hair, pulled it into a ponytail high on her head and slipped an elastic band off her wrist and onto the bundle. It was no shock her eyes were reddened; they felt dry and scratchy.

"I'm sure they are, but that's no reason to not paint your room. We'll get it done so fast we'll have time to move your stuff back into place before lunchtime."

"I don't think so."

"The room isn't huge. Sure, we can do it." She pulled one of her uncle's faded old t-shirts from a drawer. It already had paint splatters on it and would do just fine.

"You're not getting it, sister."

She turned. It wasn't like Julia to put off such negative vibes. And the scowl on her face wasn't typical, either.

"What gives?"

"I hate to be the bearer of a psychedelic funk, but we think it's best if you grab your get-out-of-Dodge gear and get while the getting is good."

"It's too early, and I'm too hung over for riddles. What's going on?"

The hammering never stopped. Endless banging followed by a short pause, followed by banging. Over and over, background music to the morning.

Jerking a finger to the ceiling, Julia said, "That's going on. Neil and his storm cloud." She sighed. "I don't know what happened between you but whatever it was, it had to be some heavy shit. I mean, real heavy. That guy is not the Neil we all know; he looks as if he hasn't slept in days. He smells like he swam in Old Granddad, the rotgut only the craziest drink. And he's just too ornery for words. Every look he gives has a dagger behind it. It's just not good."

Chloe backed up to the window seat, bent her knees and sat down.

She wanted to think the other woman exaggerated but Julia never exaggerated. Never.

"It's that bad?"

A hard nod. "Worse."

"Wow. I never figured he'd act this way. I mean, I knew he'd be upset, but I wasn't prepared for this." She met the other's gaze and shook her head. "I never saw it coming. My mind is numb, I think."

"Grab some stuff. I'll go out and talk with him so you can get out of here without having to see the guy. By the time he hears the bike, it'll be too late for him to stop you. Honestly, you look like you need a day away from whatever's going on, too."

She got moving. She switched the old shorts for a pair of jeans. A peasant top, blue with a paisley design, hung on the back of a chair so she put it on.

Draping her brown leather purse over her shoulder, she went to the door and gave her friend a hug.

"Thanks."

"No problem. Just take care of you today, okay? Walk away from your life and get some perspective."

It sounded divine. "I will. Are you sure you'll be okay here, though? You know, with the man with the hammer?"

"Definitely. Reva's home." She opened the

bedroom door. The look of understanding she gave tugged at Chloe's heart. "Remember, he's pissed at you, not the rest of us. Whatever's going on? It's between the two of you. It's…ah, it's big, isn't it?"

She nodded. "The biggest."

"Figured as much. Why don't you call later on? We'll give you the update. If the coast isn't clear by then, we'll figure something out."

They exchanged another quick hug before she went downstairs. The hammering was louder on the first floor, and even more so when she slipped out the front door. She walked the bike down the street a ways before getting on and driving off.

Exercising caution when dealing with angry men was a professional tactic she never expected to carry into her private life. The comparison was minimal but gliding off undetected gave her a glimpse of what women like Jackie, and all the rest they met and helped, dealt with.

It made her even more determined to find a way to make the women's home a reality.

Chapter 31

Nothing compared to riding a motorcycle on a hot, summer day along a winding coastal road. The wind against her cheeks, glimpses of ocean peeking between shake-shingle cottages perched on the edge of land and the sun warming her bare head were enough to dispel uneasiness from a woman's mind. Almost as soon as she'd hit the big sign at the edge of town that read "Lobster Cove—If You Lived Here, You'd Be Home Now" her shoulders felt lighter.

Ordinarily her days off were spent on the house. It did not seem so by looking at it, but she used every extra hour either doing yard work or trying to slapdash some inside job. Fixing the unfixable, it seemed.

A day to herself? It was almost as if the genie had come and granted at least one wish.

Yesterday had been payday, so she had a few bucks in her bag. Two towns down the coast, her favorite small boutique. Browsing for a little while—or all day, if she wanted—was a treat so she set Vintage Treasures as her destination and let the hum of tires on asphalt chase the truths of her life away.

Lobster Cove was the quintessential historic beach village. Others along the Maine coast were nice, each in its own way, but none compared to the Cove. It was a fact, universally accepted by anyone familiar with the state.

Summertime brought tourists from around the country, and sometimes from across the globe, so the spillover ended up in the smaller towns nearby. Their motel and cabin owners benefited from the visitors who couldn't find rooms in Lobster Cove proper. Places like the one where Vintage Treasures did business owed most of their revenue indirectly to the place it could never be.

Still, summer days in neighboring towns were never as chockfull of visitors as her hometown, so Chloe did not mind parking a block from the shop. She wandered past a row of colorful houses. Gardens dotted side yards, with tomatoes ripening on vines and melons sprawling onto lawns.

The shop occupied the first floor of one of the grand old ladies. The Victorian was painted a bright purple, with gray shutters and pink trim, and looked like a birthday cake more than it did a place of business. A varnished oak door was propped wide on the front porch, which meant the place was open, so she climbed the steps and walked inside.

Time stood still in Vintage Treasures. Literally. Several mantel clocks, ornate mixed with gaudy, had their hands pointed straight up to twelve. Each one told the same incorrect time. It was a quirky place; the clocks were just one of many interesting oddities.

The woman who greeted her wore a beehive hairdo that gave her a full foot of additional height. It looked glued in place but coordinated with her navy blue sweater, pencil skirt and spectator pumps. The sweater was so tight it was incredible the woman could draw a breath.

Chloe couldn't help herself. She stared at the

torpedo-shaped breasts snugged into the blue wool.

"I know." The clerk pushed her chest out and waved a hand down her ensemble. "Those Rosie the Riveters, they were tough broads. Everything, including girdle, stockings, garters and industrial-strength bra, are original. Just as the day they were sold, with prices attached. The strings holding the prices were nearly dust, but the pieces themselves were beautiful."

"Forties?"

"You know it. Not my usual vibe, but every once in a while a woman's got to go out on a limb." She stopped, surveyed Chloe's jeans and top. "Pretty. Suits you but…"

"But?"

She followed when the woman walked toward a selection of dresses hanging on a far wall. How she found them, amidst the juxtaposition of decades in a series of connecting rooms was a mystery.

"But some of these will look amazing on you." She pulled a form-fitting, violet wrap dress off the rack. Holding it up, she looked from Chloe to the dress, then smiled. "Oh, yeah. This will make any man drool."

"I just came in to browse." The drooling man bit ticked her off. This excursion had nothing to do with men; it was hers and hers alone. Actually, with the way Neil was behaving, she wasn't sure she wanted anything to do with *any* man for a while. "There's no man."

The Rosie wannabe pulled a face. "Listen, there's always a man. Unless…is there a woman?"

"No! Neither! Just me, okay?"

The clerk must have realized she'd pushed too many buttons because she hung the dress on a hook and raised her hands. "I'm sorry. I just thought that someone as pretty as you are, with that petite body and gorgeous head of hair...Honey, you're a fox. And if you don't have a man, there's no hope for the rest of us."

A bell went off, the sound coming from the front doorway. A sensor, perhaps, to alert the staff to the presence of newcomers. It was a lifesaver for Chloe, because the woman dashed away.

Free to peruse, she took her time with the racks of old-fashioned clothing. Poodle skirts hung in a row, like a flounced dog show, with coordinating sweaters and neck scarves nearby. A line of evening gowns, some in protective plastic see-through wrappers, made a dazzling display. Below the gowns, velvet pumps and rhinestone sandals waited. Some clothes looked almost new, tucked in among the older items.

She found a peasant top, not too unlike the one she wore, for a fraction of the price she expected to pay for it, so took it to the front counter.

"May I leave this here?"

"Of course." The clerk waved to a couple on their way out. The woman wore a pair of striking beaded earrings and the man carried a stack of books beneath one arm. In one room, there was an assortment of odds and ends, mostly furniture, but some books—if there were any left. "Did you try that dress on yet?"

She shook her head. She'd looked at it a number of times. Run a fingertip over the silky fabric. Admired the garment. But no, she hadn't tried it on.

"I don't have anywhere to wear something like that," she admitted. "I work with battered women. No boyfriend to speak of. No place fun to go. No need for a pretty dress."

Merchandise pressed in on them, a cocoon of color and fabric. The clerk looked around, but they were alone.

"Can I tell you something?"

"Sure."

"I wasn't always what you see now. Believe me, my life has changed. The women you help? I was one, once."

Abuse did not wear a sign to identify where it touched.

"I'm sorry." Chloe put a comforting hand on the woman's arm. "I'm glad you worked your way out of it. You are certainly a testament to the strength of women, aren't you?"

A sheen made the brown eyes darker when they met her gaze. "No. Don't give me all the credit. I'm the one who married a jerk and stayed with him for a year while he used me as a punching bag. It was women like you who gave me the opening to get out of the nightmare. Without them, I think I'd be dead." She sniffed, gave a shaky smile and patted the beehive. "I certainly wouldn't be where I am now, wearing a whole bottle of White Rain hairspray!"

"You might need a whole bottle of shampoo to get the stuff out. I wouldn't smoke, if I were you." There were cases in her files of men who used beauty products to hurt others. Propellants in spray cans were highly flammable.

"I won't. I learned my lesson about smoking. Used to do it, but don't now. I set a fingernail on fire once— you have no idea how scary it is to look down and see your finger's a tiny torch."

She shuddered. "I can't imagine."

"Cured my smoking habit." She pointed to the fitting rooms. "Listen, do a sister a favor. I get a discount, and I'll pass it on to you. Go try on that dress. If it works for you, take it home. Give me faith that someday I'll find a nice guy, settle down, have a kid."

"How's my buying a dress with a very generous discount going to do that?"

Her new friend shrugged, pulling the sweater so tight her breasts almost poked holes in it. "Like I said, if a pretty lady like you doesn't have a fella, there's no hope for the rest of us. Please, give a girl some hope—go try on the dress."

Chapter 32

Shopping only killed so much time. Even after exchanging phone numbers with Madge, the store clerk, and promising to keep in touch, Chloe still had a lot of day left to fill. Compared to Lobster Cove, there was nothing much to see after she'd explored Vintage Treasures, so she headed back the way she had come.

The excursion had been fruitful. Tucked into her backpack were three items, each one a find. The top, which was practically new and would jazz up her work wardrobe. Madge had been right about the dress. It fit like a dream and made her feel special. With a nice pair of shoes, it would be the ideal date ensemble. It was an optimistic purchase, buying it in hopes of being asked out so it would get worn. The clerk's discount made the dress practically free, so it was impossible to say no.

The final item was an impulsive move. She'd been about to check out when she saw the pink, flowery fabric. It brought her instantly back to her childhood, to a time when life seemed a whole lot simpler than it was now. No worries other than whether the ice cream truck would pass by on a hot summer evening.

When she reached the If-You-Lived-Here sign, she nearly blew past. Too early to go home. Besides, the freedom of being without any responsibility was too attractive, even if it was only a short-term situation.

Main Street was bustling by comparison to where

she'd just come from. Tourists posed for photos near the big ship bell on a corner. Parents guided children up the wide stone steps to the Historical Society building. Young love was in full bloom, sending couples walking hand in hand along the sidewalk. The village was alive, and thriving, and not a bad place at all.

She tried to see things from a visitor's point of view. It was a small town, with a Gomer Pyle feel, where the sea shimmered like diamonds in a jeweler's window and life proceeded at a slower pace than in most other places.

If she didn't live there, she might visit, too.

Matinees began early in the old theatre just off Main Street. She parked behind the big redbrick building, got off the bike and looked up. The sun was high, right about noon. Perfect timing for the earliest—and cheapest—show.

The Muppet Movie wouldn't be her first choice of films but a comedy featuring Fozzie Bear, Kermit, and Miss Piggy was enough to take anyone's mind off of real life. She bought a ticket at the window then headed to the concession counter. There was no line, so she ordered a large popcorn with plenty of butter and an Orange Crush.

She got change from her five, thanked the teenager behind the counter and grabbed her goodies. When she turned, she froze.

Debra had her hand on the little girl's shoulder. She smiled. "Hi. I like your taste in drinks. Beats coffee any day, right?"

"Uh, hi." Her gaze went to the big hazel eyes staring up at her. "Hi."

The voice was sweet. "I like Crush, too."

The bottle in Chloe's hand was icy cold. She held it out. "Here, you can have this one."

"Really?"

"Really."

Debra hadn't said a word. When her niece turned a hopeful gaze on her, she tugged the thick ponytail and nodded.

"It's okay. Just remember to say—"

"Thank you." Penny held a hand out, and Chloe passed her the soda bottle. Their fingers grazed, and it hit her that it was the first time since giving birth to her that she'd touched her daughter.

Her daughter. The immensity of it almost made her dizzy.

"You're welcome."

Debra watched them with a keen eye. She was behind the girl, so she raised a questioning brow when she caught Chloe's gaze.

There was no answer to the silent question. Instead, she turned to the kid behind the counter and ordered another soda. "Want anything?"

Debra shook her head. "No, thanks. We just had lunch, actually, then I happened to look over and see you. I wanted to say hi, and introduce you to my niece, Penny."

"Hi, Penny." Chloe lifted her bottle in salute.

"Hi. You going to see the Muppets, too?"

"I am. And it looks like we'll pretty much have the whole theatre to ourselves. I think everyone must be at the beach because they're not in here with us, are they?"

Penny appeared to be a happy child, despite what had happened to her. She was clean and well-groomed, and did not look like she'd recently suffered a traumatic experience.

"We should sit together, right?" Debra did not try to hide her eagerness. "Right?"

"Right." Chloe asked Penny, "Do you have a favorite side in a movie theatre? A place you like to sit?"

"In the middle." She skipped to the door leading into the auditorium. "Right in the middle—and never, ever behind a lady with big hair."

They followed the little one down the aisle. They let her choose their seats.

In an undertone, Debra asked, "She's sweet. A great kid, right?"

"Yes, of course. She's wonderful."

"So, you've given it some thought? You're going to do this, right?"

Penny had chosen a row near the front, where no one could block their view. She went to the seats directly in the center of the row. Looking back over a shoulder, she waited for them to join her. She was drinking the soda so quickly she was sure to need to go to the restroom before the previews were over.

Chloe looked at the child. Her child. It was a gift she never thought to have, this connection with Penny. It was a huge complication in an already-complicated life but there was no way around that.

She met Debra's gaze. "I am."

Chapter 33

It was early afternoon when the movie ended. She had made a strategy of sorts with Debra, all spoken in undertones during slow parts of the film. Chloe needed a day or so to make plans and rearrange her life a bit. The focus was on Penny's well-being, so rushing headfirst into something without thinking it through was not an option.

Debra did not mind keeping her for a while longer. She loved the child but admitted she was not the one to care for her properly. Besides, she wanted to respect her sister's wishes, and return Penny to her natural mother.

She nearly invited them to go to Quinn Beach with her, but it was clear by the whiny tone in the child's voice that it was naptime. Debra promised to call later on, after putting the girl to bed. It was a hard goodbye, but maybe it was good that she had some time to herself.

A child was a tricky situation, even when planned. An unplanned six-year-old was a major complication—and was entering into an already-tangled state of affairs.

Well, it will just have to work out, she decided as she walked down Main Street. She'd changed into her bathing suit in the cinema restroom and planned to sit on her towel on the beach, all alone with her thoughts. Maybe the sun would shine ideas down on her. If not? She'd get a killer tan.

Locals tended to be amused by vacationers who lugged so much to the beach they looked ready to go on safari rather than beachcombing. Mothers, canvas totes slung over each shoulder, leading children dragging boogie boards, kites and snorkels, followed by puffing, red-faced fathers bent beneath the burden of woven beach chairs, insulated coolers and, sometimes, small tents. It was all comical.

Year-round Cove residents generally carried two things to Quinn Beach: a towel—any kind would do— and, if it were coming up on mealtime, something to eat. A sandwich, cheese and fruit, even a bag of Fritos worked.

Chloe's towel was threadbare, which meant it rolled without too much trouble into her backpack. She shook it out, placed the worn blue-and-white stripes on the sand, and dropped her backpack beside it.

Kicking off the flip flops that were also part of her backpack essentials, she folded her legs and settled down onto the towel. The sea was calm, white caps in the distance breaking up the shades of blue with ribbons of foam.

Teenagers frolicked close to the shore, just in from where a line of submerged rocks hid. They were hard to miss, being the noisiest group on the beach. Three couples, all laughing, splashing and swimming. Every few minutes, someone went under, victim to a playful dunking. They were fun to watch, so she observed them for a while.

She had been that young once. That carefree. That innocent.

It seemed a dream, almost, being so unencumbered by obligations.

The ocean called, so she left her cares on the towel and walked to the edge. Skirting a toddler and what looked to be his grandmother, she put her feet in the water. The baby came close, waving a chubby fist her way. He wore only a diaper covered by clear plastic pants and his bare skin was sand-caked. He held up a seashell, babbling around four teeth.

"He's a honey." She leaned down and smiled at the baby. "That's a pretty seashell you've got there. Very pretty."

"He's not big on conversation yet, but we're getting there." The older woman had varicose veins that stuck out so far from the legs not covered by her skirt that Chloe winced. Getting old didn't look like a picnic.

"How old is he?"

"Jamie will be two next week. Time flies, you know. I remember when his father, my son, was this age. We brought him here to see the beach, too." She met Chloe's gaze with a wistful smile. "What can I say? We come all the way from Vermont—Benton, a small town—to Lobster Cove, just to give him the same experience we gave his father. My husband, Sol—may he rest in peace—he loved the beach. We came every summer." She shook her head. "Now? It's just me. A man who loved the ocean so much shouldn't have passed on a farm, but what can you do?"

"I'm sorry."

The grandmother picked the toddler up, seashell and all. "Ah, what can you do? I'd better get him changed and put some clothes on him. His mother has such fair skin, and she's passed it on. He'll look like a lobster in fifteen minutes if I'm not careful."

"Nice to meet you."

"You, too. Enjoy your swim."

When she began to walk away, Chloe went further into the water. The woman's voice stopped her.

"Miss? You have any kids?"

Water swirled around her knees. Seaweed brushed her calf, and the urge to dive in without responding was as powerful as the tug of ocean against her legs.

"Kids?" She took a deep breath. "I do."

It wasn't as hard as she thought it would be, so she added, "A daughter."

It seemed to please the woman, because she nodded her approval before she made her way up the sand with the little boy.

She dove into the ocean, let the water hold her weightless, and tried not to think too hard about how drastically her life was about to change.

She swam for a long time, going out past the line of submerged rocks. They had been the cause of many shipwrecks over the centuries and she kept in mind that the space she enjoyed was above a watery grave.

The Historical Society had many intriguing artifacts from some of the countless wrecks. An enormous mermaid from the bow of one ship hung suspended from a ceiling, piles of Spanish coin, pottery and utensils, ballast and even some clothing in moisture-controlled cases were among their best pieces.

Sometime in the eighteenth century, the captain of one of the ships lost off the beach lived in Uncle Ted's house. There was a mystery about the man, Sam Fisher, which had never been completely unraveled. Some said he was a pirate; others insisted he was a ship's captain. It was, like so many tales told around lobster pots, pointless. What mattered is that he lived, and was still remembered.

When her limbs grew weary, she headed for the shore. She walked the last yards, shaking her hair out as she went. When she looked up she saw her humble beach towel had been invaded.

"This is cool, finding you here." She dropped to the towel, rolled onto her stomach, and rested on her elbows.

Uncle Ted's beach chair sat in the circle of shade created by the umbrella. With his long, tanned legs stretched out before him, hands crossed on his flat belly and a smile on his face, he looked like he hadn't a care in the world. Beside him, Reva sat on a beach towel and held a big book on her lap.

Reva met her gaze and smiled. She searched her eyes for a sign of anything amiss, but there was nothing to see.

"Pretty cool finding you here. You're the one who's usually too busy to laze about the beach."

"Look who's calling the kettle black, Ms. Bring a Book!"

"Ladies, ladies—don't make me separate you two." Uncle Ted grinned. They all knew the teasing was pure fun. "Listen, I have a roll of Life Savers in my pocket. Anyone want one?"

They both accepted the candy and sat in quiet contemplation for a few minutes.

Simple pleasures make life special, Chloe thought as she swirled the cherry flavor across her tongue.

She checked Uncle Ted's face. His eyes were open and when he saw her look over, he winked.

"What's up, my dear?"

"Am I that transparent?"

Reva smirked. "Like a pebble in the bottom of glass of water. I'd say that's pretty transparent."

"We all know you and Neil had a scuffle last night, honey. And we saw his face this morning—damn, that man looked like he could have chewed his arm off, he was so pissed." Uncle Ted looked over the top of his aviator sunglasses. "Why don't you get it off your chest, whatever it is?"

"It's something good. I think it is, anyway." She sat up, took a t-shirt from her backpack, and put it on. Something this momentous shouldn't be blurted out when half naked. She opened her hands wide, palms to the cloudless blue sky. "I have a daughter."

The book hit the sand. The pages snapped closed with a leaden thump, but the almost-lawyer didn't bat an eye. "A daughter?" Her gaze dropped to Chloe's flat abdomen. "When are you due?"

She looked at her uncle, who hadn't said a word. "Six years ago. July 10, 1973, to be exact."

He broke into a grin. Slapping his hands together, he declared, "I'm a great-uncle—now that calls for a celebration!"

Chloe laughed when Reva grabbed her and hugged her. Then, she went on the examination stand.

"Is it Neil's?"

She nodded.

"Now we know why he's so angry. He didn't know?"

With a sigh, she shook her head. Wet tendrils stuck to her neck, so she pushed them away. "I gave her up for adoption. I didn't tell him."

Reva pursed her lips. "On the birth certificate? Father's name?"

"I left it blank."

"Ah…so, he's really pissed."

She looked at her uncle. "He wants me to marry him."

"He's always wanted that. Tell me something I don't already know." He pulled the candy from his pocket and chose the top one for himself before handing her the roll. She took it but did not select another Life Saver.

"I don't want to marry him, Uncle Ted. I just don't."

He straightened. "Motherhood must've clogged your ears, honey. I said, tell me something I don't know. Neil is a nice guy—for someone else. He's not the right man for you. Never has been, never will be."

"But Kyle…" Reva grinned. "Now that's another story, isn't it?"

Yes, Kyle was in a class all his own. She'd given the relationship they were building a lot of thought last night, and again today. It was wonderful, and full of promise, but sadly it might fizzle before it took off.

"Yeah, he's pretty cool, but I don't know how he's going to feel about Penny."

"Penny. I like that." Uncle Ted smiled so broadly she forgot about Neil and Kyle. The excitement radiating from her uncle's eyes pushed every niggling doubt from her mind. "So when do I get to meet my great-niece? I'm so happy I could dance—"

"No dancing!" Reva put a hand on his arm when he looked ready to push out of the chair. "Please, no dancing."

The truth will set you free—isn't that what the great man had said? So many times, she had used those very same words with the women who came to the agency, assured them they would feel less bogged down by whatever life had hit them with if only they'd stand up and tell the truth. Help themselves, so others could help them, also.

Time to tell her own truth. It was, again, not as easy as she'd believed when she was on the other side of things.

"Tomorrow. I want her to meet everyone."

"And everyone wants to meet her, I'm sure." Reva grinned. "Where does this little doll live? Nearby, I hope."

It was her turn to grin, so she let herself breathe and turned the shine on. "Yeah, nearby. Like, in a few days…with us."

Chapter 34

When they returned home, they found Gabby and Julia in the back yard. It was still well before five o'clock, but both women held highball glasses. They sat around the fire pit with their chairs turned toward the house. When the trio walked across the grass, the pair raised their glasses.

"What gives, girls? Tough morning at the Ponderosa?" Ted had brought his guitar, picking it up when he passed it in the house. Now, he sat in the Adirondack chair he favored and began to strum.

Julia and Gabby exchanged looks.

"You could say that." Julia took a sip, then gave the glass a thoughtful swirl. Ice clinked softly. "Why don't you guys get something to drink?"

"You're gonna need it. And make Chloe's a double." Gabby sighed, then drained her glass. "Forget it, I'll make the drinks."

She rose and took Julia's glass as well as her own into the house. They watched her sidestep the big lilac bush, swear as she caught her hair on a branch, then disappear inside.

Uncle Ted strummed a bit of Janis Joplin's Piece of My Heart. "I've got to trim that bush before it eats someone. Thing is older than Methuselah, though. Kind of hate to mess with something that old."

"We've got more on our plates than that old bush."

Julia pointed one finger to the sunroom roof. "Notice anything new about the place? Anything at all?"

When she looked up, Chloe's gut tightened. Seeing was one thing, but believing was something else entirely. The disaster was almost unfathomable.

"No way." Reva put a hand over her mouth.

"Way." Julia scraped paint off the chipping wooden chair arm with a cherry red fingernail. She did not look at any of them.

She glanced at her uncle. He'd stopped plucking the guitar strings. He stared at his house, a hard line between his eyebrows.

Yesterday, the roof's progress was wonderfully evident. The rotten mess had been piled high beside the walkway, ready for removal. Sheets of new plywood, rolls of black roof paper and bundles of shingles stacked and ready for use. On the roof, Neil had installed a half dozen new beams, with sturdy plywood decking over top of them. They'd removed the plastic protecting the interior, because it was basically sealed up.

Now, the sunroom was completely open to the elements. The fresh plywood had been butchered, cut in places and smashed in others. Whatever black paper had been attached to the wood was no longer nailed down. Most of it littered the ground beside the house. Some hung in spirals, into the sunroom and from the roof's edges like crazy black streamers.

"I-I..." There were no words in her mind. She'd known he was angry but never imagined he would be destructive. He'd made the roof worse than it was when she fell through it. "I-I just—"

Gabby walked over, carrying a tray holding

glasses. She stopped, balanced the tray with one hand and selected a glass. She pressed it into her hand. "Here. Don't try to talk, just drink."

Chloe raised the glass to her lips. The liquid was cold, and slid down her throat in four gulps. She couldn't pull her gaze from the horrendous mess. When ice crashed against her teeth, she put the empty on the tray. Her friend hadn't moved, so she reached for a second highball glass. She paused, glanced over and was relieved when the other woman said, "Go on. You deserve it."

Gabby went to the others, delivering drinks. Uncle Ted got a tall glass, which he preferred, with more tonic than gin in it.

They looked at the mess for several long, silent moments. When her knees began to tremble, she sat in one of the webbed beach chairs scattered about the space. She closed her eyes, put her head back and tried to still her mind.

Reva had chosen a spot beside Julia. Gabby sat nearer Uncle Ted, who looked less taken aback than any of the women.

"You okay?" Reva's voice was calm. Steady. She was a woman to inspire trust, and was going to make an incredible attorney.

She opened her eyes. The oak branches seemed to hang lower with each passing season. The tree was so heavy and full of leaves that it blocked out the sky. Not a bit of blue showed past the layers of foliage.

"No." She rolled her head from side to side against the metal tubular chair frame. "I'm not okay. Not at all." She sat up and pointed. "Do you see what that jerk did to our house? How the hell am I going to get that fixed? How am I going to bring my daughter home to this mess?"

Gabby was crossing the lawn with another tray of glasses. She nearly dropped the tray when she heard the outburst. "Daughter? What daughter?"

Uncle Ted chuckled. "My great-niece! I'm an uncle—again—isn't that a blast?"

Julia turned and grabbed Chloe's arm. "A baby? What do you think you're doing drinking like a fish? Give me that—"

Gabby let out a screech. "I didn't know you're pregnant!"

"No, it's fine." Reva's was the voice of reason, so they paused. She stood and held up her hands in the air, above her head. Her glass was, luckily for her, only half full. "She is not pregnant. Penny is six, and she's coming to live with us. Isn't that the best news ever?"

Gabby and Julia hugged Chloe so tightly she had to wiggle from their grasps. "You guys are going to choke me." She laughed, gesturing everyone to their seats. "Yes, it's true. I have a daughter and that's the best thing in the world but really, has anyone seen that roof? What the hell was he thinking?"

"Not a thing." Uncle Ted shook his head. "He was angry. Probably hurt that you refused to marry him—yet again. And he must feel foolish. I mean, that man has spent his whole life loving someone who doesn't reciprocate. If it were me, I'd feel pretty awful."

Silence descended as they contemplated how to deal with the chaos Neil left behind.

Finally, they gave up thinking. For a while, anyhow. No one had a solution, and the events of the day had tired everyone.

Julia asked if there was any chance she could get some time playing guitar with Ted. He did not hesitate; the man loved playing almost as much as a man can love anything. Her guitar had dried without warping, so she ran to the house and retrieved it.

The music was soulful. They strummed, sang, strummed some more. They went from James Brown to James Taylor to Janis Joplin. Then, The Knack's My Sharona, with its classic riffs.

Gabby and Reva stood, walked to the house, and began to make order from some of the turmoil. When Chloe started to rise, thinking she would help, they both insisted she stay put. She was on her third drink, which was slightly more watery but still mind-numbing, so she watched while they nailed plastic sheeting over the holes.

Julia stepped back to survey their handiwork when Gabby went inside to grab some trash bags.

"Doesn't look bad." She wiped a hand down the leg of her jeans. They were grimy from crawling on the remaining roof rafters. "We can figure this out tomorrow."

"If I didn't see irrational behavior every day at work, I wouldn't be able to handle this. It just doesn't make sense—he took out his aggression on a house. I just can't even begin to imagine how furious he must have been." Holding tears back was getting harder to do.

"He snapped." Julia put a hand on her hip and waved the other to the house. "Much better he went crazy on that than on you."

"Good point."

Gabby came out of the house wearing a frown.

"We just got a call from Chris, Neil's sister. She's really concerned about him—was kind of hoping he'd be here. Apparently he was supposed to pick Allen up from camp today but never showed. Chris said he's never done that, left the little boy hanging."

Neil doted on his nine-year-old nephew who had lost his father in Vietnam. He felt it was his place to step in and do what he could for the child. Leaving him at camp without a way to get home was completely out of character.

It didn't matter what had gone wrong between them, Neil was part of Chloe's life. She stood, looked at the others and said, "Something's happened. I've got to find him."

Chapter 35

Reva, Julia, and Ted stayed home. There was a possibility Neil might return, and if he did someone should be at the house. Whether the plan was to protect the house or help Neil, no one was sure but it was a logical arrangement. She didn't want her uncle alone, not when there had already been so much destruction to his property. Besides, a house was one thing. Who could tell what an out-of-control man might do to a sick veteran? Better not to take any chances.

Chloe and Gabby flew through the house and off the front porch at a run.

Gabby's car was as polished as her fingernails were. Sunset sent shards of color dancing along the buffed white paint. The Camaro had been a gift from an old boyfriend. When they broke up, she'd kept the car. Now, she jingled the keys and sprinted to the driver's side.

As she backed out of the driveway, she pointed to the glove compartment. "In there."

Chloe looked up every driveway and down each street they passed. "What's in there?"

"A bag. Listen, chickie, I was making those drinks, remember? You've had a lot, and I don't recall hearing anything about dinner, so just in case you get the urge to lose some of that gin, use the bag."

She was too frightened to be sick. "I'm fine. Where

the hell can he be? He'd never forget about Adam—never."

"Allen."

"Hmm?" She rolled down the window and poked her head out a bit, trying to see down a side street. There was a truck, but it was maroon, not red.

"Chris's little boy—his name is Allen."

"I know that. Did I call him something else?"

"You did, but it's fine. We're all upset. Let's just find Neil and send him home."

She had an excellent imagination that was unfortunately beginning to get to work. Big time. Lobster Cove wasn't so large that a car crash could go undetected. If he'd rolled his truck taking a curve on the ocean road, someone would have noticed. Someone would have helped him. She hoped.

But what if he had left town? Just gotten into his shiny truck and driven off into the sunset? So many times she'd seen women walk away from their own lives, feeling no alternative was open to them. And how often had she toyed with the idea of walking away from all the problems of her life? It was a common enough notion.

With all the rage he exhibited, she couldn't discount the possibility he would hurt someone. Totally out of character for him, but with the damage he'd inflicted on the roof, he was fueled by anger, not reason.

As if she read her mind, Gabby asked, "You don't think he'd hurt anyone, do you?"

"I was just wondering that very same thing." She tried to snap her fingers but they were not cooperating. "But it's not like him. He's usually so kind and—but wait, he called me a hooker last night. That wasn't like him, either."

Gabby swerved when she looked across but quickly corrected. They were on the ocean road, headed south. "Tell me he did not say that!"

"Oh, but he did. He was furious. I disappointed him, so many times. It must be awful to be Neil right now. Awful—and I'm to blame."

"Keep looking for his truck." She slowed when they passed a convenience store. A few cars, but no trucks in sight. "Listen, you're not to blame. You're half in the bag, but that's my fault."

She did feel pretty tipsy. If Neil hadn't gone missing, the buzz would be an enjoyable one.

"You think?" She tried not to giggle but she was forced to admit—in her own mind, and to herself only—that the gin had gone right to her head.

"I know. And what I also know is that sometimes things don't work out. The whole couple bit? Sometimes it's wonderful, all glittery dreams and stuff, but a lot of times it's a drag. I got this boss car because my ex felt sorry for me. He fell out of love, cheated, and I got the Camaro. End of story. With you and Neil…well, it's not so cut and dry."

"Tell me about it."

Driving further from Lobster Cove was futile. He wouldn't go away from everything he knew. Everyone he loved. The places he felt most comfortable in. It wasn't like him. Even in the gin haze, she knew that.

Then, it hit her.

"Turn the car around—Gabby, turn around!" She twisted in her seat, a speedier movement than was wise, and practically screamed. "But first, pull over."

They were lucky there was a shoulder on the winding road at that point, so there was room to get the car off the road, and time enough for her to push the heavy door open. Most of the gin came up in one rush. To their relief, she did not get any of it on her or in the car. And as soon as she was done being sick, her head stopped spinning. Almost.

"Feel better?"

She wiped her mouth on the tissue Gabby offered. Her hands trembled and her head was beginning to pound, but it was preferable to the woozy sensation that had been building ever since the car had begun to move.

"I do, actually." She sat a moment, studied the chrome button on the dash as twilight set in around them. "I know where he is. I'd bet my last greenback on it."

Gabby waited until both lanes were clear before she u-turned and headed back the way they'd come. They drove for a mile or so without speaking. The silence was welcome and gave the fuzziness in Chloe's head time to clear. She hung her arm out the window, let the breeze pull her curls out in a thick stream behind her and contemplated what she was going to say when they found him.

Not one damn thing came to mind. How was it that she had known him for practically her whole life, yet she had nothing to say to him? It made no sense...and it made complete sense.

If they had been "right" for each other, this night would not be taking place. But it was, because they weren't. Only now, there was someone else to consider. They weren't the only ones with an interest in how their lives moved forward.

She slapped a hand over her eyes.

"You okay? Need me to pull over again?"

The car slowed, but she waved a hand. "I'm fine. Don't stop. We've got to find him and maybe talk some sense into him." She peeked through her fingers, looking to the sky for inspiration. "I just don't know what to say to make it right, is all. He can't act like a jerk, not if he wants to be part of her life. I won't allow it—he's got to straighten up or hit the road."

"Which works best for you?"

The big welcome sign came into view. One more gentle curve, and they'd turn off the main road to enter the village.

"It's not about what works for me anymore. Penny is the one who counts." She swallowed, wishing she had Uncle Ted's hard candy to erase the bitter taste on her tongue. "It's about doing what's best for her. And I think, if it's at all possible, that having a father in her life is a good thing. For her. And for him."

They were coasting down Main Street. They passed the park, where the sailor statue stood sentry, and the shops which had closed for the night. There were no tourists vying for position near the big anchor. And, no traffic to slow them down.

"Mind telling me where we're going?"

"The spot where we conceived our daughter. Quinn Beach—that's where he is."

Chapter 36

"That's his truck." Chloe pointed as they pulled into the parking area leading to the beach path. There were two cars near the far end, beside Neil's truck. It hadn't been parked so much as abandoned. Had there been others hoping to use the three spots he'd taken, it might have attracted attention. But with no one to see, it was no disturbance.

Gabby pulled in beside the front bumper. "Who parks like that?"

"He's still not thinking."

They got out of the car and went to the truck. She opened the driver's door, sending light spilling from overhead. The keys dangled from the ignition, so she removed them, and stuck them in her pocket. Gabby had gone to the other door, opened it, and stood peering in.

"My God, how much did he drink?" Bottles littered the cab. Wild Turkey, nearly empty, on the floor. Crushed cans of Miller High Life spread across the seat. The sweet scent of pot hung in the air. "There's enough booze—the bottles, anyway—for an army."

"I don't know what to say. We've got to find him. If he drank all of this, he's got to be sick."

"Or dead."

The thought had crossed her mind, but she'd squelched it.

She turned away, scanning the parking area. No sign of him, not even a passed out body which was what she really expected.

The pounding in her head ratcheted up a notch. All that gin on an empty stomach had been an error in judgment. Harmless at the time but she was paying for it now.

She met Gabby's wide-eyed stare. No need to ask what she was thinking; it was clear she thought the worst. "Please, help me find him."

"That's why I'm here, sister. Let's get a move on—but where do you think he'll be? Does he take long walks on the beach road? Go down to the scrub at the far end and look for stuff, like shells and beach glass? I mean, this is a big area—where do we begin to search?"

Gabby had a point. There was a lot of territory to cover. And, it was growing darker by the minute. Soon they'd been in pitch blackness, making a search even more impossible.

Even with her mind clouded, her gut was spot on. "The beach."

They ran for the path leading over the dune. They paused when they hit the top and looked in both directions. Dusk closed in around them and made it difficult to see much.

"I don't see him." Chloe peered into the gloom as her heart began to beat overtime. How were they going to find him?

"Me, either."

A couple walked toward them. They had little grins on their faces. He carried his shirt and something lacy—her bra, perhaps—in his free hand.

Chloe hated to disrupt their post-coital mood. She

called, "Hey, have you seen a guy?"

The woman giggled, leaned against her partner and said, "I sure have, sister."

When they came abreast of the couple Gabby pressed them. "Really, a guy? Alone? Did either of you see him?"

A look passed between them.

"Did you see him?" Chloe wanted to go right up in his face but knew better. "It's a matter of life and death—please, help us."

The guy turned serious. "We wondered if there was something wrong with him. We were busy, you know, but he was hard to miss. Staggering, like he was stoned or something. Then, he took off his clothes."

"Yeah, that was something we couldn't miss…even though we were, you know…"

So Neil had been such a spectacle that he aroused interest even when the couple was having sex?

"What'd he do then?" Gabby asked. Chloe was already moving in the direction the lovers had just come from. "What'd he do?"

"Swimming." The man followed them, so his date followed him. "Oh, shit—the cat's in the water!"

Chloe saw clothes strewn at the water's edge. Something—his shirt, maybe—floated, on its way out to sea.

Facedown, just a few yard further away, a still form. She knew it was Neil—she'd seen that body too many times not to recognize him.

Behind her, the woman screamed. She heard the guy shout for her to take his car and call for help. She heard Gabby's low moan, a sad sound that cut the warm air.

And she heard the sound of her heart shatter.

Her knees hit the sand hard. Salty water splashed around them. "Neil!"

She grabbed him, pulling him backward with the weight of her body. All she could think to do was get his face out of the water, but he was too heavy for her to move. The other two arrived seconds after her. The guy grabbed Neil under the armpits and dragged his body out of the water.

"Neil? Can you hear us?" Gabby took one of his hands in hers. "He's cold!"

They placed him on his back. Chloe dropped her head to his chest.

"Damn it, don't do this!" She grabbed his face in her hands, put her forehead against his. "No—this cannot happen! No!"

"Let me roll him on his side," the stranger said. "Maybe he'll puke the water up—watch out—"

He turned the still form, gave him a few hard slaps between the shoulder blades and yelled in his ear. "C'mon, man—we're not letting you get away just yet. C'mon, puke it up!"

She met Gabby's gaze. There was no need for words. They'd learned the drill to keep Ted alive. Now, it was time to put theory to practice.

Gabby elbowed the man and positioned herself on the other side of Neil.

"I'll do the chest compressions—you breathe for him. Chloe—can you do this?"

Of course she could. Tilting his head back and opening the airway, she put her fingers near his nose and listened to Gabby count. Each count matched a chest compression.

"One, two, three, four, five…" Eventually Gabby yelled, "Go!"

She covered his mouth with hers and blew. It was not the same at all as when she'd practiced on the rubber dummy. And, it was nothing like kissing.

A second round of chest compressions. Then, she blew into his mouth again.

The third time, she thought she felt a response. When he didn't revive she waited while Gabby did her part, then leaned close to breathe for him. Before she put her lips on his, he coughed.

"Turn him—on his side!" The guy helped Gabby roll him, and she put her hand on his neck.

His body gave up the sea in a torrent. Water gushed from his mouth, so she held his head for him. Then Neil gasped, great, gulping sounds. His eyes opened, and he met her gaze.

Sirens in the distance, coming closer. These past weeks had brought enough sirens and hospital visits to last a lifetime.

He gave her a loopy grin. "There's my honey…"

At least—for the moment—he wasn't angry. She smiled back at him, avoided the effort he made to pull her down and kiss her, and waited for the ambulance. It threw circles of light as it bumped over the sand toward them.

The man had kindly placed his shirt over Neil's genitals. He sat back on his heels, looking as if they'd saved the world instead of one irritated drunk man.

"Damn, that was something, wasn't it?" The guy put an arm around Gabby's shoulders in a quick hug. "You two saved the guy—and I got to watch the whole thing. Far out, man…"

Gabby gave a shaky laugh. "You helped. He was so heavy, I'm not sure we could've gotten him this far without you."

She heard them, but her mind was on the man staring up at her. The grin had faded, and he looked worse for the wear. Bloodshot eyes, matted hair, remorse pulling his features into an unrecognizable blur. She had never seen this side of Neil. Somehow, she always suspected a darker mood lurked beneath the smiles and optimism, but she had no idea it was this deep.

His voice was rough. "I really screwed up big time, didn't I?"

The ambulance pulled up and its doors flew open.

Softly, just before the medical team took over, she said, "We both did."

Chapter 37

After the crew put Neil on a gurney, covered him with blankets, and strapped him in place, they lifted him into the back of the ambulance. He went in and out of consciousness, unable to answer questions or speak a coherent sentence. The last thing he'd said that made sense was the comment on the beach, and Chloe wasn't going to share that information with the medics.

"He hasn't spoken yet?" The guy asking questions was about her age, with a surfer's squint that revealed a web of white lines running from the corners of his eyes across his tanned face. He gave her a big smile, then a wink. "Anything at all?"

It might be vital, so she nodded. "A little. But nothing important."

He held a clipboard, and made a fast note. He wasn't wearing a wedding ring. It didn't matter; he wasn't her type and even if he was, she wasn't looking. All day long she'd wondered what she would say to Kyle. Even as she supplied answers to the medic about Neil, she had the doctor on her mind.

"I'm not sure what exactly he drank. There are a lot of bottles in his truck." She hated ratting him out but they probably already knew the story. They'd seen it before. Neil couldn't be the first guy to get wasted and go swimming. "I'm pretty sure he smoked some weed, too."

Another notation on the board. "Common for him? Getting high like this?" The pencil hovered over the information sheet.

"He hardly ever drinks at all. This is unusual."

The other two men called to them. Neil was secure in the vehicle, and they were ready to go.

"I'm riding along." She did not ask because there was no way they were taking him anywhere alone. "To the hospital—I'm going with him."

A casual shrug was the answer. He snapped the file closed, stuck the pencil behind his right ear, and held out his arm. "Watch your step—the first one is high. Grab the bar and pull yourself up."

She grabbed the metal bar on the inside of the door and hoisted herself into the vehicle. The rolling bed was fastened to the left side. A man sat near Neil's head, where he watched the IV line dangling from a ceiling hook. He nodded to the bench running the length of the opposite wall, so she sat.

The door slammed so loudly she jumped. Neil, however, didn't move a muscle. She gave the attendant a questioning look.

He shook his head. "Just passed out. I can't be sure, but this guy has had a helluva lot to drink. No surprise he's out."

"Oh. I just thought…"

"No, no worries there. His vitals are strong. He's doing well, nothing to be afraid of." He adjusted the flow on the line, ran a hand down the tubing. "All good. But he wouldn't be, if it wasn't for you and your friends. You do know you saved his life, don't you?"

It was warm inside the ambulance. They had begun moving, bumping over the sand at a snail's pace. Neil really couldn't be too critical because they weren't racing to the hospital. The heat and motion weren't great on her stomach or pounding temples.

A chill swept over her when his words sank in. She looked over. Neil looked very comfortable, all bundled up the way he was.

"I-I…ah, I just…we just…"

Her tongue tangled, her mind searched for words in a blank space.

"You saved his life. That's what you did." He waited a beat. There still weren't any words in her head, so she stared at him without speaking. "Hey, are you feeling okay?"

The man was kind, and reached out a hand to check her pulse. She pulled her arm away, not to be rude but because she knew that if he was too nice to her, made too much of a fuss, she was going to cry. Not little, sniveling tears, either. The emotions fighting for freedom inside her weren't small ones by any means.

He was smart enough to pull back. "Okay, then. You've had one huge shock. Why don't you just put your head against the wall behind you—it's got some nice, thick padding on it—and take a breather. I promise, I'm here, he's going to be okay. We'll get him to Bar Harbor just fine. You've done your job. It's my turn now."

The key to being ready for the next challenge was knowing when to rest after surmounting the last one. She put her head against the padding and closed her eyes.

They'd made the road, so it they'd be at the hospital fairly soon. If Neil regained consciousness, she would leave him to the staff's capable hands. But if he didn't wake or something even worse happened, she would stay with him. No matter what happened between them, she wouldn't leave him alone.

The ride was, thankfully, uneventful. The patient slept the entire way—although she wasn't sure if being passed out in an alcoholic stupor was the same as sleeping.

When the heavy double doors swung open she took a look at Neil. No change. The man by him shook his head and gave her a friendly smile.

The ambulance driver reached in and offered her his hand. "Miss?" She placed her hand in his and let him help her out. "Careful, that last step's a doozy. There, you've got it. If you want, you can head inside. We'll be right behind you."

She went through the wide glass doors. They slid open noiselessly, and led not into the waiting room but a hallway. Cubicles lined both sides. Some had curtains closed around them, but a few were open. She waited, not knowing which one they would occupy.

The gurney rolled through the doors. Neil must have begun to rouse when they moved him because he mumbled from his white cotton cocoon.

A nurse appeared, her starched uniform and rubber-soled shoes bright in the crowded hallway. She pointed to the nearest cubicle, speaking to the ambulance crew. "Number Five, guys. Near-drowning victim, is it?"

Neil saw her as he was wheeled past. He stretched out a hand to her, so she took it and walked beside him. His skin was clammy, but his grip was firm. It had to be a good sign, that he was able to grasp her so tightly after his experience.

They rounded a corner into what she thought was an empty cubicle.

A voice, so familiar her heart squeezed when she heard it.

"Water victim—give me a check of vitals and start an additional IV of—Chloe!"

She turned and practically bumped noses with Kyle. His gaze shot from her to the patient, who refused to let her hand go even when she gave it a small, and hopefully unobserved, yank.

The nurse snickered. "What was that, Doctor? An IV of what?"

He ignored her. He also ignored the paramedics who were signing off on the paperwork and preparing to leave. And, he paid no attention to the patient, unless a furrowed brow and scowl at the man's grip counted.

"Kyle." She ran a hand through her hair, conscious she looked a sight. And, after the side-of-the-road pit stop to toss the gin, she probably smelled dreadful. While he, as usual, was polished. Professional. In complete control of his emotions.

In complete control of his life, while hers was a mess.

They were oil and water. Fire and ice.

Just looking at him made her insides quiver. An hour ago, she would have attributed that sensation to the alcohol. But the way he looked at her, even now when he was not as pleased to see her as he usually was, made her want more. She stared into his eyes and believed, for the first time in her life, that she deserved more.

"Doctor?" The nurse's toe tapping made a squeaking noise against the tile.

Kyle walked past her and spoke to Neil. "Sir? I'm Doctor Brown. Can you understand me?"

She liberated her hand and stuck both in her pockets, out of reach.

"He didn't say much in the ambulance," she offered.

He scanned the chart when the nurse handed it to him. He snapped it closed and put it on the foot of the bed, then took a stethoscope from his coat pocket. "He's ingested a large quantity of alcohol. We may need to pump his stomach."

"Do what you have to do."

"You know this man? He's a friend of yours?"

Neil had been quiet, but he must have heard the line of questioning. With a grunt, he pulled himself partway to a sitting position, tangling his IV tubing around the rail of the hospital bed and letting the sheet fall to his hips. It was no secret he was naked. And, he made no bones about what he thought of Kyle's questions.

Waving an arm in the air, the tone was all belligerent drunkenness. "Hell no, she's n-not my friend! Sh-sh-she's the mother of my child!"

The air left her lungs in a big whoosh.

Kyle's gaze met hers, and he must have seen the truth because he did not ask any questions.

She felt her world crumbling around her, and the pain in her chest could only be her heart breaking. Chloe refused to cry—not here, not now.

Behind them, the patient waved a frantic hand. "H-h-hey! Hey—I, ah, I think I—oh, no…"

The nurse anticipated his need with astonishing accuracy and speed. She held the blue plastic bucket while Neil was sicker than anyone ever should be.

Chloe didn't feel one shred of pity for him as she turned and walked out of the cubicle.

Chapter 38

Leila could be insistent when she chose to be. "Go home. You look like—and I'm not trying to be mean here, just saying the gospel truth—a dried turd. It's obvious you didn't sleep more than an hour, if that. We love you, but you're no good to anyone in this rough shape. Go the heck home, put your feet up, and take a load off. I'm right, ain't I, Jade?"

The other woman nodded her agreement. As usual, they were all seated around their desks. Or, in Leila's case, perched on the edge of hers. Today she wore a magenta skirt whose pleats were stretched to the limit, paired with a scoop-neck blouse and funky earrings. The outfit would have looked ridiculous on another woman but simply made Leila look exotic.

Chloe scrubbed a hand over her face. She did not take offense at their frank assessment of her appearance. She'd done all the right things: showered, deodorized, brushed and dressed but it didn't matter. If she looked half as bad as she felt, she did, in fact, look like a dried turd.

"I hate to bail on you like that." She didn't remember the last time she had taken a day off or called in sick. It wasn't her habit to do those things. "What if the place starts to jump? What then?"

Jade smirked. She closed her eyes and shook her head ever-so slightly. "Don't flatter yourself. We're all used to working single shifts. Even after you leave there'll still be two of us. We can handle whatever comes through the door."

"And it's Thursday. We all know it's the slowest day of the week." Leila swirled her mug around, stirring the leaves in the bottom of the cup. When she finished the tea, Jade was going to read them. "Go home. Or, go to the beach. Or to dinner. Or to that sexy doctor. Just go somewhere."

The beach held some bad memories today. They would dim, but right now she had no desire to set foot on the sand at Quinn Beach. Not even a toe.

Jade, the philosophical one, took a break from buffing her fingernails. "I don't think you realize just how vulnerable you are right now. You finally met a guy who you dig, and who digs you right back. Should be groovy, right? But the old flame is a drag. He's wearing you out. And when the past comes calling—in the most amazing way ever—it's great but stressful, too. The mama gene just doesn't turn on because we want it to. Believe me, I know."

"Amen, sister." Leila nodded her agreement the whole way through the rundown. "Listen to Jade here, that mama gene is a tough nut to crack open. You've been able to forget about that beautiful child to an extent. I know you must have had her on your mind a lot, but the day-to-day of it is all going to take some getting used to. For all of you."

It had not been hard to confide in these two. They had been a sturdy support system as she cared for her uncle and the house. She knew Penny would have two new aunties who would probably spoil her rotten unless she put the kibosh to it.

"When did you say Penny is coming to the house?" Jade resumed working on her manicure. Thursday, the day for taking it easy in the office, made up for the days when they were so busy they had to scramble for bathroom breaks.

"This afternoon. After her nap and before dinner. I can only imagine what the girls have on the menu for tonight."

They informed her she had no chores, no obligations and certainly no worries while she was getting to know her daughter. Dinner, cleanup afterward—it was all on them. She loved their excitement over having a child in the house, even though it was going to be a time of transition for everyone.

"I'm going to take your advice. I need some chill time. My head's a little fuzzy."

"Not going over to the hospital to see Neil, are you?" Leila's tone told what she thought of that idea.

His sister Chris arrived in the waiting room shortly after the ambulance last night. Gabby had gone to tell her the news, rather than let her get a phone call from some random nurse. She'd even driven Chris to Bar Harbor, and back home after Neil was settled in a room. They'd all had a late night.

"No. I'm sure his sister is there. It's her job now, to deal with the situation." She stood, stretched her arms above her head and failed miserably when she tried to stifle a yawn. The phone on her desk rang as she was about to pick up her backpack.

"No—do not get that." Leila punched buttons on her phone, transferred the call, then picked up. "Good morning, Anchor Women's Services, Leila speaking."

A pause. "Certainly. Hang on a minute, please."

She held a palm over the mouthpiece. "It's for you. Kyle Brown." She flashed a million-dollar smile as she handed the phone over.

"Good morning."

She heard him take a deep breath. "Hey, I wonder if we can get together. Soon. I think we need to talk."

His willingness to discuss what happened last night was wonderful. He'd hardly looked at her after Neil began to vomit, concentrating on his patient and avoiding her as if she were contagious.

"Yes, that's a good idea. When?"

"Well, I just finished my shift. I know you're working—"

"Leaving early, actually. Like, right now."

He chuckled, and the sound warmed her heart. Maybe there was hope for them, if he wasn't so upset he could be amused.

"Serendipitous. So, how about coffee on the dock? I'll bring the coffee."

"Sounds perfect. See you there."

Chapter 39

Sitting dockside was nice but Chloe preferred the small pier in Lobster Cove to the wider, longer one in Bar Harbor. Although she had to admit the yachts gliding past were more impressive than the lobster boats she was accustomed to.

Wooden benches lined the pier. Kyle was nowhere in sight, so she chose a bench and waited. A deep breathing exercise to steady her nerves and a slash of lip gloss comprised the full preparation for the meeting. A far cry from the primping she'd undergone for their first date.

But this wasn't a date, really. Was it?

More like an it's-been-nice send-off. He seemed considerate enough to end things with a civil parting.

Coffee to hit the road by, she mused.

"Sorry to keep you waiting."

Kyle looked great even after working all night. He had on tight blue jeans, worn around the knees and loafers, scuffed at the toes. The light blue button-down shirt was unbuttoned at the neck and rolled up on his arms. Dark sunglasses.

He held two Styrofoam cups. "Okay, since I wasn't sure which way you take your coffee, you've got first pick. In the left hand, black. In the right, light and sweet. What'll it be?"

"I don't want to take the one you want for

yourself."

"I'm a doctor. I'm used to drinking the mud at the bottom of the pot in the doctors' lounge. It makes absolutely no difference to me—they both contain caffeine, and that's the selling point in my world. So, choose."

"Light and sweet." She took the cup he handed her. "Thanks."

"My pleasure." He uncovered his cup, tasted the dark brew and nodded. "Just the way I like it—strong enough to keep a man awake but not so nasty it'll send him to the moon."

She tried hers. "Perfect."

It was hard to know how to begin the conversation, so she put her full attention on the beverage. It went down smoothly, soothing the scratch in the back of her throat. She attributed that to the screaming she'd done last night.

The thought he might be waiting for her to inquire about Neil crossed her mind but she had no intention of doing so.

"I don't want to put you on the spot, so I'm going to say what I need to say first, if you don't mind."

She turned and met his gaze. Even with the sunglasses she could see his eyes. They were genuine, as they had been since the first time she looked into them.

"Okay. I know I've got some explaining to do…"

Kyle shook his head. "Not necessary."

Her spirits fell. This *was* the kiss off. If not, he'd want to hear her side of things.

Better get it over with. "I'm listening."

"All my life, I dreamed I'd meet a woman who—

and I know this sounds stupid—would make my heart jump. I know, I know…I'm a physician. I'm aware hearts don't jump, but it's the truth. I've been around, dated my share of women, but no one caught my heart's attention. Not saying they weren't nice. Just saying they weren't enough to make my heart respond."

A yacht, *This Is The Day* painted across its stern, passed into view. A flying bridge and three decks made it impossible to miss. Bikini-clad women sunned themselves while a trio of bare-chested men wearing white shorts raised bottles in greeting to those watching.

"Would you like something like that someday?"

His question did not logically follow the conversation so she was surprised. Pointing with the hand that held her cup, she asked, "Like that?"

"Yeah, a luxurious, attention-grabbing queen of the seas…see yourself in one?"

"Not this girl. I'm not the yacht-lifestyle kind of chick."

"Good to know." He finished his coffee, put the empty cup on the dock beside his feet and turned to face her. "Listen, I'm trying to say that I never met a woman who made my heart jump—until I met you."

The coffee she'd just sucked into her mouth went down the wrong way when she gasped. She choked, sputtered, and coughed. Her eyes teared, and she couldn't speak.

Doctor training kicked in, because he was unperturbed by the display. The first thing he did was take the cup from her and place it beside his. He spoke in a reassuring tone as he pulled a pristine white handkerchief from his back pocket and handed it to her.

"It's okay…you'll be fine. No, don't try to speak, just wait a minute, you'll be breathing again in a second. Hold on, you're doing just fine…"

Had she heard him correctly? Or had she finally gone off her rails?

Chloe dried her eyes with the handkerchief. It was monogrammed, and felt expensive, but her nose was dripping so she dabbed at it anyway. When Kyle handed her the coffee, she took a sip. It had gone cool, so she took a big mouthful.

She finally managed to speak. "Did you say what I think you said?"

He smiled. "It shook you up, didn't it?"

"I'd say so. But, Kyle…"

He pushed his sunglasses up on his head. "Did I mean it?" She nodded. "Yeah, every word of it. Chloe, I'm crazy for you in a way that I've never been for anyone else. When I'm not with you all I can think about is being with you. When we're together…" He swallowed, shook his head, and met her gaze. "I never want it to end. Do you understand what I'm saying? It's fast, but I knew how I felt the first day you were in my ED. I just knew…what can I say? It was like a bolt of lightning—one I've waited for a long time to hit me."

It was crunch time. Her whole life, she'd wanted to be loved by a fabulous man. Here was her chance. She could either leap or be a coward and regret it forever.

"Me, too."

He raised a questioning eyebrow. "Are you saying…?"

"I am. And, I do—too. I have, since that day. It's been—" She put a hand over her mouth to stifle the giggle that bubbled up from her throat. Fortunately, he was grinning, so she said, "I'm babbling."

"Yes, as a matter of fact, you are. But I kind of like it. I worried…well, I worried you don't feel the way I do."

She shook her head at the absurdity. How could he not know how she felt?

"I do—I have—oh, Kyle, it's been a dream come true, to meet someone who makes me feel this way. Couldn't you tell when we were on the beach? I practically threw myself at you."

He took the cup from her hand. Placed it beside his again. Then, he closed the gap between their bodies, and put an arm around her shoulders. "Sex isn't what I'm looking for. Yeah, of course, it'll be great when we're ready but I want a real relationship. Marriage. Family. All that square stuff—it's what I want."

"All that? It's exactly what I want, too." She tilted her face to receive his kiss. It was the type of kiss to seal fates, a soft, soulful moment when they claimed their feelings without words. When he broke the connection, she kept her eyes closed for a full minute longer. She leaned against his strong shoulder and savored the moment.

There were still matters to discuss, though.

She looked out to sea. She couldn't even believe she was going to risk ruining this but two lives didn't become one without a foundation of honesty.

She looked over and found him watching her.

"Your turn."

A sigh. "I know." She tugged the elastic out of her hair, shook it loose and ordered her thoughts. The truth. The only way through anything was with the truth, so she began with the biggest one. "I have a daughter. I got pregnant on graduation night, and when I realized I couldn't care for her properly, I decided on adoption. Right from the hospital. Never saw her before this week. It's wrong, but I didn't tell Neil." She watched for any sign he was upset, but there was none.

He rubbed the palm of his hand against her shoulder, a reassuring touch that worked the knots out. "I bet she's beautiful. Like her mother."

A flash of pride brought a smile. "She's adorable. Her name is Penny and…" She took a deep breath. "She's going to come live with me. Starting tonight, probably."

Pulling her close against his side, he put his lips to her head and kissed her temple. Murmuring against her hair, he said, "I can't wait to meet her."

A tear rolled down her cheek. "I thought…"

"Shh, I know. Last night, I thought the same thing." He kissed her temple again. "I had quite a talk with Neil, and he set the record straight. He's a good guy who just wants what's best for you, and for his daughter."

She wiped the tears away with the back of one hand and turned to meet his gaze.

"He's Penny's dad, so he'll always be part of our lives."

Kyle didn't flinch. "I'm adopted, remember? I know how important it is for a kid to have a family. It's great, I think Neil should be involved with his daughter. And I want to be involved, too." He paused and gave her a reassuring smile. "I love her mother. I'll love her, too."

Chapter 40

Chloe did not know what to expect when Debra dropped her daughter off. The exchange was a fast one, with a pink backpack and brown paper grocery bag the only luggage. The child kissed her aunt goodbye, but there were no tears.

Penny enchanted the adults in the house, and she did it quickly. Within twenty minutes, she was in the kitchen, helping prepare dinner.

Gabby had put one of her t-shirts over Penny's clothes. It reached past her knees but kept her from wearing the ice cream she helped churn. She'd mastered the art of splashing, and they all had spots of cream dotting them.

Julia flipped burgers at the stove. "How do you like your burger, honey?"

"With cheese, please." She cranked with rugged determination, her lower lip between her teeth. "This is gonna be some good ice cream when we're done."

Uncle Ted reached around and helped turn the handle. "It sure is. But why don't I give you a hand with that?"

"Harder than it looks." She relinquished the churn but kept an eye on his progress. The pointer finger on her right hand made circles beside his hand, her method of directing.

Reva removed a tray of tater tots from the oven.

She took them and a big casserole of macaroni and cheese out to the picnic table beneath the oak. It was set beautifully, with festive paper plates, colorful napkins and a red-and-white checked tablecloth. The girls and her uncle had gone to a lot of trouble to make this evening perfect.

It was a blessing being loved so thoroughly. Uncle Ted and Penny both declared the ice cream ready for the freezer at the same moment. It was a good thing, because Julia announced, "Burgers are done. Let's get to eating."

Penny took her hand when they all stood and headed outdoors. Their fingers seemed to fit together as if they'd been made from the same mold.

Once they gathered around the table, dinner was a blur of laughter. Spilled grape juice. Silly conversation. Too many tater tots, and ketchup on a sneaker. It was one of the best meals of her life.

When the food trays were picked clean, Gabby clapped her hands together and stood. She began to gather the dishes. "Who's ready for ice cream?"

They all were. Uncle Ted and Penny gave nearly identical singsong "Me!" responses.

"Good. We'll just deep six the paper plates, napkins and cups, and grab some fresh ones from the house."

Chloe rose, but Reva pushed her back down. "Sit a spell. We've got this, sister."

Penny looked over her shoulder at the woman. "Sister? So, you're my aunt?"

Without missing a beat, the legal eagle folded the paper plates in her hand and nodded. "That is an affirmative. We are family. We're all close as sisters, so yes, I'd say you've got three new aunts. How do you feel about that?"

The girl looked from one to the other. A smile spread across her face, lifting her ketchup-smeared lips. "Groovy. Very groovy."

Reva leaned down and brushed a kiss across the child's brow. "We think you're very groovy, too. Now, we'll be right back with the ice cream."

Uncle Ted looked at the sky. "Hope we don't get rained out. Those are some pretty big thunder clouds coming in from the ocean."

She looked up. Gray clouds scudded above them. In the distance, they turned black. "Looks like we're in for a storm."

"Good thing the roof is secure. That plastic should hold against whatever Mother Nature dishes out." He'd taken the damage well after the initial shock wore off. They all had, because done was done, and there wasn't much they could do about the mess other than deal with it. Not hard to take something in stride when there was no other choice.

"It should hold. I hope it does—but I'll make sure nothing of importance is under the plastic. Definitely not Julia's guitar."

Penny inched closer on the bench. "I don't like storms."

She put an arm around the small body. "I understand. When I was your age, I didn't like storms, either."

"What changed?"

"Well, I lived here—"

"You did?"

"Mmm hmm, I did."

"With your mommy and daddy and Uncle Ted?"

Chloe met her uncle's gaze across the table. He watched silently as the girl climbed onto her lap.

She looked into the big hazel eyes that reminded her of her own and sighed. The secrets had to stop sometime. Now was that time.

"No. I lived here with Aunt Ginny and Uncle Ted. My parents weren't alive when I was little. So my aunt and uncle took good care of me."

Her daughter considered the words, putting a finger beside her lip, and tapping it. Lifting the finger, she said, "My mommy and daddy aren't alive anymore either."

"I know. I'm sorry for that, honey."

She endured a serious stare from those pretty eyes. Penny's voice was soft when she said, "Aunt Debra says you're my mommy, too. Is that right? Can a kid have two mommies?"

Conscious that the answer would have a lasting impact, she chose her words with care. "Yes, it's true. I am your mommy. You actually had two mommies and two daddies. When you arrived as a little baby, I was very young. I couldn't take good care of you then, so I gave you to your other mommy and daddy—because I knew they would love you and keep you safe. So yes, I am your mommy."

There. It was out. She held her breath, waiting for the all-important reaction of the child she'd loved, lost and now loved again.

Penny put her arms around her neck and snuggled her sweet head onto her shoulder. Wrapping her in a hug, she held her tight, the feel of her girl's heart beating against her own almost too perfect to bear. She swallowed her tears, not wanting to ruin the moment by crying.

Penny pulled her head back. "Did you say I had two daddies?"

"I did. And, you did. Your mommy and daddy who are in heaven now, and me and your other daddy—the one who was like me, too young to take care of a tiny baby."

"Does he live here? My other daddy?"

"No. He has his own house. If you want, you can meet him tomorrow. He said he'd come over whenever you want to see him."

"Tomorrow's good." The child kissed her on the cheek, then rubbed her nose against Chloe's. Her peripheral vision gave her a shot of Uncle Ted wiping his eyes. "Tonight is for us. Just us, at my new house. With my new family. And my Mama. That's enough."

"I agree, it's enough." A fat raindrop splashed on Penny's head. Then, another landed on the hand she put over her daughter to shield her. "I think we need to eat our ice cream inside. What do you say, Uncle Ted?"

He rose, picking the last two cups up from the table just as the rain started to fall harder.

"I say we run for it if we don't want to get soaked!"

Chapter 41

Situated on the coast of Maine made Lobster Cove prime real estate for nor'easters. Those who made their homes there were hardy people and endured storms with stoic New England grit. The gale was furious, but not much different from others they'd weathered.

"Wind's picking up." Reva spoke quietly, so as not to be overheard. "Hear it howl?"

But for once, Uncle Ted's hearing problem was a blessing. He and Penny were watching Diff'rent Strokes in the living room, with the television so loud Arnold and Willis sounded as if they were in the house, too.

"I'm just glad she hasn't noticed yet. It's hard enough to move in with people she only just met, but to do it on a dark, stormy night? Ugh."

Reva put the last dish in the plastic drainer and let the water out of the sink. Chloe put the cup she'd just dried in the cupboard. Julia wielded the other dish towel. She took the final dish, gave it a swipe, and stacked it on the counter.

"I'm a lot bigger than she is, and I hate storms like this." Julia lifted the stack and carried them to the cupboard. With a grunt, she lifted them and put them in place. Slamming the door closed, she asked, "How did that happen? We used paper, so where did all those plates come from?"

"Preparation. We used them when we cooked." Reva wiped the sink out, hung the dish rag on its hook and wiped her hands on the hem of her shirt. "I am bushed. Really, truly tired."

"Last night did a number on all of us." Chloe hung the dish towel on the cupboard door knob closest to the sink. "I'm with you, sister. It's going to be an early night. As soon as that show is over, we are going to bed."

The lights flickered.

They looked up at the ceiling. Then, at each other when the lights came back on.

"That might be sooner than you think." Julia went to the pantry. They kept a supply of candles, flashlights, and batteries there, so she grabbed three flashlights and one candle. She put them in the center of the kitchen table, then put a Bic lighter beside the candle. "Just in case."

"Good thinking." Reva went into the pantry and grabbed two more flashlights. She stuck one in her back pocket and handed the other to Chloe. "Might need this. Especially up on the third floor."

Thunder rumbled, so loud the house shook. They looked at each other, then jumped when lightning flashed just outside the kitchen window. The yard was momentarily illuminated, as light as if it were high noon instead of nearing nine o'clock.

"Did you see that?" Again, Reva kept her voice low.

Tree limbs were down in the yard. The chairs usually grouped around the fire pit were overturned and scattered.

"Going to be a mess to clean up in the morning."

Chloe had tomorrow off, courtesy of Jade who offered to work her shift so she could spend time with Penny. "Whatever it is, we'll put it all back to rights. Not as if we haven't seen a storm before."

"You're right." Julia crossed her arms and leaned a hip against the kitchen table. "Whatever Mother Nature throws, we've just got to keep on truckin'."

"Mother Nature needs a Midol right now." Reva jumped when thunder rumbled again. It was surprising that someone so logical could be so illogically affected by weather. "I hate this. I really, really hate this."

"C'mon. It's just a little storm. We get 'em here, you know that." Julia put an arm around the shaking woman's shoulders and gave her a reassuring hug. "Imagine being out on a boat in this. Now that's got to be hell."

"I can't begin to imagine how awful that must be." Reva trembled visibly when there was another near-miss lightning bolt. "I'd die. I'd just literally die, on a ship in the middle of this mess."

The phone rang. Chloe was closest, so she picked the receiver up. "Hello?"

Static hissed on the line.

"It's Neil."

"Reception is really bad. Are you okay?" He'd been released from the hospital that afternoon. She'd suggested he stay with Chris and Allen for a few days, but he went home to his own place. It was large, and he lived alone, which was fine as long as he didn't go on another bender.

"It's okay...I'm okay. Not singing the blues, just checking to see you're all safe. This is one big storm, I hear. Fast-moving, but hit hard just south of us."

"We had no idea anything was brewing until we were caught out in it." The lights flickered again.

"Want me to come over? So you're all not alone over there?"

"We're fine, thanks. Stay put, that's much safer. I think we're all turning in early." Another rumble of thunder that seemed to go on and on. "Do you hear that?"

"How could I not hear it? Shook the whole damn house."

"Here, too."

"You're breaking up, Chloe. Listen, the storm's going to pack a wallop, then head up to Bar Harbor. It's just riding the coast, so hunker down."

It was sweet of him to care how they fared. And it was nice to know the track of the storm. Usually she was on top of that, but with Penny's arrival, she'd missed listening to the forecast.

"We're hunkered. You, too."

"Will do. See you tomorrow."

Before she could reply, the phone line cut out. Not even a dial tone when she hit the bar, so she hung up.

"No phone."

The lights went out. No flicker, just blackness. Suddenly the house was silent except for the tempest's roar.

From the living room, Uncle Ted's steady voice reassuring Penny. Then, they appeared in the kitchen doorway, the child held close to his chest. Chloe crossed the room and put her arms out. Penny came willingly.

"I think it's bedtime." Chloe nuzzled Penny's cheek. "What do you say? Want to see your new room?

Gabby's up there, putting nice sheets on your bed."

"No, Gabby's not up there." She came into the room from the hallway. "Gabby was halfway down the stairs when the lights quit. Made me wish for headlights above my eyebrows."

Penny giggled. "That's silly."

"Yeah, well Aunt Gabby is the funny one around here. Hey, kiddo, sleep tight."

They all hugged the little girl, took flashlights, and headed upstairs. Except for Uncle Ted, who called a final reassurance to the child before he went into his room near the kitchen. "Remember, honey, there's nothing to be scared of. Just a little storm. Tomorrow the butterflies will be flying and the birds will be singing."

She put Penny down at the bottom of the first flight of stairs. Reva went ahead of them, with Gabby and Julia close behind. They all trained their lights on the treads, and Chloe held her daughter's hand.

"Hold the handrail, and take your time. We're all here with you." She gave her hand a squeeze as they began to ascend. At least there were no windows beside the staircase, although the thunder was deafening.

"Follow me, Penny." Reva moved slowly.

"We're right behind you." Julia hummed when the thunder rolled.

"Oh, that Neil Diamond is dreamy." Gabby sighed, and they all giggled. "What are you laughing about? Forever in blue jeans? Anytime…"

They made the second floor.

Reva asked, "Are you sure you don't want to sleep down here with us tonight? We've got room for two more, don't we?"

"Always." Julia pointed to an open door. "An extra bunk in my room."

"I could go sleep with Julia so you can have my room," Gabby offered. "I don't mind at all."

She left the decision to Penny. "What do you think? Want to go up to our room? Or do you want to stay in Aunt Gabby's room for the night?"

Her daughter had spunk. Visibly nervous, she shook her head. "Our room. My first night, I should sleep in our room. Don't you think?"

"I do think." She smiled. "Thanks, sisters, for the great offers. But we're going up to our room for the night. We're not afraid of a silly storm, are we?"

"Nope."

The others stood at the bottom of the steps leading to the third floor and shined their lights so they had no trouble finding their footing. She'd considered bringing a candle up with them, but fire might not be a good idea with a child in the house.

Gabby had done a beautiful job arranging the room. They'd brought a twin bed in, rearranged the furniture, and hung pretty white lace curtains. The change made the space more inviting.

She pointed with the flashlight. "That's your bed. The one with all the pretty pillows. And, the pink fuzzy bear."

"I love it!" Penny lifted the small stuffed animal and hugged it to her chest. "I will call him Herbert. That's a good name for a bear, right?"

Right. Her aunt's word. But she'd have to learn to like the affectation, since it was likely the only piece of Debra the child had to hold onto.

"Right. And, your bear is just like mine." Chloe

reached for the bear that lived on her bed. It was identical to the one she'd picked up in Vintage Treasures. Only, hers was not in pristine condition, the way the new bear was. "I've had Norton since I was your age. A little bit younger than you are, actually. He's slept with me every night."

"Herbert will sleep with me forever, too."

She helped Penny change into pajamas. They brushed teeth. She tucked her into bed, kissed her goodnight and left the flashlight under Penny's pillow.

"I'm right over there if you need me, okay?"

"Okay…'night…"

Chapter 42

Sleep eluded her. No matter how many sheep she counted, or how many times she flipped her pillow over, Chloe could not fall asleep. The steady, sweet sound of Penny's breathing was a lullaby that should have sent her off to Dreamland, but it didn't.

Instead, her mind raced.

The fact she had a second chance with the marvelous child across the room was almost too good to be true. Part of her—a big part—didn't think she deserved this chance. She'd blown it the first time with Penny, giving her away instead of seeing her for the gift she was.

She'd failed so many times in life. What made her think she was cut out for motherhood? Maybe it was egotistic to believe she would be any good at being someone's mother.

The wind picked up, rattling the old windows in their rickety frames. The house shook, as it had for the last two hundred plus years. It was old and had seen better days, but it was solid. The roof on the main section was new, so they were safe. She hoped.

There had been enough storms through the centuries since Lobster Cove was founded that if there was one thing they knew it was that after rain, comes sunshine. Making it through the night could be challenging but somehow they'd manage.

She shifted gears, hoping to lull herself to sleep with happy thoughts.

Kyle Brown. *Doctor Dreamy*. The man who made her feel all warm and fuzzy inside.

Now, that was something to take her mind off…everything.

Lightning flashed, sending a glaring burst of light into the room. She looked over. Penny was curled up on her side, close to the wall. One of Herbert's pink ears poked out from under her arm.

Thankfully, she slept.

Kyle wasn't on duty tonight. She wondered how he was faring in the storm. He owned a house—the one with the flower garden—but she had no idea just where he lived. Someday soon she would like to see it for herself. Check out his garden. Maybe pick a rose or two.

The air seemed charged as a bolt of lightning tore the darkness outside the window. A thunderous burst shook the house so hard it felt as if they'd been hit by an earthquake. A split second later, there was a massive boom.

Then, he house did more than shake. The sound of wood splitting and beams crashing woke Penny. She sat up and screamed.

Chloe threw her covers off, jumped out of bed, and ran across the room. Plaster rained down in big chunks, but she kept running. Her daughter hadn't moved, so when she reached her, she pushed the child back against the bed and covered her with her body.

Something hard fell on her back, but she held tight to the child. Even when something sliced her skin, she did not release Penny.

"Mama! Mama—what's happening?"

"Shh, honey, shh—I'm here. We're going to be okay, I promise."

The crashing seemed interminable. And, it got much louder before it began to taper off.

The whole damn place is falling in, Chloe thought. Even as she murmured to Penny, trying to comfort the shaking child, she waited to be swallowed by the house.

"Mama!"

"Honey, listen. Listen to me. I'm here. Don't you feel me? I'm right here, you're not alone. We're going to be okay. I'm going to get us out of this mess."

"The crashing! What's happening—"

"Something fell on the house." Rain hammered on her back, cold and stinging. Something hard lay across her ankle. She bit back a shriek as she wriggled from beneath whatever pinned her.

In the distance, she heard screaming. Not hers. Not Penny's.

They had to get out.

"Honey, put your arms around my neck. Hold on tight."

Placing a hand on the back of Penny's head, she pressed the child's face against her chest and got to her knees. She used one hand to push a big tree branch off her, shimmied out from beneath another branch and stood. The darkness was cut by the lightning, which came through the gaping hole above them.

Chloe didn't waste any time. She held onto her daughter and climbed over the mess. Every step brought sharp pain. The floor was covered with wood, glass, roofing, and tree parts.

Penny clung to her like a monkey to its mother,

wrapping her legs around Chloe's waist. "Hold tight, honey. Don't look up, we're almost out."

She didn't want the child to see the nearly-crushed bed. Things were still falling, and lightning was so close it raised the hairs on the back of her neck.

When she made her way to the stairs lights shined below.

"Chloe! Penny! Oh thank God you're okay." Julia's voice came from the darkness.

"Don't fall—the steps are crushed!" Gabby screamed when they were all outlined by a fresh wave of lightning.

Part of the oak tree sliced the house in two. It lay on the steps, and into what used to be a hallway. Everything it hit had been devastated, including the way out. Too risky to try to negotiate the bits of treads left. Alone, she would have gone for it. But taking a chance with Penny was out of the question. Unfortunately, so was staying where they were. The house shook, and things crashed below.

"We've got to get out of here. The whole place is going to go." Julia waved her flashlight beam along the ragged edges of what used to be the staircase. "How about if we get a ladder to a window?"

"Not enough time." The floor beneath her feet tilted. She grabbed what was left of the wall beside her. "I'm coming down the tree."

Penny lifted her face, meet Chloe's gaze, and sniffed. She'd stopped crying but her face was wet, her hair streaming rainwater.

"It's raining. In the house."

And the floor is moving, she thought. She wanted to run but that would scare the little one even more.

"That's why we're getting out of here. Listen, can you hold onto my back? Like a piggyback rider?"

A nod, then they changed position. Small legs wrapped around her waist, and slender arms around her shoulders.

"Don't let go—no matter what, don't let go."

It was dark. And wet. And lightning felt right inside the space with them. She had to get out without killing them.

She reached out, grabbed wet wood, and climbed onto the huge tree branch. Leaves plastered to the bark sent her left foot slipping along slimy moss when she stood. One heart-stopping slide as she fought for balance was illuminated by a sharp bolt of lightning flashing dangerously close.

No time to contemplate falling. Not a moment to spare if they were to escape with their lives, so she forced herself to move. The lacerations on her bare feet stung, but she concentrated on putting one in front of the other and balancing in the center of the bark.

The two women below kept their lights trained on the branch. She tried not to look over the side of the tree. There was a dark drop where the steps should have been. It wouldn't take much to fall into the hole.

When she reached the bottom, Julia put her arms out and called to Penny. "Come on, honey. I'll catch you so your mom can climb down."

The child hesitated. "It's okay. Go to Auntie Julia, just for a minute. I'm right behind you."

She complied, reaching out, and letting Julia take her. Chloe scooted down the last few feet of tree bark, stepped over the empty space where the steps should be and into the second floor hallway. Here, too, the walls were crushed and the floor littered.

Gabby hollered to be heard over the storm. "Reva has Ted in the car. It seemed the safest thing—he's not happy about it, but we didn't give him a choice."

"Thanks." Penny was in her arms the minute she reached the hallway, so she followed Julia and concentrated on getting out before more of the house caved in. "He's okay?"

"Fine." Gabby pushed a piece of the banister out of the way.

The other staircase was intact, so they took the steps quickly. The old house groaned, almost as if it chased them from within its walls.

They ran out the front door, into the storm. Julia ran to Reva's car.

She took Penny to the Camaro. It was closer, so she pulled the door open and jumped in.

"Oh my God. This is a killer storm!" Gabby put her hand over her mouth.

Her daughter had been silent—too silent, she thought, so she checked her eyes and put a hand to her cheek. "Are you okay? Honey, talk to me, please? Are you all right?"

From beneath her arm, Penny pulled the pink bear. He'd gotten dirty and was somewhat soggy, but he had made it out.

"You saved me. I saved Herbert."

Chapter 43

They weren't in the cars for more than ten minutes before they saw lights. There was debris in the street, but the big truck wove from side to side and made it to the driveway. Chloe looked in the side mirror.

"Neil."

"That's crazy—he shouldn't be driving yet. And in this weather? Guy's nuts!" Gabby had found Tootsie Rolls in the console. Now, she unwrapped one and handed it to the youngster.

"I've got to talk to him. Can Penny stay with you for a minute?"

"Of course she can." A huge smile for the child as Chloe moved forward and placed her in the seat. "We're having a midnight picnic."

She smoothed the hair off Penny's forehead. "I'll be right back. I'm just going over there, to that truck." She kissed her soft eyebrow before opening the door and dashing out into the downpour. She closed the door then ran to Reva's car. Uncle Ted rolled down the window, so she leaned close. "Are you okay?"

"Fine. You and Penny?" He grabbed one of her hands in his. "Is she okay?"

"She's fine, Uncle Ted. Eating candy with Gabby. I'm going to talk with Neil."

She tripped over a downed branch as she ran to the truck but managed to keep from falling. The door swung open from inside as she neared, so she climbed in. A strong gust held the door wide. She pulled with all her might but could not close the door. Neil reached across, put his hand on the door handle and muscled it shut. They got drenched in the minute they fought with the door.

He ran his forearm across his face, wiping rain away. "Haven't seen a storm this bad in years. Are you okay?"

The t-shirt she'd worn to bed stuck to her body like a second skin. She pulled it away but as soon as she let go, it exposed her assets.

He reached behind the seat and came up with a denim work shirt. "It's wrinkled, but clean."

She put it on over the wet shirt but that was useless so she slipped off the t-shirt and pulled it out one of the arms of the button-down. "Ugh, it's soaked. I don't know what to do with this—"

Neil took the dripping shirt from her, tossed it over his shoulder and grinned. "Problem solved." He pointed to the house. "You all got out okay?"

"Yeah. It's a mess in there. Your house, any damage?"

"No power, and a few small trees snapped in the side yard, but nothing like this." He held his hand out, motioned to the destruction around them. "And it's not over. Phone lines are down everywhere, so there's no telling how bad it is further north. It's supposed to head that way, though—and if it hits there like it's hit here, we're all going to be cut off for a while."

Her heart hadn't stopped thudding since the moment the house was struck. She took two deep breaths, holding both before releasing, but the pounding didn't ramp down. Neither did the deluge. Rain lashed against the vehicle while it swayed in a volley of powerful gusts. Around them, branches smashed against the earth.

"I need to get back to Penny."

He put a hand over hers when she reached for the door handle. "Wait a minute. You can't go back out in this."

"I can't leave her."

"She's fine, you said so yourself. Besides, we need to get everyone to safety. Staying in these cars in the driveway makes us all sitting ducks. It's just a matter of time before a tree hits one, or a light pole comes crashing down."

He had a point. But she'd run out without anything. No wallet. No shoes. Nothing—except the most important pieces of her life, her family.

"Where can we go?"

"My place. It's big, and when I left it was still standing. I'm going to tell Gabby she can come with us, and let Reva know to follow closely. The intersection is flooded, but we'll make it." When he started to open the door, she reached for him. Before she could speak, he nodded. "Don't worry. I'm going to bring Penny back. She belongs with her parents."

Neil was swallowed by the storm the instant he left the truck. Straining to see past the wall of darkness was futile so she attempted to quiet her heart. Being wound up when he returned would not help her daughter.

Deep breaths, only now she realized it hurt to breathe. Shallow was fine, but anything more stung. Not inside, but on the surface.

Sitting forward, she reached a hand up under the

baggy shirt. She was soaked to the skin almost everywhere so when her fingers encountered moisture she wasn't alarmed. But it was a different kind of wet...sticky and warm. Chloe took her hand away, knowing before she even looked what was making breathing painful.

The door opened beside her. Neil thrust Penny into her arms, then slammed the door. She grabbed the child with one arm and pulled her close.

"You okay?"

Herbert endured a tight embrace. "We're good. Wet—we're wet."

Neil climbed in and started the truck.

"I thought you were going to get Gabby, too?"

"Won't come. Doesn't want to leave her car to be crushed. I hope it clears the flooded part." He turned to her and said, "The lap belt. Fasten it—wide, so it goes around both of you. There's no telling how bad the road's gotten since I've been here. Let's be cool, take no chances."

The belt dangled beside the seat, so she reached down and located the strap. Sliding her hand to the metal part, she tugged but it was so rarely used it wouldn't slide.

"I can't—Neil, it won't get any bigger."

He took it from her and forced the buckle to move. When it was wide enough, he stuck his hand down into the seat and pulled out the other end of the device. Jamming the buckle home, he tightened it so the child's body was snug in Chloe's arms.

"That should do it." He'd turned the overhead light on so they could see the unfamiliar seat belt. "Hey—do you know you're—"

She curled her hand into a fist. "I know."

"From where?"

"Just get us to your place, please. We can deal with it there."

"You sure?"

She wiped her palm down the side of her leg, hoping the raindrops washed enough blood away so she wouldn't get any on Penny. "I'm sure."

He backed out, and waited for the other two cars to pull in line behind them. They could just manage to see the headlights as he started creeping away from the house.

Neil hadn't exaggerated. He skirted trees and downed power lines. Rain continued to pound against the truck. She held her child against her chest securely in case something hit them. She had just found Penny— it would take more than Mother Nature's fury to pull the girl from her arms now.

The intersection was a raging vortex. The headlights illuminated what appeared to be a stream, debris swirling and heaped against the road signs. A VW Bug, tipped on its side, was partially submerged in the center.

He read her mind. "Empty. I checked on the way in."

Reva and Gabby weren't going to make it with their cars. It was not even worth trying.

"We'll have to leave the cars." He put the truck in neutral. "I'll go get everybody—no time to waste. Be right—"

The wind let up just enough that the rain stopped blowing sideways for a moment. She saw something in the maelstrom that terrified her.

"Neil—look! Standing on the roof of the car—do you see him?"

"Crazy fool—he'll get killed that way." He pointed to the power lines dangling perilously close to the water's surface. "Won't take more than another gust or two to send those into the water."

"We've got to get him—please!"

He was already out of the truck. Penny had gone silent, and Chloe didn't encourage her to speak. Better to keep her head down, and stay close, than to see the horror before them.

Neil jumped back inside. He shook his head, sending water flying. "Want to stay with Gabby? I can take you to her if—"

They had precious few minutes before the cherry red Mustang was either swept away or the man standing on top of it fell into the whirlpool. Or, before the power lines electrified the whole mess.

"We're going with you."

Her world was wrapped up in the cab of the truck, and the doctor clinging to his car in the intersection. There wasn't any bit of it she was willing to give up, even if it meant sacrificing everything.

Chapter 44

Two days later, folks in Lobster Cove were already calling the storm The Big One. It was almost too incredible to believe, but no lives had been lost. Property damage tallies continued to rise, but whatever the total was mattered not one bit to anyone. It was, they all agreed, chump change gladly paid in exchange for everyone's lives.

Chainsaws buzzed from sunrise to sunset. There would be no shortage of wood for winter's fires. Tow trucks removed flood-damaged vehicles, and town workers hit the streets before the rain ended. Damaged signs were replaced and orange cones warned of hazards. Two roads were cordoned off until they could be repaired. Power and telephone crews installed new poles and were busy restoring services.

Lobster Cove wasn't the kind of place to languish after a storm—not even The Big One.

The old house had been the only one in the Cove that was a total tear-down. Others had sustained roof losses, broken windows and an assortment of other structural ills but all were going to be fixed.

The old oak had damaged their home beyond repair.

Penny and Ted hadn't been back in the house, but the others had ventured inside. They'd salvaged whatever they could and moved it all to Neil's place. So much had been lost, but they kept reminding each other that they were alive, and the rest were just material possessions.

Easy to say, but the reality of the situation scared the hell out of Chloe. For the first time in her life, she was homeless. Along with the rest of her family. It was an overwhelming realization.

The Lobster Cove cemetery sent a backhoe to disinter the remains from beneath the oak tree. Most of the tree had fallen, but a part remained. It was better to move the dead before the heavy equipment required to raze the house and take away the tree could destroy whatever survived the centuries.

So far, Leah and Ned Sweet had been recovered. Their plots yielded little, but the bones and wood leavings, as well as a good quantity of surrounding earth, had been placed in concrete vaults on a flatbed truck.

A smaller box, amazingly nearly intact, had been removed. Its lid had been carved to read *Zeke Smith, Beloved Brother.* That, too, had been transferred to a vault.

They sat on what remained of the back steps. The overgrown lilac bush was bedraggled but would probably live. The steps had been pulled from the house by the wind and deposited near a side hedge. They made a wobbly spot to sit but few options presented themselves. The lawn chairs had all been torn to shreds or smashed by the tree.

Kyle cleared his throat. His voice was hoarse, from shouting into the wind and rain, but that didn't stop him from speaking. "Two more buried there, you said?"

"That's what we were told. Ned and Leah's

descendants are in the cemetery, so they would have been the last buried here. With Zeke out, that leaves two."

"Who are they?" He took her hand in his and rubbed a slow finger across her knuckles.

"Lizzie Sweet—Ned's mother. And Sam Fisher. Depending on who you believe, he was either a pirate or a sea captain." John, the backhoe operator, gave a shout. The men on the ground, charged with keeping lookout in the holes he dug for signs of human remains, got down on their hands and knees. "Looks like they found another one."

John got out of the cab, peered into the hole he'd just dug, and nodded. He climbed behind the controls again and started scooping earth into one of the empty vaults on the truck.

"Does it matter to you whether Sam was a sea captain or a pirate?" Kyle bumped her with his shoulder, but it was a gentle touch. "Who turns you on, hero or villain?"

"I've always figured Sam to be a good guy. He came to Lobster Cove and stayed, that's got to count for something. In the 1700s it must have been a hard life, so we're sure he was stubborn, which, as you know, is a trait I obviously find endearing."

Only a stubborn man would disregard the weather bulletins and drive into a horrific storm. And, when he saw the devastation, refuse to turn around. When they spotted him on his car, he had been preparing to swim across the intersection.

Since the storm, they'd had a friendly debate regarding his character. Chloe knew he was probably the most stubborn man alive, to have tried such a thing.

He, on the other hand, insisted it was determination that sent a man into a storm.

They both knew it was love, but the discussion lightened the mood and amused the family, so they kept it up.

"My kind of guy." He leaned in for a quick kiss. It was interesting what a near-death experience did to hasten a relationship along. They hadn't rounded home yet, but they'd reached third base—very carefully, given the damage her back and shoulders had received when the tree branch sliced it—and it had been fantastic.

"I figured you'd say that." She watched the lid being secured to the vault they just filled. The backhoe moved backward about three feet, then began to dig again.

"You know you're all welcome to stay at my place if you want. There's enough room for everyone."

Neil had graciously moved in with Chris and Allen. With nowhere to call home, they were all grateful. It would do for short-term living, but long term? Chloe had no idea what was going to happen to them.

"Thanks, but we're settled at Neil's. The insurance company is expediting the process, so I'm hoping they cut us a check soon. I'll have to come to terms with the bank on the roofing loan, but aside from that, the funds are ours. It won't be nearly enough to rebuild—but I can't think about that yet."

She shrugged, which was a mistake. Pain reminded her she'd very nearly lost a kidney in the storm. Kyle had stitched her back when they were all safe at Neil's place—after Gabby, Reva, and Julia put Penny to bed and Uncle Ted snoozed in an armchair wearing a pair of

Neil's pajamas.

Kyle put a hand on her forehead. "No fever. When was the last time you took pain meds?"

When she didn't reply, he shook his head. "You should take them. It will help."

"I can't have my mind clouded by drugs—legal or otherwise. Don't you see?" She waved a hand toward the collapsed building. The tree had cut it nearly in two. "I don't know what the hell I'm going to do."

Neil walked around the side of the house. Kyle stood, and the men shook hands.

"What you're going to do about what?" He gave her a smile, then crossed his arms and watched John dig.

"Everything." The backhoe stopped again, and the men fell to their knees and leaned into the fresh hole. "No, that's wrong. Not everything. Just the house, I guess."

His generous spirit knew no bounds. "Hey, you know you can stay at my place for as long as it takes. You've all got a home, so don't waste energy thinking you're homeless." He turned, met her gaze. "You'll never be homeless; do you hear me?"

He knew her too well.

The lump in her throat kept her from speaking. That had been happening a lot since the storm. Kyle said it was nothing to worry about but the vulnerable feeling was new to her. She couldn't wait for it to go away.

"Listen, I want to thank you for loaning me your car. Helluva nice thing to do—first you save my life, then you let me use your wheels. I don't know what to say, man." Kyle had thanked Neil more than once since the storm. The two had formed an interesting friendship. It made Chloe's life simpler, and Penny had already fallen in love with both men, so it was cool that they were on good terms.

"No sweat. Hey, you saved my life. Now we're even." Neil gave him the thumbs up, sealing the deal.

"Yeah, now if Chloe could find her happy place, we'd be all set." Kyle sat beside her again. He put a hand on her knee and asked, "Why don't you decide what you want to do? That'll cut the stress by a ton, just knowing what kind of home you want."

Neil stopped watching the cemetery workers. They'd begun filling the fifth vault with earth and remains. Hardly something a man who'd nearly died a few days ago wanted to witness. He turned his back on the action, squatted before her and met her gaze.

"You know what you want. You've always known."

He was right. But wanting something and having it were two different things. She didn't point out that he, of all people, should know that.

"I don't know if I can do it."

"Of course you can do it. You only have the limitations you set on yourself. All your life, you've given to the rest of us. It's time you take what you want—long past time, really."

Kyle cleared his throat.

She turned and gave an apologetic smile. "Didn't mean to cut you from the conversation. Sorry."

"No worries. But I would like to know—what is it you want?"

Neil answered before she could open her mouth. She glared at him, but he smiled and she could not be angry. He was just trying to fit in, to build a bridge between all of them. It was his way, and there was no malice in his actions. She knew him well enough to know that, so she let him explain.

"She wants to open a home for women who need a safe place to stay. Women who are escaping abuse. Women who are pregnant and unwed, and need support. Women who have no place to go, or just need a break to turn their lives around. It's what she's always wanted. It's been Chloe's dream for longer than I can remember." His tone was serious when he met her gaze and added, "You should do it. Grab the dream of a lifetime and do it."

"Is that what you want, really?" Kyle asked.

She nodded. "It is."

"Neil's right. You should go for it. We're all here to help." He looked up at the workers, then back to her. "We only get one go-around in life. None of us should forget that."

She put her palms over her eyes and rubbed. They were still itchy from all the plaster dust that covered her when the third floor collapsed. She stopped, looked each of them in the face and said, "Have you forgotten it's not just about me? I have a daughter to consider now, remember?"

The men exchanged glances.

Kyle shook his head. "Have you forgotten about the rest of us? We're here to help. You're not alone in that."

Neil's gaze didn't falter. "You've forgotten who you are. You've always been the one to believe the impossible was possible. That shouldn't change—ever. Think about this—a month ago, Penny didn't have parents and we…well, we were a mess. Now, we're moving forward, and she has parents. Three parents, to be exact. I'd say there's no better example of making fact from fiction. So, go for it. Realize a dream."

She wanted to. Oh, how she wanted to…

"Even if I took a leap and built big enough to open a home, the truth is the insurance check isn't going to cover all of that. It's not enough money." She would have some cash to spend, but it would never build a house big enough to shelter the family plus take in needy women.

"A mortgage?" Neil wasn't giving up.

"Won't work. I'd have to charge the women to stay here in order to make the monthly payments. They can't afford to pay, so that's out."

Kyle spoke. "A personal loan? From someone who loves you and wants to help?"

"As much as I want to accept, I can't. It's wonderful of you to offer, but if I do this, I have to find a way to make it happen without putting myself in debt. Thank you, though."

"Offer stands if you change your mind."

She took his hand in hers and nodded. "Thanks."

Shouts went up near the backhoe.

Chloe looked up in time to see John wave them over. She hadn't wanted to approach the old graves, not while they were digging, so she shook her head.

"You've got to see this! Before we pull it up—come on, it's incredible!"

They stood and headed across the lawn. Some of the debris had been pushed aside by the backhoe when the crew arrived so they followed the cleared path.

Every man was grinning from ear to ear. And,

when she got close enough, John grabbed her hand. He tugged her to the side of the hole.

"Move over, guys! Let the lady through!" He took her right to the edge and pointed. "Look! I felt something hard when I dug the last one out—something peculiar, don't you know? We shoveled a bit and look! Look at that!"

Chloe's knees bent and she dropped to the muddy ground. The hole was only four or five feet deep, but nestled in the mud was the thing children's dreams are made of.

"A pirate's chest." Goose bumps rose on her arms. She leaned into the hole, reached a hand out and ran her fingertips along the hard metal surface. "It's real."

Kyle knelt on one side of her, and Neil on the other.

She looked from one to the next. Both wore similar expressions of utter disbelief.

"Let's get it out of there." Neither responded so she said, "Hey, guys—can we get it out of there?"

"Sorry—I think I'm just in shock." Kyle reached in and brushed the dirt from one side of the chest with his fingertips. "There's a handle over here."

Neil jumped into the hole, knelt beside the chest and dug with his hands until he uncovered a matching handle. He looked at the other man when he spoke. "How about if I lift it out and hand it to you?"

"Good idea." Neil lifted but the box did not move. "Need some help?"

The men around them were taking bets on what was in the chest. They all congratulated her on her luck, but until she saw what was in the box, she wasn't counting her chickens.

"Thing is heavy. Yeah, maybe you should come in and help."

"Thought you'd never ask."

Kyle joined Neil in the hole, and for one insane moment, Chloe realized that the only two men she'd ever loved now stood side by side in a grave. A creepy thought, so she pushed it aside.

While the cemetery men cheered, they lifted the chest and placed it on the grass. Both men climbed out wearing big grins on their faces.

"It's heavy." Kyle wiped dirt from his hands onto the legs of his jeans.

"Real heavy." Neil agreed.

The pirate's chest was a thing of beauty, even after being buried. It resembled the replicas sold to tourists in gift shops, only this one was much nicer. The leather straps had deteriorated, but the buckles were intact. There were scenes hammered into the metal along the front and side panels. Pirate ships. A skull and crossbones. Swords. A mermaid. A date.

1743.

"Well, anyone going to open that?" John and his men had fallen back when the chest was lifted but now they moved closer.

"It's up to you." Kyle traced a finger over the mermaid's hair. "But I've got to admit, I'm pretty curious about what's in there."

Neil raised a dubious brow. "You're not going to wait, are you? The suspense will kill me."

Two men, both of the same mind. And, the ones gathered around all looked as if they were ready to jump from their skins, the anticipation was affecting them so.

Chloe grinned. She looked at each of them in turn, savoring the magical moment.

"If I'm dreaming, don't wake me up."

"It's no dream, honey." Kyle accepted a hammer and screwdriver one of the men brought over. He held it up. "Well?"

"Let's open it!" She moved aside and gave him room to work.

Every man had a suggestion about how to break the lock.

Neil gave it one good tug. "Solid, even after centuries. I bet a couple of hard ones where the mechanism is should jar something loose."

Kyle put the screwdriver against the lock, to the spot where the other had pointed as being the likeliest to spring.

"Wait." She heard the chorus of groans but did not care. "You don't think there's a body in there, do you?"

"No way. It's too heavy." Neil shook his head.

"Okay, then. Do it."

It only took one whack with the hammer to make the ancient lock pop open. Kyle moved aside. He looked at her, swept a hand toward the chest and said, "It's yours, Chloe. You should open the pirate's prize."

A shiver of anticipation shot up her spine. Impulsively she leaned over and kissed him. Then, she reached for Neil and gave him a fast hug.

Her fingers trembled as she took the lock off. She dropped it on the grass, and placed her hands on the metal chest. She took one deep breath for courage, then swung the top up.

Gold doubloons, silver cups inlaid with jewels and dazzling gems came into view. She gasped as the others began to cheer. Kyle picked her up and swung her in a circle, holding her so carefully that for a moment she thought she was flying.

When her feet touched ground, he kissed her. Passion, promise, hope…so many things, and all at once.

"A pirate's prize, my love. It is the answer you've waited for. Now, you're free to do whatever you wish." Kyle's eyes were so filled with tenderness she felt the power of his love.

She tilted her head back, looked to the sky and laughed.

Then she shook her head and met his gaze. "The pirate's legacy? We'll put that to good use. But what I've waited for is love. Laughter. Light. That's what I've waited for—and now, my wait has ended."

A word about the author...

Sarita Leone loves adventure, whether it be in a distant continent or her own backyard. When she's not off exploring the world, she keeps busy writing, reading, and dancing beneath the stars. Always a fan of happy endings, she's fortunate to have a job which allows for so many of those!

She loves to hear from readers. Easiest way to connect? Check out her Facebook page, where all the latest news hits the screen.

Thank you for purchasing
this publication of The Wild Rose Press, Inc.

If you enjoyed the story, we would appreciate your
letting others know by leaving a review.

For other wonderful stories,
please visit our on-line bookstore at
www.thewildrosepress.com.

For questions or more information
contact us at
info@thewildrosepress.com.

The Wild Rose Press, Inc.
www.thewildrosepress.com

Stay current with The Wild Rose Press, Inc.

Like us on Facebook

https://www.facebook.com/TheWildRosePress

And Follow us on Twitter
https://twitter.com/WildRosePress

www.ingramcontent.com/pod-product-compliance
Lightning Source LLC
Chambersburg PA
CBHW060525260626
47161CB00003B/763